Shadowed Eden

I0674067

Katie Clark

Shadowed Eden

Scripture quotations, unless otherwise indicated are taken from the King James translation, public domain.

Cover Art by *Nicola Martinez*

Watershed Books, a division of Pelican Ventures, LLC
www.pelicanbookgroup.com PO Box 1738 *Aztec, NM * 87410

Watershed Books praise and splash logo is a trademark of Pelican Ventures, LLC

Publishing History
First Watershed Edition, 2016
Paperback Edition ISBN 978-1-61116-489-3
Electronic Edition ISBN 978-1-61116-480-0
Published in the United States of America

Dedication

To Micheal, Emma, and Ashlyn; and to the greatest big
brother I ever had, for all the brainstorming help.

What People are Saying

"Shadowed Eden is a unique and intriguing tale that will keep the reader guessing and turning pages to find out the secrets of this mysterious story, and the suspense doesn't stop until its surprising end! I highly recommend it." ~ Melanie Dickerson, award-winning YA author of *The Merchant's Daughter*

"A truly original premise, *Shadowed Eden*, is an exciting supernatural adventure filled with danger, redemption, and a cast of teenage characters that I grew to love. I enjoyed Clark's story and look forward to seeing what she comes up with next." ~ Jill Williamson, author of *From Darkness Hid* and *Captives*

Part 1

Genesis 3:1
"Now the serpent was more subtle than any beast of the field which the Lord God had made."

1

Avery

Avery watched from the tarmac as the pilot taxied down the dirt runway. The same plane had just brought her and the rest of the youth group to Iraq, and it was already leaving them behind.

Warm air from the jets sent her dark, wavy hair flying, and she brushed it from her face to keep from missing the takeoff. Once the plane was gone, they would be stuck here. Stuck in Iraq with only a few vans to cart them around.

The airplane roared into the sky, and even the locals on the airstrip stopped to watch.

Avery should have felt nervous at being left behind. Being stuck in a foreign country with no way out. Instead, she smiled. No one at the mission would keep their distance because of her past.

"Can I carry that for you?" a man asked. His accent was thickly Middle Eastern, and his caramel-colored skin glistened with sweat.

He reached for her bag but Avery pulled back. "That's OK. I'll carry it."

The man lifted his eyebrows but nodded. "As you wish." He sidestepped to the next student on the mission trip, and Avery glanced around for Daddy. He'd made it clear she was to ride with him. Avery had insisted on coming on this mission trip, in spite of his objections. He would chaperone even if she didn't come, and he didn't want her in danger, or so he said.

Putting up a fight wasn't her usual persona, but she was glad now she'd done it. Getting away from home was exactly what she needed to get a fresh start, and the desert area of Iraq was about as different from the rolling green hills of Alabama as she could imagine. Instead of cookie-cutter grocery stores and brand new cars, tarps covered roughhewn poles where locals sold fruits, clothes, and meats. A few vehicles dotted the space around the measly airport, but the newest model looked as if it debuted at least a decade ago. Besides that, there was the humidity—or the lack of it. Already the dry desert air was frizzing her hair and drying out her pores.

Chad, the youth leader, stepped to the front of the group. "Load up!"

Avery hauled her luggage to Daddy's van, and the man from earlier took it from her hands. He quirked an eyebrow—probably wondering why she hadn't let him have it to begin with. She wasn't sure herself, except this was her chance at freedom. At doing things her way without feeling ashamed.

"Hey buddy, here you go!"

Avery turned in time to see a boy from her group toss a duffel bag at the luggage guy. The man reached for it, but he was too late and it toppled into the other stack sitting on the pavement. It knocked the neat pile into a mess.

Bradley cackled and turned away, and Avery shook her head. Unbelievable.

Turning back to the luggage guy, she moved to help. "I'm sorry about him. He's an idiot."

"Thank you," the man said.

"You're welcome." She smiled and restacked a few pieces while the man arranged them on top of the van.

After making sure her luggage was secure, Avery climbed inside the fifteen passenger van and found a seat at the window in the second row. Other kids piled in behind her, last of all a girl from her group.

Mallory looked around for a seat, her red hair frizzing as badly as Avery's. The van was almost full. Their eyes met and Avery managed a smile. She pointed to the empty seat beside her, but Mallory's eyes darted away. She moved to sit on the first row with the other girls.

Avery sighed and turned back to the window.

The driver—the same man who'd loaded her luggage—climbed inside and started the vehicle.

Avery smiled as the van revved up, and the rest of the group broke into an excited chatter. Daddy still hadn't made his way to her van. Maybe he'd be riding in the other vehicle after all. She readjusted herself to account for the empty seat beside her, but just before they pulled away, the door opened and Daddy climbed in. He smiled at her and maneuvered into the empty seat.

"Everything's been squared away," he said. His eyes glowed with some kind of excitement that she wasn't used to seeing in him.

Avery opened her mouth to answer him, but Bradley's voice broke through. "How long until we're at the village?"

Daddy twisted toward the back seat and held up two fingers. "Two hours. You guys are in for a treat."

Avery managed a weak smile before turning toward the window. People might warm up to her if her own father didn't ignore her. And if he hadn't practically institutionalized her.

This trip would change all that. She would prove to him she could make it in his world.

They pulled away from the airport and started down a pockmarked, dirt road. A few of the others had brought ear buds, but Avery's were still packed in her suitcase.

She took a deep, cleansing breath. The ear buds didn't matter. She was too busy dreaming of all the things the next two weeks would hold. Today was the beginning of her "start over."

She sighed as they rumbled into the desert. The jostling of the huge vehicle over the rough roads rattled her teeth, but she didn't have the strength to move. This trip had been way too long. Her muscles ached, her eyelids drooped, and a huge yawn erupted from her lips.

"Tired?" Daddy asked.

Avery turned enough to give him a small smile. "Unlike you, oh, mighty archeologist, most of us are not used to travelling the globe."

He smiled and patted her leg. "Get some sleep. I'll wake you up when we get there."

Avery relaxed against the side of the van, but she kept one eye on Daddy. He'd said more to her in the last two days than he had in the entire year before.

She glanced at the other van in the entourage. It drove behind hers on the crazy, unregulated Iraqi road.

"I thought there were checkpoints and stuff around here. Where are all the roadside bombs?"

Leave it to Bradley to ask such insensitive questions. Avery kept her eye roll to herself.

"There certainly might be bombs on this road. We could hit one at any moment." The driver's deadpan answer silenced the entire van.

Except Avery. She snickered.

The driver caught her eye in the rearview mirror and winked at her.

Chatter resumed a moment later, and Avery tuned it out to watch the desert pass. The sun had begun to sink closer to the sand, and the reflecting light played tricks on her eyes, making it seem as if the sand moved.

No, it wasn't the sand. It was almost as if the air moved—like she could see the wind. She shook her head and blinked, and when she opened her eyes everything was back to normal.

She glanced again at the other vehicle. Some of the occupants were teens in her own youth group, but others had come from churches across Alabama. The *Mission: Education* trip was a statewide effort.

Luca was in that other van.

Avery worked to calm the storm his presence put inside her.

The road turned suddenly, and the van jerked to follow it. Avery gasped as it rocked hard, and her head hit the window. The sun glared off Luca's van, blinding her, and she turned away.

"My apologies," the driver said in his thick accent. Dark eyes met hers in the rearview mirror, and she looked down.

"The wind is picking up," Daddy said.

Avery followed his gaze. Clouds of sand whipped through the air.

"Only a mild sandstorm," the driver said. "It happens all the time."

Avery listened to his carefully spoken English. It was impeccable. She'd been taking Spanish for four years and still spoke it in a broken lilt.

Daddy spoke seven languages—which he reminded her of often. He never failed to let her know all the ways she disappointed him.

The van jerked a second time, making a few of the others shout.

Avery held on to the seat handle for support.

The radio on the dashboard crackled to life. "Driver two, come in."

Avery craned her neck but there was nothing to see. Too bad it wasn't like a GPS where she could read the information for herself.

"I'm here," their driver said.

"The storm is getting worse ahead. How would you like to proceed?"

"Pull over," Daddy said. "Let's discuss this away from the youth."

Avery glanced at him. Of course the drivers would do as he said—as the only one of the group who had ever been to Iraq before, he was the unspoken leader— but stopping in the desert in the middle of a sandstorm didn't seem like a great idea to her.

After a few moments, both vans had stopped in the road and the adults gathered in between them.

Avery watched the road ahead, scanning the sandy street for oncoming cars. She hadn't seen a single one pass ever since they left the airport, but how would they know if one came upon them now?

Sand swirled around them like dirt tornadoes. The drivers had pulled thick scarves over their faces and sunglasses over their eyes. Daddy followed suit, ever prepared. But the other chaperones dodged sandblasts by jerking away or holding their hands over their faces.

At this rate, they would never reach the village

before dark. Her sweater was packed away on top of the van in the towering bundle of luggage. How would she survive a cold desert night?

The group of adults moved toward the other vehicle, and Daddy climbed into it. Someone else climbed out and darted through the sandstorm. Avery's van door pulled open, and Luca appeared in front of her. He took the only open seat, which just happened to be the one beside Avery, the one Daddy had left unoccupied.

This wasn't good.

"The other driver knows the area better," Luca said. Of course, he knew she wanted to know what was happening. "Your dad is riding ahead with him, and we're going to follow."

Avery stared at him, still working to control her emotions at being near him again.

Luca watched her curiously, probably trying to give her time to comprehend what he was saying. "He needed my seat, which is why I'm here."

Finally, Avery talked her brain into responding. "Oh." Brilliant. He probably thought she'd lost her mind in the three months since she'd spoken to him.

Their driver climbed back in, shaking sand from his clothes. It sounded like rain as it hit the hard, plastic floor of the van.

Avery scooted as far away from Luca as she possibly could—which was way too far and still not nearly far enough. She watched through the swirling sand as Daddy's van pulled into the storm. A moment later, their vehicle jerked into gear, and they were off again.

"Does this thing have a GPS?" Benny asked. He leaned up from the back seat, his arm brushing against

Avery's shoulder. Avery let the touch go—Benny had no sense of personal boundaries. She'd learned that long ago, since they'd started going to youth group together in seventh grade.

"I don't know, Benny. Maybe you could ask the driver." She caught Luca's scowl pointed at Benny's arm, and she almost laughed. She scooted away from Benny's wayward arm, which unfortunately put her closer to Luca.

A violent gust of wind smacked into the van, rocking it back and forth. Some of the girls screamed, and Avery gasped as she crashed into Luca.

"Sorry," she muttered, untangling her long, brown hair from his seatbelt.

He helped her up silently, his face serious.

The van continued to rock so hard it felt as if they were back on the plane and flying through rough turbulence.

"Maybe we should pull over," Erin, the youth leader's wife, said. She had to raise her voice above the sound of sand hitting the side panels outside. "We could wait it out and then catch up."

The driver glanced at Erin in the rearview mirror. He took a deep breath, which sounded more like a sigh of frustration to Avery, then pushed the radio button. "Driver one, come in."

Static filled the air.

"Driver one, do you copy?"

Crackle.

Avery frowned, her stomach dropping. She glanced out the window, but now she couldn't see anything of the road. The billowing sand was so thick it was like driving straight through a sand dune.

The van took another violent hit, and Avery

tightened her seatbelt. Where was Daddy? Why wasn't the other van answering?

Vibrations rocked them again, starting as a slow rumble but growing into what felt like an earthquake.

Awkward or not, she reached out and took Luca's warm, strong hand. He didn't protest, just held on tight, his eyes wide with confusion and maybe even fear.

Some of the girls began crying, and others put their heads between their knees.

Avery was on the verge of tears herself when suddenly the rocking stopped.

Even the sand had stopped blowing. Everything was still.

Luca leaned forward and squinted toward the window. A frown turned his full lips down. "Do you see that?"

Avery turned to the window, and her jaw fell open. Before them sat a massive green jungle.

Everyone stared out the window, taking in the foliage in front of the van. Avery gaped at the swaying trees, draping vines, and deep green backdrop of leaves.

Her gaze swung to the driver. "Where are we?"

The driver's eyes were still glued to the jungle. He shook his head, muttering an answer in his native language. Obviously, this place was as new to him as it was to everyone in their group.

Avery scanned her memories of Daddy's maps, trying to remember a large jungle anywhere near the airport, but she couldn't think of any. She watched the jungle for a few moments, but she'd had enough sitting. She pushed past Luca, climbing over his legs and making her way to the door.

"You're going out there?" someone asked. "Are you crazy?"

Avery winced, but she let the comment go.

"What are you doing?" Benny climbed out of his seat, stepping on a blonde girl in the process.

"Watch it!"

"Sorry," Benny muttered, still working his way to the doors.

Avery pushed through the door, and waning sunlight greeted her. Benny climbed out, followed by everyone else in the van.

The jungle stretched in front of them for as far as Avery could see. Trees rose toward the sky, nearly blocking what was left of the sun. The tree line bulged and dipped in places, rolling like the waves of the ocean. Jungle sounds drifted on the small breeze that blew—a jungle clatter that grew louder with each passing second.

"Look," someone said.

Avery turned to the blonde girl from earlier. Her permed hair hung just below her chin, and she had a full, round face. Those features were almost invisible compared to her sparkling green eyes. Avery followed the direction of the girl's pointing finger. Several inches of sand buried the van's tires.

"Were we blown here?" Avery asked. That was impossible. Wasn't it?

Erin pushed through the group with the driver close behind her. "How did this happen?" she demanded.

The driver's face still showed disbelief. Finally, he said, "I don't know."

Erin sighed and looked around. Avery followed her gaze. A jungle rose before them, but miles and miles of desert stretched out behind them. If there was or had ever been a road, it was gone now.

"Wait," Avery said. "Where's the other van?" It was the first she'd realized they were alone. Daddy was nowhere to be seen, and Chad, Erin's husband, wasn't at her side.

Everyone in the group looked around, searching for the missing van.

"It is possible they were able to stay on the road," the driver said. His accent was much thicker in his nervous state, and it took Avery a second to understand what he was saying.

"You mean they could have made it to the village?"

He glanced around, taking in the emptiness surrounding them. "It is possible."

He wasn't convincing.

Avery scanned the wide span of desert. No sign of a sandstorm stirred in the distance.

How had they ended up here?

The blonde girl started crying. "I'm sorry," she blubbered. "It's just that I've never been away from home before, and now this."

Poor thing.

Avery looked to Erin for help, but the youth leader's wife still stared absently at the desert. Avery took in their group.

Thirteen teens and two adults—it should have been three adults except Daddy had switched seats with Luca.

Erin was useless, and the driver wouldn't be any help in comforting anyone. That left Avery. Daddy was in charge of this trip. It only made sense that Avery would step up. It wasn't like she wasn't used to fending for herself, and when they found the other van, Daddy would see she wasn't as useless as he treated her.

She moved quickly to the girl and wrapped her in a hug. "It's OK to cry. We'll be fine. When the other group reaches the village, they'll see we're not there. They'll come find us."

The others in the group nodded, comforted by her explanation. It was better than the cold shoulder she usually got from them, even if she didn't know what she was talking about. What if no one came to find them?

She shook off the thoughts. "We're probably going to have to sleep in the van."

Luca stepped forward and hopped onto the van's bumper. It wasn't a far jump considering the van's sunken state. "We need to get out sweaters to keep warm, and if you brought any snacks you can eat them for supper. The other group will probably be here at first light."

Everyone snapped to action, moving to get what they needed from the luggage as Luca pulled pieces down. He stood like a born leader with his head held high, and his shoulders pulled back. He was poised and ready to make things happen. He caught her looking and smiled.

Avery smiled back her thanks. She could put their past behind her—at least for now. It was good he'd been the one to switch with Daddy. Of course, if Daddy hadn't switched then Avery wouldn't have had to step up at all.

"What's your name?" Avery asked, turning to the blonde.

"June," she said, blubbering. "June Sanderson. I

was named after my grandmother."

Avery smiled and squeezed June's shoulder. "It's nice to meet you, June. I'm Avery."

June sniffled and wiped her tears with her palms. "Are we going to be OK?"

Avery looked at Luca. Some of the others had begun helping him get the luggage. Even Erin seemed to have snapped out of her funk. They could do this. Maybe.

Avery glanced back at June and smiled. "Yes. We're going to be fine. You'll see."

2

Luca

Luca tightened the last rope in place, re-securing the luggage to the top of the van.

The driver smacked the bags and gave the ropes a solid tug. "This is good. Strong."

Luca nodded and climbed down. Everyone had what they needed to get through the night—sweaters, snacks, magazines. He'd even hauled down Erin's thirty-two pack of bottled water.

He had nothing, since his bags were on the other van. A cold, desert wind hit him, and he rubbed his arms to keep warm.

Most of the group huddled around a fire someone had managed to light. Lighters and matches had specifically been on the "Do Not Bring" list. Whoever brought them probably wouldn't admit it. The heat took away the chill as he sat with the others around the fire.

Each face stared at the flames. No one said anything.

Not that Luca could blame them. They were lost in a desert a million miles from home. He slid his thumb across his phone one last time, but no bars still meant no signal. Why did he even keep trying?

He shouldn't be here. Coming on this trip was the last thing his family needed to shell out money for, and now he was stuck in the middle of nowhere. He could be at home fixing their leaky roof or looking for a summer job. Or a permanent job. Movement to his right caught his attention, and he turned.

Avery stumbled her way through the sand and finally found a seat next to the blonde girl. She looked up when she had arranged her legs—Indian style—and her eyes met his. She looked away. Up, down, around. It didn't seem to matter, as long as she wasn't looking at him.

She was avoiding him, just like she'd done the entire trip. If she was surprised he came, Luca didn't know why. They had committed together when Chad and Erin had first brought the idea to the youth group. Of course, that was nine months ago; six months before he and Avery broke up.

Now Erin sat on a box in the sand, eating crackers and staring into the flames like everyone else. Luca had hauled the box from the back of the van for her. There were two of them, one filled with medical supplies for the village, and the other filled with food. At least they'd been stranded with the van that had the food.

His thoughts moved back to Erin. Was she going to step up and take care of the group? So far it seemed like the answer was no. She'd done nothing but stare into space for two hours now.

Avery had told everyone that help was coming first thing in the morning. Sure, that was a great thing to hope for, but they were pretty far out.

He looked again at the huge nothingness around them. Empty sky and land stretched for miles on end, rising and falling in waves of sand. No buildings, villages, or roads.

Help might take more than a night to come. While

some of them were used to fending for themselves, others like that blonde girl looked like they needed a chaperone telling them what to do.

Luca cleared his throat and called across the small space. "So Erin, what's the plan?"

The youth leader looked up, her eyes glowing in the firelight. "What?"

"The plan? For the night? What should we do?"

Her confused look cleared, and she sat up straighter. "Oh. Right. I guess we'll have to sleep in the van. Girls in the back and boys in the front." She threw in the last line with a glance between Avery and Luca.

Luca looked to Avery for her reaction, but Avery only stared at the sand. If Erin's insinuation meant anything to her, she sure didn't show it.

He ground his teeth and kicked at the sand. If it wasn't so cold, he would get as far away from the group—and her—as he could. How were they supposed to survive the next two weeks if she acted like he had some sort of disease?

"Maybe we could sing," the blonde girl said.

"Nobody feels like singing, June." Benny rolled his eyes and looked around for support.

Benny was getting on Luca's nerves already. He'd sat beside Luca on the plane, showing him the differences between his old phone and his new smart phone. For fourteen hours. "Actually, I think singing is a good idea."

The blonde girl—June—smiled at him. "Thanks. We always sing at my church."

That reminded him he didn't really know her. Wasn't anyone else from her group on their van? There were a few other kids he didn't know, but they didn't flock to June's side like Avery did when June had her breakdown earlier.

June started singing a praise song that he recognized from church, so he joined in. After him, a few others piped up, too, until most of them were singing.

The harmony carried in the clear night air, and Luca started to relax. Singing did that to him, and in the deserted—literally—area, it felt like God himself could hear them.

When the song ended, June launched right into another one. Nobody hesitated this time.

Luca sang along as he scanned the area. Finally, his gaze landed on Avery. She still stared at the sand. Her lips didn't move.

After a second, she stood and stumbled back through the sand, away from the group and toward the van. The faint sound of the van door closing carried through the air.

Luca sighed.

After a few more songs, Erin stood and held up her hands. "Let's get some rest. We'll get out of here in the morning."

Luca waited until everyone else had wandered away. He stomped on the small fire until it smoldered out, and he made sure no one had left anything behind, then he climbed into the van and took the last remaining seat—the front seat across from the driver.

A few of the girls huddled together under sweaters. Most of the guys were turned as far away from each other as they could get. Avery curled into a corner, alone. Her eyes were closed and her chest moved up and down, slowly.

She'd probably looked that way since everyone else climbed in. They probably all thought she was asleep.

She wasn't, though. Her breaths were too shallow, and she lay too still, like she was trying not to move.

Luca turned around and tried to get comfortable in his seat. The driver was already snoring beside him. No wonder the passenger seat had been empty.

He stared at the ceiling and did a mental run-through of what needed to be done tomorrow. If he was right, no one would make it to them for a while. That meant they needed food and water. There had to be a water source close by with that huge, green jungle behind them, and there had to be fruit. Two groups could go out; one for food and one for water. Everyone else could stay back and wait for help.

Out of the thirteen teens there were six guys and seven girls, even though Benny wasn't exactly a dependable choice when it came to any hard labor. On the other hand, Luca would trust Avery to get any job done, so maybe that evened things out.

They could split the teams, half guys and half girls. Avery was with him, whether she liked it or not. Who knew what kinds of animals lived in that jungle? She could go back to ignoring him once they were rescued.

As the night wore on, Luca glanced around. Almost everyone was asleep. A few people looked out the window. He twisted further to check on Avery.

She watched him but must not have expected him to see her because she quickly turned around.

He grinned as he faced forward. He knew she'd been awake earlier. He knew her better than she knew herself. Maybe this trip wasn't as big a mistake as he thought. She'd actually smiled at him once or twice. There might still be hope.

He kept himself awake until the last passenger nodded off, and sometime in the darkest hours of the night, he fell asleep, too. He woke up when the blinding desert sun shone in his face. The others were already climbing from the van and cold air blew in from outside.

He twisted around. Avery was already out.

Too bad no one had left their sweater behind. Bracing himself against the cold, he hopped out with the others. A few of the girls stuck together, huddling for warmth. Avery wrapped her sweater more tightly around herself, looking anywhere but at him and standing alone.

His gut clenched at seeing her by herself, and he wanted to move toward her. Protect her. Make everything better for her. It'd surprised him when he found out she was still coming on the trip herself. She'd signed up in a flurry of independence, but Mr. Miles usually stomped out those flames pretty fast.

The sun rose toward the sky behind her, towering like the huge ball of fire it was.

One day she'd learn how strong she was on her own.

"Hey, where can I go to the bathroom?" Benny's face blocked his view and Luca punched him in the arm.

"Dude, go find a tree."

"In there?" His voice went up an octave.

Luca rolled his eyes. Maybe Benny should be on the team that stayed behind.

"You want someone to hold your hand?" He meant it as a joke, but when Benny's eyes lit up, Luca shoved him. "Get out of here."

Benny skittered away and Luca glanced around.

Avery was gone.

He huffed and scanned the crowd for Erin. He needed to tell her his ideas and try to get her on his side. She wouldn't let anyone go trekking across the jungle if she believed help was coming any minute.

Erin stood near the spot where they'd gathered around the fire last night, and Luca made his way toward her. He scanned the area as he moved—a habit from all his years spent hunting in the woods—and he had almost reached her when he froze.

Something moved at the tree line. Something white.

Whatever it was, it was fast and it looked about his size, maybe bigger.

He frowned and stared for a second, trying to get another look.

Just then, Benny came strolling out of the jungle.

"Are you OK? Luca?" Erin's voice broke into his thoughts.

He looked to her then back to Benny. The white image couldn't have been Benny. The kid had on a red jacket.

He swallowed and turned back to Erin. "Yeah, I'm fine. I just wanted to talk to you."

He glanced one last time toward the jungle. Whatever it was, it was gone now.

3

Avery

Avery nibbled on a peanut butter cracker June offered. Her stomach was an empty pit of hunger, and she hadn't brought a single snack. She'd kept it to herself last night—she'd gotten used to her isolation, and talking to someone even to ask for food was way out of her comfort zone. She would have continued keeping it to herself this morning, but June commented on Avery's stomach-rumblings and offered to share.

"Do you want another one?" June asked.

"No, that's OK. This will hold me over until the others get here." But really, she wanted to take the whole pack and shove it into her mouth. She smiled to prove her point, but her stomach growled again and June laughed.

"Here. Take one more."

Avery chuckled and rolled her eyes as her cheeks heated up, but she took the cracker and made herself eat it slowly so it would last longer.

Most of the kids huddled in groups, watching the silent desert around them, but not even the sand stirred. Where was the other van? Luca stood with Erin and they looked like they were deep in conversation. Erin and her husband, Chad, had been there for her when Mom left. Avery definitely felt comfortable enough to approach.

She shuffled over to them. "What's going on?"

Erin looked to Luca.

He paused like he was waiting for Erin to say something, but when she didn't, he turned to Avery. "I think we're going to be here for an undetermined amount of time. I mean, look at this place. We're in the middle of nowhere."

Avery frowned and looked around. He was right—she'd been thinking about the emptiness of the desert herself—but she hated hearing him say it. "So, what are you suggesting?"

"We need to find water and food, but no one is going to like it." He paused, watching her face before going on. "Are you on board with this?"

"Absolutely." Her words came out much braver than she felt. Inside? Inside the thought of going into that jungle and looking for anything at all scared her to death. The only thing that prodded her forward was the fact that she'd come here to remake herself. She could do it. She had to.

Luca nodded once, his brown hair falling onto his forehead. He pushed it back and turned to look at the group. "We need to split up into three groups; one to stay here, one to look for water, and one to look for food."

"OK. That sounds good to me. How will we pick the groups?" Avery glanced at Erin who kept her eyes glued to Luca. Erin should be the one doling out the instructions. What was wrong with her?

Luca cleared his throat. "I kind of already did."

"Great. Then let's get to it. Who do we tell first?"

He watched her for another second. Did he expect her to argue? Finally, he nodded. "Right. Benny can stay here with Erin, that blonde girl—"

"June?"

"Yeah, June, and the other two girls who aren't from our group." He stopped and pointed to a huddle of boys and girls. Most of them were from Avery's own church group, including Tasha, Mallory, and Brittany—otherwise known as the best friends—and David. He was more of a quiet guy, but he seemed nice enough. "They can look for food and the rest of us can search for water," Luca said.

The rest of us. Meaning she would be tromping around the jungle with Luca.

He did this on purpose. She could call him out on it—which she definitely wouldn't—or she could act like a grown up, and just do it. After all, she could ignore him just as well in person as she'd been doing for the last three months by avoiding him.

She pushed her shoulders back and raised her chin. "Fine. Let's tell them."

Luca led the way and did all the talking. Everyone listened to him like he was the adult instead of Erin. The only person who had a problem with it was Benny. Of course.

"I can look for food and water too," he said.

"Benny, you wouldn't even go into the jungle to use the bathroom by yourself," Luca said.

Ew.

Benny turned four shades of red and frowned. "I did go, thank you very much. Why do I have to stay behind?"

Luca looked to the sky and growled. "Fine. Do you want to go? You can help look for food."

"Why does he have to come in our group?" Bradley asked. He was the captain of the football team back home, and he always acted like the leader of everything. Funny how he hadn't done much to help out here.

Avery rolled her eyes and turned away from him. "This isn't dodge ball at summer youth camp. We need food and water. Benny can come with us."

Luca shot her a look. "Fine. Let's just go."

Avery hurried after Luca as he stormed toward the jungle. She glanced back at Benny who followed them with a mix of relief and irritation on his face. Poor kid. He didn't know he was totally annoying.

Well, maybe he did know, but he couldn't always help it.

The others followed behind them, but when they reached the tree line, everyone paused.

"What do you think's in there?" Avery asked.

Luca scanned the area, his eyes narrowed.

"I haven't seen any animals," Avery said. Of course, that didn't mean they weren't there, but talking about it wouldn't help.

Luca frowned and looked deeper. "I haven't seen any animals either."

Something in the way he said *animals* made Avery pause. She looked into the jungle and gulped.

Luca turned to Benny. "Did you see anything while you were in there this morning?"

Benny turned red again, but he shook his head.

"OK. Let's go." He took the first step in, and Avery was right behind him. She had to show everyone that she believed in him—that he was right. Boy, she hoped he was wrong about the rescue group, though. Staying here much longer wasn't on her agenda. Sure, she wanted to prove herself, but not in a place full of who-knew-what.

The jungle leaves swished and crunched around

them as they marched through the foliage. The group forged ahead, carving a path with nothing but their hands.

"Watch out," Luca said, ducking under a thick vine.

Avery moved just in time, but she shuddered. What if it was like the Jungle Book, and one of these swinging vines was really a giant snake?

"You OK?" Luca asked.

"Yep." She didn't look at him, but it was hard. In fact, the last three months had been hard. If only he would just forget about her. Or maybe learn to control his stubborn temper.

"How do we even know there's water out here?" Benny asked. "We're in the middle of the desert."

"Have you ever seen trees grow without water?" Luca asked.

"No, but what if it's like some underground spring or something?"

Luca shrugged. "We have to try."

The hot jungle air seemed to cling to their every step. Avery took off her sweater and tied it around her waist. "It's hot in here."

"We're in the jungle," Luca said with a grin.

Her face burned—again—and she looked away. The ground went on forever, and everything was green. She could barely see ten feet in front of her. How was she going to spot water?

They hiked farther inside, and Avery struggled for fresh air. It was like a sauna, steamy and damp. Her vision blurred and she wiped her hands over her face, but her hands were sweaty and it made everything worse.

For the first time she realized she hadn't had

anything to drink since she got off the plane yesterday. Her throat was swollen and dry, and her head had begun to spin. No wonder it was so hard to see. To think. Avery took a deep breath and closed her eyes for a moment.

She could use her ears instead. She needed to listen for the babbling sound of water running in a creek or river.

She focused on her senses, listening for birds or water—or snakes. Then she opened her eyes and scanned as far ahead as she could. Something caught her eye and she squinted. Just like back in the desert when she thought the air was moving, something pale and green appeared on a tree branch. Was that what she thought it was?

"Luca, look!" She pointed to their left where small, green fruit grew on a tree. "Are those pears?"

He stopped and scanned the trees then he changed directions. "Yeah, I think they are." He plucked one off the branch and rubbed it on his shirt before biting into it.

Avery's stomach went crazy in protest. She grabbed one, too, and bit in.

"Shouldn't you wait to see if I, like, die or something?" Luca asked.

"They're pears. They have to be OK," she said around another bite.

"Miss supper?"

"And breakfast."

He grinned and she grinned back.

"You can break up the love fest," Benny griped. He pushed past them and grabbed a pear. "Besides, I thought you guys were over."

Avery's face burned and she backed away. She

looked around, trying to act like his words hadn't bothered her. And she refused to look at Luca.

"There has to be water around here," she said. "You can't grow a fruit tree without water."

The others grabbed pears too, and then they continued their search. Her head felt much clearer after eating something, especially something juicy, and her vision had cleared. She kept her eyes and ears open but still didn't see anything. This was useless. They might as well go back to camp.

Sweat dripped down her forehead and her back. She had a tank top in her luggage on the van, which she would be grabbing as soon as they returned.

"This is bogus," Benny said. "I'm going back."

"You can't go back alone," Luca said.

"You didn't want me to come anyway. And I'm hot."

"So you're going to cool off by sitting in the sandy desert?"

Luca made a good point, even though Avery wanted to go with Benny.

Benny rolled his eyes and turned around anyway. He stomped several feet away, dodging branches, except he was going in the wrong direction. Avery was about to call out to him when he screamed. He lost his footing, his arms flailing in the air like something in a cartoon. His legs finally gave out, and he landed with a thud on the ground and disappeared from view.

Weak cries came from somewhere below them.

"Benny!" Avery said, rushing forward.

Luca grabbed her arm, but she jerked away. "We have to help him!"

"We will," he said. "But we don't know what made him fall. Let's walk a little more slowly."

She huffed, but he did have a point. She slowed down, stepping lightly every inch of the way. "Benny, can you hear us?"

"Guys, look!" Benny's voice floated back up to them.

They got closer and Avery realized it was a ledge. He'd slipped down an embankment—a muddy one.

Benny sat at the bottom, grinning from ear to ear, in the middle of a rushing creek bed.

"Water! Benny, you found it!" Avery laughed. This must have been how Daddy felt every time he found something new on one of his digs. No wonder he was always off looking for another adventure.

Even Luca didn't stop his smile. He braced himself on an exposed tree root and slid down the slope on his feet. Avery grabbed a loose vine and made her way down after him, and the others quickly followed.

The water was clean and clear, bubbling along the large creek bed. It was perfect, and suddenly her mouth felt the same as when she had to take antibiotics for strep throat—dry and bitter. She leaned down and scooped up a handful. It was cold and wet, and it tasted like heaven.

"You're tossing caution to the wind today, aren't you?" Luca asked.

She paused, not sure if he was talking about more than just the pears and water. She shrugged and smiled. "Maybe I am." After the water, her head cleared completely. She didn't even feel sweaty and hot.

They helped Benny up and quickly made a plan to mark the path so they could come back with containers, but it turned out that they didn't need the plan. The path back to the van was easy to follow—it looked like elephants had trampled through the jungle.

Avery smiled as she glanced around at their group. It wasn't a bad effort for a bunch of kids who had never been in the jungle before.

Her gaze landed on Luca and she paused to amend her thought. They may not have been in the jungle before, but Luca had spent a lot of time in the woods. Maybe some of the others had, as well.

June raced to meet them at the tree line, and Avery grinned, waving. As June got closer, though, Avery paused. Something was wrong. Tears raced down June's cheeks and panic was written all over her face.

"What happened?" Avery asked.

"The other girls—the ones who stayed behind—they're gone."

Luca frowned and stepped forward. "What do you mean?"

"They said they had to go to the bathroom, but they never came out."

Avery glanced past June and saw Erin. The youth leader's wife frowned toward the sand and paced back and forth at the driver's side of the van.

The driver stood at the driver's side door, frowning and gazing toward the jungle.

"What do we do?" Avery asked, turning to Luca.

He watched Erin for another few moments before he sighed and pulled himself up straighter. "Simple. We find them."

4

Luca

Luca turned his back on the group, searching the jungle they'd just come from. How could two girls disappear? They had to have known the way out, and surely, they'd only gone a few trees deep. The jungle was thick, but the sun coming in from one side was obvious.

The flash of white from that morning bugged him. It might have been his imagination, but what if it wasn't?

"Luca, wait." Avery grabbed his arm and he tried to ignore the way his skin buzzed when she touched him. The jungle was no place for thoughts like that.

"We have to find them," he said. "The faster we get in there, the better our chances."

"Shouldn't we wait for the food group to get back?" she said. "We need a more solid plan; some guidelines to follow so no one else gets lost."

"You stay behind and explain to them that no one should go into the jungle except in groups. I'll be back."

Her eyes flashed. "What? You can't go in there alone. You have to follow the same set of rules as everybody else so that you don't get lost, too."

He gritted his teeth and looked back at the trees. The longer he waited to go after them, the further in they could wander. He wasn't losing anyone or leaving them behind, and he wasn't worried about getting lost himself. Dad taught him to track, even if he hadn't done any other good for Luca.

But when Luca looked back at Avery, his decision was made for him. She stared up at him with her sparkling blue eyes, and he knew he wouldn't go against her. "Come on," he said. "We need to come up with a plan."

Everyone followed him to Erin and the driver. Erin still stalked next to the side of the van, staring a hole through the sandy ground.

"We need to go in after them," he said.

Erin looked up for a second but then went back to pacing. She took a swig from one of the water bottles she'd brought from home. "You're right. Why haven't they come yet?"

"They could be lost," Avery piped up.

"No." Erin stopped moving and frowned in their direction. "I mean the other van. It's been hours since the sun came up. Why aren't they here by now?"

"They'll be here," Luca said. "And that's why we need to find the other girls. What are their names?"

"Gabby and Katelyn," June said. "They came from my church."

"Good. You can help us go in and look for them. Benny, you and the others will stay with Erin. You can wait for the other group, and tell everyone to stay put until we get back."

"What about me?" Avery asked.

"Do you want to come?" She would say yes. There was nothing Luca wanted more, but at the same time, he needed to focus on finding the other girls and not worrying about Avery's safety.

"Of course," she said.

"Fine. From now on, no one goes into the jungle except in groups of three or more. And no one goes exploring. You go in for essentials only."

"What about the water?" Benny asked. "We need water."

This would be so much easier if Erin would help make some decisions. "We'll take a few containers with us and try to bring water back."

The others nodded and Luca readied to head back in.

Avery jogged to the van and grabbed a stack of empty water bottles and a backpack. She shoved the bottles inside the pack and started to put it on her back, but Luca stopped her.

"I'll take them. Ready?"

"I am," June said. It was the first time she didn't look like she was falling apart. She had dug up a rubber band from somewhere and tied her hair back from her face, and her eyes blazed with determination.

Luca looked to Erin. "We'll be back."

She nodded and went back to pacing.

Luca turned to June. "Do you know where they went in at?"

June pointed toward a dip in the trees. "Over there."

Finally, someone had some useful information. He stepped toward the trees, and Avery and June followed him. Hot air swarmed him as soon as he was under the leafy canopy. The moisture took his breath away. He pushed out the thought of water for now and tried to focus on the missing girls. "We need to find their trail. We should be able to tell which direction they walked in. The brush will be pushed aside."

Avery began searching through the leaves, looking toward the ground. Her dark hair hung over both shoulders, framing her face.

It took a second to realize he was staring at her. He forced himself to look away. "June, can you look over there?"

She nodded. "Of course. What do I look for?"

"Broken branches, squished leaves, pushed down grass; it's no different from tracking deer."

"Right." She turned and started looking, but she was looking everywhere except toward the ground.

They would never find anyone at this rate.

He walked straight ahead, searching for any sign that someone had passed this way. So far, he hadn't seen anything that looked disturbed. Every tree was perfect. Every vine hung low and untouched.

They looked for what felt like hours.

Maybe June was wrong about where they'd come in at.

Luca knelt close to the ground and began inspecting the dirt when Avery called to him.

"Over here! There are several broken branches."

He pushed through the brush and stood beside her. A clear path had been stomped into the jungle. It was about time. "Good. This is the way they walked."

The path moved in a straight line for several paces, but after a while, it started to turn to the right. He veered along with it.

"That's the path we took to the creek." Avery pointed further to the right, and their earlier path stood out like a parade route. "Maybe they found our path and followed it back."

Luca studied the ground. It had clearly been walked on, making a bridge between the two paths.

"But did they go toward the creek or back toward the camp?"

And why hadn't they just stayed put like he'd told them to do? They were supposed to be waiting for the rescue van.

"We can check the creek first," Avery said. She stepped toward him, talking softly, her eyes understanding. She knew this was frustrating him, and she was trying to keep him calm like she always had.

He took a deep breath. "OK. We'll fill up the water bottles, and then we'll head back to camp. Maybe they'll be there."

It didn't take long to retrace their steps to the water. The gurgling creek was music to his ears. He filled up a bottle and downed it in one long drink.

Avery grabbed the bottle from his hands and did the same. Luca watched her, almost unable to believe they were here together. He'd wanted nothing more than to talk to her—to apologize for screwing things up—for so long, and now they were together, but they still weren't talking. Not really talking.

"Can I have some?" June asked.

Luca had almost forgotten she was there. "Here. We'll each fill a few."

He handed out the bottles and they hurried to fill them. The clear water rushed over the rocks and reminded him of the woods around his house back home. He'd give just about anything to be back there again.

As everyone handed back their bottles, he tucked them inside his bag. It felt like a lead weight.

"It doesn't look like they came this way," Avery said. "There are no fresh footprints in the mud."

"Let's check the camp." The two paths had run

into each other, and the creek was deserted. Camp was the only other choice.

"I really hope they're there," June said. "I don't know what they'll do otherwise." Her voice was smooth like a musical instrument. No wonder she liked singing.

"What do you mean?" Avery asked, pushing her way back through the brush.

Luca wondered, too. Something in June's tone tipped him off.

June glanced at them and frowned. "Well, because Katelyn has asthma, and I have her inhaler. She asked me to hold it at the airport. She didn't have any pockets."

Great, so she could be having an asthma attack right now, and there'd be no help for her.

They tromped through the hot jungle, and by the time they reached the desert's edge, sweat ran down Luca's back and his shirt stuck to him, making it uncomfortable to move. He sure wished for that cold morning air, now.

He adjusted his pack and stepped out of the cover of the trees. The rest of the group stood around the van, and Erin sat on one of the boxes of supplies. At least she'd given up the death march.

"Are they back?" he called.

Benny turned around and jogged toward them. "Nope. The food group came back though. They found fruit. Not pears this time. Pomegranates. Want one?"

Luca stared at the greenish-reddish fruit. It did look good, but he couldn't eat right now. "They didn't come back?"

Benny held out the fruit another second before he got that Luca didn't want it, and he dropped his hand.

"No. We haven't seen them."

Luca looked toward the sky. The sun was already moving toward the trees. Before they knew it, they would be in the pitch-black desert again. And it would be cold.

How were the girls going to survive in the jungle, by themselves, at night?

"I'll take that," June said, pointing to Benny's hand.

Benny handed over the fruit.

"Are there more of them?" Avery asked.

Luca glanced at her. She'd practically devoured the pear from earlier, but now that he thought about it, he hadn't seen her eat anything else since they got stranded. "I have chips and stuff if you're hungry."

"Oh, I'm fine." She said it way too fast. She wouldn't even look at him.

"Avery, quit trying to be a hero and eat. Come on." He almost grabbed her hand to pull her toward the van, but he stopped himself just in time. She would freak out if he did that.

She only hesitated for a second before following after him.

"You're lucky I grabbed my backpack from the other van when I switched seats with your dad." He handed her the half eaten bag of chips.

She grabbed it and started eating as if she hadn't eaten in days.

He turned away while she ate. Watching her was way too painful. In fact, being with her at all was painful. It'd been easier at home when they'd only had to see each other at school, and even there it was easy to focus on getting his school work done, so he could get a job over the summer.

A job. It was something he still needed to do. Mom needed the money now more than ever.

"Where do you think they went?"

Her words pulled him back. "Gabby and Katelyn? They're in there somewhere. We just have to find them."

"What if some kind of animal got them?"

"We haven't seen any animals." His argument was weak and he knew it, but what else could he say?

She didn't call him out on it. "What about my dad's van? Do you think they made it to the village? What if they got lost, too?"

He could pacify her and say they were fine, but this was Avery. She would see through it in a heartbeat. "I don't know. The driver said it was possible they made it, but he didn't seem like he believed that."

"No, he didn't."

She held the bag of chips out to him.

"You didn't eat very many."

"We may need to start rationing."

Smart girl.

She frowned. "If you don't have your luggage, where did you get a sweater last night?"

He shrugged. "I'm fine without one. I'm always hot."

"Luca, it was freezing out here last night."

He was much more interested in keeping her safe and warm than he was in keeping himself heated. "I was fine."

She huffed but let it go. "Are we going back in there?"

He glanced at the trees again. It was even darker now than twenty minutes ago. "I think we'll have to wait until morning. It's probably too dark for us to see anything else tonight."

Avery looked away, her eyebrows puckered the way they always were when she worried, but she didn't say anything.

"I wonder when everyone will figure out we're not getting rescued today."

Avery turned back toward him. "I think they already did."

He frowned and followed her gaze. Three girls from their own church sat in the sand crying. Now June was the one hovering over them, trying to make them feel better.

"Do you see Erin anywhere?" he asked.

Avery glanced around. "There."

She stood at the tree line, staring into the jungle. Luca growled. "What is she doing?"

"I don't know. She's seemed really out of it since we got here. You want to talk to her? I'll go see what's wrong with the others." She headed off in the sand, her feet shifting with every step.

He watched Avery until she reached the group, then he started toward Erin. Whether Avery knew it or not, they made the perfect team. She just needed reminding.

Maybe he could show her before they made it home.

5

Avery

Brittany, Tasha, and Mallory sat sniffling in the sand. June had them mostly calmed down, but tears still dripped from their chins. Taking a deep breath, Avery stepped forward. They probably wouldn't listen to her. None of them had spoken more than a dozen words to her all school year. Still, she'd come to Iraq to help people, she might as well get to it.

"Anything I can do to help?" she asked.

"I'm hungry," Tasha said. "And hot."

Avery studied Tasha's face then looked at the others. Now that Tasha mentioned it, everyone's skin was an angry red color around their eyes, noses, and foreheads.

"Did anyone bring a hat?" Avery asked. "I brought sunscreen. Maybe we need to get them both out of the luggage."

"Why would we need those?" Bradley asked. He sat on a broken log near them, kicking at the sand. "The other van's coming, right?"

Avery swallowed hard and glanced around for Luca. He was better at explaining things and demanding a little respect. "It's best to be prepared. Besides, I don't want to end up miserable because I have third degree burns."

"Avery is right." June stepped forward and stood

next to her.

"Thanks." Avery gave her a small smile. She could use some backup, even if it was June who didn't actually know her. She turned back to Tasha and the others. "You guys found fruit, right? So we can eat that along with any of the snacks everyone has left. The other van will be here soon, whether that means tonight or first thing in the morning."

"I ate all of my snacks for breakfast," Mallory said. Her red hair was pulled into a tight ponytail on her head, and her pale skin glistened in the sun. She looked miserable.

Avery grabbed the backpack of fruit beside the girls and began passing it around. "We can share. It's important that everyone has enough while we're stranded here. We can survive without our cheese crackers and snack cakes once we get to the village, but right now we need them."

A few people grumbled, but they began passing around their snacks, and Avery wiped her forehead. This heat was enough to make anyone crazy. They'd all be tearing at each other's throats soon, if they didn't do something to stop it.

Avery turned to June and smiled wearily. "Thanks for your support."

June shrugged. "It's no big deal. I want to get home, too, but until we can go we might as well get along."

June's help meant more than Avery could say. The urge to get to know her better was strong, but before she could say anything else, Erin and Luca approached from the tree line and Luca stepped toward Avery. "I think we should move closer to the trees so we can stay in the shade and out of the direct sunlight."

It was amazing how much they were on the same page.

"You want us to go inside the jungle for protection?" Benny's voice went up an octave.

"No, not inside." Luca pointed to the thick line of shade at the edge of the trees. "We can stay at the edge and keep out of the sun."

"I think that's the best idea," Avery said quickly. "I also wanted to get sunblock and any hats from the luggage."

Luca nodded and stepped onto the van's bumper. "Come over and get your bags."

Avery was the first in line. She had something she wanted to get out besides sunblock. A few others stepped up behind her, and the line moved slowly.

"Why are we doing any of this?" Bradley stepped forward, his arms crossed.

Luca pulled someone else's luggage off the top and handed it down. He glanced at Bradley. "You want to bake in the sun?"

"I wasn't talking about that." Bradley took another step, his jaw working back and forth as he leaned dangerously close to Luca.

Avery braced herself. Luca had been taking care of himself way too long for him to take orders from Bradley.

"I meant why aren't we getting ready for the other van? Why pull down more luggage and lounge in the shade? Let's get inside that jungle and find those girls. Let's work on this van and get it running."

Luca's eyebrows shot up. He swept his arm toward the van. "Your dad's the mechanic. Work away."

Bradley rolled his eyes and stepped even closer.

Avery swallowed hard and shifted in the sand. Luca would win any fight, if it got to that point, but the last thing they needed was two guys punching each other.

A thump and a movement from the inside of the van drew everyone's attention. The driver climbed out of the driver's seat, his eyes widened in a hopeful look. He pointed at Bradley. "You know engines?"

Bradley's face froze, his eyes wide. "What?"

"Engines. Maybe I could help you. I know some."

Bradley backed away and shook his head, but it was too late. The driver moved to the front of the van and popped the hood. He waved Bradley over. "Come on. I'll help you."

Bradley's face fell, and he glanced around. No one piped up to help him. Why should they? If he could fix the van, he should be trying. In fact, this was exactly what they needed to do—start looking for a way to save themselves.

Save themselves?

Fear knotted in her stomach, and she looked across the desert. If Daddy was out there looking for her, why hadn't they been rescued? The storm had lasted only a few minutes. It couldn't have blown them that far off course.

But if Daddy wasn't out there looking for her, where was he?

She pushed the thought away, refusing to cower without Daddy's protection. He'd never been there for her anyway, only in theory. She turned back to the van.

All the boys huddled around the hood, listening as Bradley pointed and the driver questioned. Even Luca peered in.

The others in the group made their way to the

shady tree line, and June stepped to Avery's side. "Aren't we going to look for Gabby and Katelyn some more?"

Tears pooled in June's eyes and Avery hoped she wouldn't break down again. It had been a long, hot day, and Avery was still starving. She couldn't deal with anything else. "It will be completely dark soon," Avery said. "We won't be able to see anything."

"Couldn't we make a torch or something? We can't just leave them alone in the jungle all night."

Avery paused and looked toward the trees. June had a point. What would it be like to get lost in there? They hadn't seen any wild animals, but that didn't mean there weren't any. It was the jungle, after all.

"I'm sure we'll go in at first light."

June's lips quivered but she didn't argue. Instead, she shuffled to the van and climbed inside, alone.

Avery's gaze swung back to the darkening jungle and she shivered. Getting lost for hours sounded bad enough, but staying overnight would make her go crazy—something she didn't take lightly.

And speaking of crazy. Erin stood at the tree line with the others who had moved to the shade, which was everyone besides the guys bent over the open hood of the van.

The girls under the tree canopy huddled together, drinking water and glancing at Erin who paced and rubbed her temples with two fingers.

Avery grabbed what she needed from her suitcase—sunblock, a black and red cap she'd bought at Disney World a few years ago, and a sweatshirt— and stacked the suitcase next to the back bumper for Luca to put away later. She sighed as she moved to join the group.

Maybe some of them should go into the jungle. They could call out and give it one last shot at finding Gabby and Katelyn. Katelyn could be in danger without her inhaler, and what if the other van did come?

"Do you think she's OK?" Tasha asked, nodding to Erin. Tasha had apparently recovered from her breakdown earlier.

Avery looked at Erin, too, and frowned. "I don't know."

"Do you think we should say something to her?"

"I don't know if there's anything we can say."

Tasha nodded and stepped back to her clique. They had gone to church together for years, but they had different friends at school, so they never really hung out.

Avery didn't want to force her way into their circle of friends, so her gaze returned to Erin. Maybe there was something Avery could, or should, do.

Erin was the only adult in charge of their whole group. She was probably in shock and didn't know what to do.

Avery empathized with her. She stepped over to Erin. "So, what do you think of all this?"

Erin shook her head, frowning. "I can't think."

"It's good the guys are trying to fix the van, wouldn't you say?"

"I don't know." She kept pacing.

Avery frowned. What wasn't to know? "Well, I'm here if you need me to do anything. Really. I'm at your beck and call."

Erin stopped abruptly. Her gaze flew to the trees.

Avery jerked around.

Had Gabby and Katelyn found their way back?

She stood still, scanning the trees, but nothing caught her eye.

Erin slid into a sitting position in the sandy grass and leaned her head on her hands.

Avery paused. Should she say something else? But it seemed like Erin had already forgotten about her, so she turned away.

Something cracked in the jungle behind her and she looked back. Maybe that was what Erin had heard. Avery glanced at Luca, but he was busy working on the van. She looked at the sun. It moved closer and closer to the ground.

The noise sounded again.

It was almost dark, but the noise could be one of the girls needing help. She had to go. Peeking inside wouldn't hurt anything, and it would only take a moment to make sure things were OK.

Dim light surrounded her as she stepped into the jungle, and the sticky air clung to her skin. "Gabby? Katelyn?" She strained her ears, listening, but no one answered.

Her eyes moved quickly as she scanned the dense trees. The only visible path was the one they had made going in after the girls earlier that day.

She wouldn't go in farther. It wouldn't do anyone any good if she ended up lost, too. But something strange was going on here. The air seemed to shift the way it had right before the sand storm and right before she'd found the pears earlier this morning. She squinted into the dim light, stared ahead, and then blinked. When she opened her eyes, her vision had cleared. That was enough of that.

She turned to go back but froze.

It was as if the whole jungle had shifted, and the

desert was no longer a few trees away like it had been. In fact, all she could see in any direction was thick, green foliage. This wasn't happening, right? She took a few more steps, but nothing looked familiar. Spinning in a circle, she groaned.

This was just perfect. She was obviously lost. No wonder Gabby and Katelyn had gotten turned around so easily.

Standing here wasn't getting her anywhere, so she started moving. One step, two, three. After a few minutes it was clear she was going in the wrong direction. She had no light, which didn't help, and she stumbled through the huge banana leaves and overgrown brush.

She waded through a few more feet of jungle until her foot caught a vine and she tumbled head first into a thorny patch. "Ow!" She stared at her hand and the giant thorn sticking out of it. How did a thorn even grow that big?

She gritted her teeth and yanked it out. It came loose, along with a flowing river of blood. "Ow," she moaned again.

She had to get out of here. This entire trip was a nightmare. If only she could remember how to get out, or how she got lost in the first place.

Blurry images swam in front of her eyes. The green leaves, green grass, green canopy above her— everything mixed together and she pressed her eyes closed. Why couldn't she concentrate?

A twig snapped behind her. Something moved in the brush.

Avery froze. She turned slowly, keeping as still as she could. It could be a tiger, or a panther, or something much bigger and stranger.

"Don't be afraid."

The voice was soft and smooth—and definitely male. She spun toward it and spotted the speaker. He was tall, probably taller than Luca, though it was hard to tell from her place on the ground. His blond hair covered his head in short waves, and his blue eyes stood out in the sea of green jungle.

He had told her to not be afraid, but why would anyone start with that unless they were going to hurt her?

She scrambled to her feet and backed away. "Who are you?"

The guy paused. His shoulders were broader than a football player's, and he held out his large hands in a defensive gesture. "My name is Rae. I've been waiting for you. I can help you get back to your group."

She shook her head. Somewhere along the line she had started shaking. "Waiting for me? Where did you come from? How did you know I was with a group?"

"I live here," he said. "I know everything that goes on."

He lived here? That changed a few things. She cautiously stepped forward, eager for more information but afraid to get too close. "Where are we? Can you tell us how to get out of here?"

The sooner they got out of this jungle the better. Getting to the village and helping people was the whole point, but after everything they'd been through Avery just wanted to go home. Maybe she wasn't meant to start a new life after all.

Again he paused.

He.

Rae.

What did he need to think about? He lived here,

and her group didn't. He knew how to get out, they didn't. He could tell them how, they could leave, end of story.

"I'll see what I can do."

Relief washed over her, and she even forgot about the sweat and grime covering her skin. "Thank you. I need to take you to my group. We're trying to get our van fixed, and you can tell the driver which way to go."

He seemed to consider her words, something that must be a habit of his. "I can't come right now."

The boy—Rae—made no sense. "But you said you would help us." Her head began to swim again.

"I will," he said quickly. It was the first time he'd spoken without thinking first.

"Then we need you."

"You're lost, aren't you? I can help you get back, for now. Your group is that way. If you follow the path you will find them." He pointed to the area behind her.

She turned and recognized the path she'd made earlier in the day with Luca.

Besides the fact that the path hadn't been there a few minutes ago, something weird was happening here. "When will I see you again, Rae? You said you would help us."

"I don't know. It will be soon."

She swallowed hard. "Thank you for your help." She turned to go, but paused. "Wait, there are others who are lost. We had two girls wander off alone. Have you seen anyone else?"

This time he paused for a little too long.

Avery frowned. She was about to hurry away when he spoke. "I pointed them in the right direction. They'll be back soon."

Avery's frown deepened, but staying with this guy another minute was the least appealing thing ever. She hurried back, trekking in the direction he'd pointed her, but something about his behavior didn't make sense.

The further she stomped through the brush the more her mind worked and the faster she moved. This place was doing weird things to her. Hadn't she been unable to think just a few hours before? Unable to focus just a few *moments* before?

Erin had slipped into some unhappy place, and two girls had gone missing just by going to the edge of the jungle.

Avery ground her teeth and examined herself hard. Was that guy even real? Was she hallucinating?

She couldn't deny it might be a possibility. And she definitely couldn't tell anyone else about Rae.

Maybe that was what was wrong with Erin. The youth leader's wife had never been anything but on top of things, so her behavior since getting stranded was definitely out of character.

Avery picked out the path they'd worn earlier that day and she glanced back. The mystery guy was nowhere in sight, which didn't do anything to dispel her theory. Luca would have questions when she got back—he'd probably be furious with her—but she wasn't sure which facts she would tell him.

All she knew was that she needed out of this jungle, and fast.

She turned back to the path and ran.

6

Luca

"My name is Samuel," the driver said. "You may call me Sam."

He definitely didn't look like a Sam, but Luca kept that to himself.

"There." Bradley pointed toward a hose that had come loose, and Sam pulled it off. Sand poured out of it.

"Dude, how does that even happen?" Bradley took the hose and turned it over in his hands.

Sam frowned. "I do not know."

"Can we fix it?" That was the most important question, and Luca knew almost nothing about mechanics.

"Maybe, if we had any tools. But I don't see a spare tool box lying around the desert."

"Tools?" Sam stumbled through the sand and yanked open the driver's side door.

Someone gasped from inside, and Luca frowned. He peeked through the side window.

June sat inside, alone and crying.

What was it now? It didn't matter, he couldn't leave her there. He stepped to the side door and opened it just as Sam found a small toolbox stashed under the driver's seat. Pent-up heat hit Luca in the face. "How are you sitting in here? It's like an oven."

June wiped the tears off her face and shrugged. "I wanted to be alone."

Where was Avery when he needed her? Dealing with a crying stranger wasn't his thing, especially a *girl* stranger. "I think it's best if you be alone with everyone else. You'll get sick if you stay in here much longer."

She shook her head, keeping her face down. "I don't care. I think we should be looking for Gabby and Katelyn. They're alone out there."

Was she trying to stage some sort of protest?

Luca took her seriously as he hauled himself inside the van. "It's too dark right now. We'd end up lost."

She stared at some point behind him, not budging from the seat.

Luca kept his growl to himself. She needed more convincing? "We'll go first thing tomorrow."

Her eyes finally met his. "As soon as we wake up?"

"You have my word."

She sighed. "OK. Thanks."

He nodded then pointed toward the door. "You're welcome. Now will you come out and join everyone else in the shade?"

She sniffled. "I guess so. It is really hot in here."

"You think?"

June smiled at him before moving toward the others in the shade. He watched her go then scanned the tree line for any movement that might tell him where those girls had gone. Nothing caught his attention.

A small stack of luggage sat at the back bumper so he moved to re-pile it on the roof. It wasn't like they needed him under the hood, anyway.

The last suitcase was Avery's, and after he hefted it on top and tied everything down, he scanned the area for her. June had moved to sit with the other girls, and Erin paced in the sand with her head bowed. Most of the guys hovered around the van. Luca frowned and looked again.

Erin paced. June sat with Tasha, Mallory, and Brittany. Benny ranted behind the girls' backs—it looked like he was ranting to them, but they weren't listening.

No Avery.

He spun around but she wasn't at the van.

She wouldn't have gone into the jungle on her own. She was not that stupid.

"Have you seen Avery?" he asked.

The guys bent under the hood glanced up at him, but it was pretty obvious they hadn't been watching out for his ex-girlfriend.

He groaned and stomped through the sand to the tree line. His feet shifted with every step, making the short trip take twice as long. He probably looked like a big idiot.

"Where's Avery?" he asked June when he'd finally reached her.

June frowned. Her tears were gone, and she was getting comfortable with the others. "I haven't seen her since I got in the van."

Luca glanced around. Something in the pit of his stomach twisted, and he swallowed hard. He didn't like this. "I can't find her."

June gasped. "You don't think she went in there alone, do you? I asked her why we weren't going in again. I could tell she thought about it, but she said no.

That's when I got in the van."

Luca closed his eyes and held in his frustration. Avery, alone in the jungle.

The memory of the white flash from earlier that morning was all he could think about. What was that thing? And was it dangerous? "Do you still want to go in there?"

June bit her lip and glanced around. "The sun is almost down."

"I'm going to look for her, even if I have to go alone. I just thought you might want to come along."

Benny scrambled over, almost falling flat on his face as his feet slid in the sand. "I'm coming too!"

"You better not get in my way."

"I won't!"

"Fine. Are you coming?" He turned back to June.

She stood and glanced at the other girls. They didn't move. "Yeah. I'm coming."

He stared hard at Tasha, Mallory, and Brittany. "Go tell the other guys what's going on. And no one else goes in until we get back. Do you understand?"

They nodded.

Luca sighed and turned toward the jungle. This was probably as dumb as Avery having gone in. "Does anyone know who brought the matches? We should make a torch or something."

"I have a flashlight in my bag," Mallory said.

"Can I borrow it?"

She nodded, and they retrieved it.

Making his way back to June and Benny, he formed a plan. They would follow the path they had made to the creek. If Avery had gotten lost, she was smart enough to look for a path. Except she wouldn't be able to see in the dark.

"Ready?" he asked.

June and Benny nodded, and he maneuvered around them to take the lead. Stepping into the jungle at night was like walking into a closet and closing the door. He shined the flashlight in front of them, but it didn't do much to light their way.

"I think we each need one of those," Benny said, nodding to the light.

"Yeah, I think so too. Anyone know who brought the matches?"

"I think it was that Bradley boy," June said.

Luca would remember that.

They kept walking, but the flashlight beam didn't do much in the way of illuminating the path enough to tell if anyone had passed this way.

"Avery?" Luca called. "Can you hear me?"

Benny and June began calling out, as well. They paused every few moments, but Avery never answered.

A movement to the left caught Luca's attention and he pivoted around. He shined the flashlight into the mass of trees. The swishing sound continued, but he couldn't see anything.

"I—I think it's coming from the ground," June said. Her voice quivered.

Luca swallowed and slowly moved the light toward the tangly, grassy, jungle floor. The tall grass barely wavered, but it was definitely moving.

"What do you think it is?" June whispered. Her voice was high pitched, which meant one thing. She was on the verge of tears. Again.

They waited, watching.

Luca's heart thudded harder in his chest. It beat so loud he was sure June and Benny could hear it. He straightened his shoulders, determined to be a man.

A long, shiny, black creature slid out of the grass and straight for them.

June's scream bounced off the jungle canopy and pierced his ears a few dozen times.

Pain shot up his arm, and he realized she was clawing at his skin in her terror.

The snake stopped and coiled into a springy defensive position. It hissed and lunged.

Luca didn't care that it was several feet away. He shoved June and yelled, "Run!"

June took off without another thought, and Benny was right behind her. Luca brought up the rear. They ran as fast as they could through the brush, and after a few minutes he began worrying they weren't even on the path anymore. The snake had probably given up, but he wasn't about to slow down to find out.

"Are you sure you're going the right direction?" he asked. His lungs were beginning to burn.

"I think so," June panted.

A dim light filtered through the trees ahead. They were almost at the tree line. Almost back to the desert.

Umph.

Luca smacked into something solid and bowled right over it. He hit the ground, landing on top of whatever he'd run into. Terror pulsed through him, and he scrambled to his feet in case he'd upset some other jungle creature.

A whimper came from the ground, and he quickly shined his flashlight on it.

"Avery!"

Avery lay on the ground, her arm protecting her eyes from the beam of light. She moaned. "Luca?"

He dropped to his knees. "I'm so sorry, Avery.

Where did you come from?"

She moved slowly, like he'd broken every bone in her body.

He helped her sit up. "Are you OK?"

She swallowed and nodded. "I think so." Then she gave him a wry look. "You ever consider playing football?"

He chuckled and relief hit him hard. "You're OK. I was so worried about you. We came as soon as I realized you were gone."

She gently pulled away from him, and he realized he'd grabbed her shoulders and pulled her into a hug.

"Help me stand up?"

He held out his hand and pulled her into a standing position. "Why did you go in there?"

She paused, and he could see the wheels turning in her head. What did she have to tell him?

"Let's get out of here first, then I'll tell you all about it."

He nodded and waved the flashlight beam. "Lead the way."

June stepped in front of Benny and put her arm around Avery's waist. "I'm glad you're OK. I'm sorry I fell apart on you like that."

Avery shook her head. "It's OK. I wanted to find Gabby and Katelyn, too."

"Did you find them?"

Avery looked at June and shook her head again.

They reached the tree line and Luca flicked off the flashlight.

Some of the others had fallen asleep, but almost everyone waited for their return.

Erin stood near the tree line, her shoulders tensed and her eyebrows pulled together. When they stepped out and everyone saw Avery, Erin let out a pent up breath and put her face in her hands. "Thank God!" she said.

A few of the others rushed forward and hugged Avery. She smiled at them and let them touch her. They made a fuss over the cut on her cheek, which he hadn't even noticed. It felt good to see they were acknowledging her, instead of acting like she didn't exist. Avery never deserved the way the others had treated her.

Luca waited until the fuss died down, but he couldn't wait any longer. As soon as he could, he pulled her aside. "So, what happened in there?"

7

Avery

Avery licked her lips and glanced around. Everyone was listening, even though Luca had pulled her to the side. They would hear if she admitted what she'd seen—what she thought she'd seen. She threw a look behind her, back to the jungle. No one lived in there. How could they? No one could live in a funky oasis in the middle of the Iraqi desert.

"I only went in a few feet. I could see the light from the desert behind me at all times, but then I got dizzy. I closed my eyes until the dizziness passed, but when I opened my eyes, the light was gone. I was somewhere deeper in the jungle, and I don't know how I got there."

Luca took in every word she said. He watched her closely; he was definitely taking her seriously.

A tiny flicker of relief sparked through her—he didn't think she was crazy.

"That tells us how easy it is to get lost without realizing it. No wonder Gabby and Katelyn got turned around." He turned to the others, who had all heard. "No one goes into the jungle without someone keeping watch, and only go in with a group. No exceptions."

They nodded, a few wrapping their arms around their stomachs and stepping closer together. The anxiety in the air was thick enough to nearly choke her.

"Let's get some sleep," Luca said. "We'll find Gabby and Katelyn first thing tomorrow, and the other van will either come, or we'll get out of here in our own van."

Bradley stepped forward. "We made a lot of progress today."

Luca nodded and the others took it as their cue to move.

"Hey," Luca said. "Let me take those things."

Avery looked down and realized she still carried the sweatshirt, hat, and sunblock. She shook her head and handed him the sweatshirt. "Here, I got it out for you."

"I am not taking your sweatshirt."

"It's yours. You left it at my house a long time ago." She looked away hoping he wouldn't ask why she'd brought it on this trip.

He didn't, only took it wordlessly as they began walking to the van together.

Avery clasped her hands and let her mind wander back to the jungle, and her memory of Rae's face. Was he real? She didn't like this at all. How could she help anyone when she couldn't trust her own mind?

She followed the others to the van and climbed into her seat. She unwrapped her sweater from her waist, slipped her arms inside, and sat back. Her eyes slid closed and she sighed.

Aches throbbed from the top of her head to the tips of her toes, and her hands burned from where she'd fallen. Even her cheek stung. When her stomach rumbled she didn't think she'd ever been so hungry. No wonder she was seeing things.

Things would look better in the morning, and hopefully Daddy would be here soon.

She tried to stay awake, to keep one eye peeled for Gabby and Katelyn to come stumbling out of the jungle, but her eyes drooped, and she fell asleep quickly.

When she awoke the next morning, the sun had only just begun to rise on the horizon. She sat up and looked out the window, but there was no Katelyn and Gabby, and no rescue van. Everyone else still slept. Taking a deep breath, she began the climb over the others.

Tasha stirred but didn't wake up, and the others didn't notice her movement.

Avery slipped outside and pulled her sweater tight. The sun wouldn't be fully up for another hour or two, and that meant cold air. She stared at the jungle in the dim sunlight. It looked beautiful, even if it was scarier than anything she'd ever experienced.

Still, with the new day came new hope. Something would happen today—they would get the van running or they would be rescued. They could get away from this blazing prison and do what they came to do—build a school.

Her stomach growled and she hugged herself tighter. She'd be ready to go find food as soon as a few more people woke up.

Benny was the first person out of the van.

"Good morning," she said.

He waved, wiping at his hair which stood on end. "I'm going to the trees. I'll be right back." His cheeks turned a fiery red.

She nodded, quickly looking away. No reason to make him any more embarrassed than he already was. Bradley climbed out, followed by the van driver, June, and the others.

"Hey," June said. She stretched her arms and massaged her neck. "I'm ready to sleep in a place where we can stretch out."

Avery smiled and nodded, but more than a bed, she wanted food. "Was Luca awake yet?"

June frowned and glanced at the van. "I couldn't tell."

"I'm starving." It was OK to admit that now, since June had no more food to offer.

"Me too. We'll get some fruit once we're inside."

The thought of food sent Avery's stomach into a frenzied growl, and June laughed. "My grandma used to say a growling stomach was an easy-to-please stomach."

Avery opened her mouth to disagree, but she had to snap it closed. "I guess I do eat just about anything."

June grinned, and Avery couldn't stop the warmth spreading through her. How long had it been since she'd had an actual girlfriend? A long time.

Hanging onto June, even when they went home— if they went home—would be at the top of her priority list.

Everyone moved through the camp like they'd been there forever, each of them with their own duties. Bradley and the driver popped the hood and started their work immediately, and Mallory stepped in front of Avery, looking strong and sure. Her moment of complaining yesterday must have been a tiny crack in her normally solid façade. "We're ready to go get food and water. Can we go ahead and make a run into the jungle?"

Avery shifted in the sand, surprised anyone was asking for her permission.

She glanced at Tasha, Brittany, and David. There

were enough of them, and they weren't going in without telling someone. "Sure. I think that'd be fine."

"Great. We'll follow the same path we took yesterday, and we'll be back with fruit. Are you guys going to get the water?"

"We'll go once Luca is up."

Mallory nodded and hurried back to her group. They headed into the jungle, and Avery hoped Luca would wake up soon. She really was starving.

A few minutes later, the van door clicked shut. Luca emerged from the van. He wore the sweatshirt she'd given him last night, and she smiled. "Sleep well?"

"Nope, not even close."

She laughed. "Too bad. Anyway, Tasha's group went in for fruit, and I said we'd get the water. What's the plan?"

He stretched and scratched his head. "Are you sure you want to go back in there?"

Avery opened her mouth to promise him she was, but she realized he was talking to June. Avery turned to June, her eyebrows raised. "What happened?"

June shuddered. "I had nightmares about that thing all night."

"What?" Avery asked again. And why did it bother her that Luca was talking to June? She pushed the thought away, not willing to go down that path so early in the morning.

"A snake," June said. "It came at us when we were looking for you."

Luca nodded. "It's why we were running when I knocked you down."

Snakes? Avery shuddered along with June. "There really could be anything in there." She regretted saying it right away. Could there be people inside? People who lived in the jungle and could help them find their way home?

"Give me a few minutes, and we'll get going, OK?" Luca said.

Avery nodded and watched him move toward the trees. She scooted to the raised hood of the van and peered inside. "How's it going?"

"Good." Bradley's voice didn't hold the hissing frustration it had yesterday. Now his eyes were opened wide and full of excitement. "Hey, can you guys bring me back water? I need it to clean off this sand."

"Hold on, I think we have some." She reached inside the van and pulled a half empty bottle from the pack in Luca's seat. "Here, use this. We'll bring back more for drinking."

Bradley's smile grew. "Excellent."

He poured the water over the engine hoses as she turned to study the others. Everyone was hungry and thirsty, and none of them had any food. They needed to hurry.

Luca came back a few minutes later and Avery stepped forward.

June and Benny gathered around.

"I think we should bring back water before we start our search," Avery said. "Everyone needs something to drink."

Luca nodded. "That sounds great." He turned to Benny. "You sure you want to come along?"

Benny frowned. "I think I've proved myself by now."

Poor Benny. He'd never be able to prove himself.

"Come on," Avery said. "Let's get moving. Hopefully they'll get the van running soon."

Luca nodded and they began their hike into the jungle. "I don't even know where to start looking for the girls," he admitted.

"I've been thinking about it," Avery said as they moved toward the creek. "We saw their path. We need to follow it and look for any part where they might have strayed from it. A place we might not have noticed yesterday."

Luca watched her as she talked, not looking away or blinking, and heat burned her neck.

Finally, he spoke. "Yeah, that sounds like a good idea."

It took a while to reach the creek, and they took time filling each bottle. Avery drank two bottles of water, then she found the tree with the pears a few feet over. She picked one and began eating when Benny, Luca, and June joined her.

"We're going to need more to eat than fruit if we're here much longer," Luca said. He took a bite.

Avery didn't like the thought of being there much longer, but she kept it to herself.

"There's that box of food in the back of the van." The idea came from Benny, which surprised Avery. By the look on Luca's face it had surprised him, too. Benny chomped on his pear, fruit juice running down his chin. He wiped it with the back of his hand.

"I can't believe I'm saying this, but it's not a bad idea," Luca said. "Hopefully we won't have to break into it."

They stuffed a few pears in with the water and quickly headed back to the desert. As they walked, Avery kept an eye out for the path she'd taken last night. The spot where Luca tackled her was obvious—the grass and brush were all smashed to the ground.

She looked into the distance, to the place where she would have seen Rae, and she swallowed. Would he reappear? Would he speak to her?

Would anyone else be able to see him?

They reached the sand and delivered the water. The others had returned with a bundle of fruit, but Avery didn't plan to stick around to eat it.

Two girls were missing in the jungle, and it was time to find them.

8

Luca

Luca was never so happy to unload a backpack. Carrying a couple gallons of water a mile in the hot jungle was the opposite of his favorite workout. He hefted the pack onto the ledge of the van's hood. "Here's enough water for everyone for the day. We'll be back in a few hours."

Bradley nodded, his head bent toward the engine.

"We are making great progress," Sam said.

"Good." Luca nodded, grabbed a few bottles of water for their group, then it was time to head back in. He turned to Avery and the others. "Remember, we're looking for paths we may have missed yesterday." He didn't know why he hadn't thought of it sooner. It just proved more that he and Avery made a great team. He needed her.

She needed him, too. Now if he could convince her of that.

Avery, June, and Benny nodded at his instructions to keep their eyes peeled, and they started back into the inferno. They hiked straight for the fork where their two paths met. Any deviation from the path would happen there. As they walked, Luca stumbled. A large stick lay in the path. It was as tall as he was, and as thick as a broom handle. It might be useful later, so he grabbed it.

He tried to keep an eye out for landmarks, to remind him where they were at any given point. As he passed a large bush, something rattled in the leaves. Luca slowed down and glanced around. No one seemed to notice the movement, so he kept it to himself as he raised the large stick and pushed the branches apart.

Something skittered out. It was small, no bigger than a squirrel, and it stopped a few feet from him to let him have it.

Avery giggled at the screeches as the baby monkey ran away.

Luca let out a rush of air, trying to keep his fear from showing. He'd been sure it was another snake.

"That little guy wasn't very happy with you!" Avery said.

He attempted a smile. "No, I guess not."

Just then, the leaves rattled again. At first, it was a small shake, but then the entire bush rocked back and forth.

"What is that?" Panic filled June's voice.

Avery and Benny backed away, and Luca swallowed hard. Raising the stick toward the leaves, he took a deep breath and pushed the branches aside for a second time.

Nothing.

He let out another rushing breath. It was nothing. They were fine.

He began to turn when a high-pitched screech erupted from the bush. A much bigger monkey burst out from the middle of the leaves. It was a larger version of the baby monkey from earlier. It had to be the mother, and she wasn't happy.

The monkey lunged at Luca.

Luca swung the stick, connecting with the monkey's leg. The monkey cried out but didn't give up. It swung from a vine, doubling back and latching onto Luca's shoulders. It used its furry little hands to go for Luca's face.

Panic set in and Luca grasped at the monkey's arms. "Get it off me!" The last thing he needed was rabies, let alone some other strange jungle disease.

Avery grabbed his stick and beat at the monkey. Most of the swings landed on his shoulders instead of the monkey, but the monkey's grasp had loosened so Luca wasn't complaining.

He spun in circles, pulling at the monkey's arms, but his hands were slick with sweat and he couldn't get a good grip.

"Over here!" June called.

Luca turned toward the sound of her voice and—

BAM!

Lights danced in front of his eyes, then there was nothing.

Splitting pain inched its way across Luca's forehead when he woke up. The pain started on the left side of his temple and worked toward the right temple in a slow, steady line. He peeled one eye open, then the other. "What happened?"

Avery knelt over him. Her forehead wrinkled with worry and she touched a spot on his forehead.

Pain shot through his brain.

He winced.

"Sorry!" she said.

He swallowed down the sickness rising up his throat. There wasn't enough in his stomach already. He sure didn't want to throw up what little he had.

Slowly, gingerly, he pushed himself to a sitting

position. Stars flashed in front of his eyes and he blinked them away. At least the monkey was gone. When he was sure he wasn't going to throw up or pass out, he spoke. "What happened?"

Avery glanced at June and Benny then looked back to him. Her cheeks glowed red, but Luca couldn't tell if it was from the heat or embarrassment.

"I was swinging for the monkey just as you turned toward June. I knocked you in the forehead by mistake." She bit her lip, never taking her eyes off him.

He tried to think of something to say—anything—but his head hurt too bad to think.

"I'm sorry." Her words came out in a whisper.

"I'm sorry, too," June said. "I shouldn't have called to you like that. I just thought there was a window of getting away..." her sentence trailed off.

"Hey, at least the monkey's gone. You think you can walk?" Benny watched them all, shifting from foot to foot.

"Anxious about something, Benny?" Luca bit out. Let *him* get knocked in the head with a giant stick and see how fast he recovered.

"I don't want to stick around for round two with the crazed monkey, OK?" Sweat dripped from Benny's dark hair and down his forehead.

He had a point.

"Fine. Give me a minute, will you?"

Moving slowly so he wouldn't get sick, he pulled a water bottle from his pack and drank a few gulps.

The nausea disappeared and the dizziness went away. "OK. I think I'm ready." He put his hands on the bushy grass and began to push himself up, but something caught his eye. A path—grass clearly stomped down—led away from the path they were on.

"Guys, look."

Avery moved the brush aside.

The green path led ahead for as far as he could see.

"Maybe the monkey was good for something," Benny said.

Benny was making lots of good points today. Luca nodded. "Yeah, it was." He hauled himself up, bracing for the dizziness, but it didn't come.

"Are you all right?" June asked.

"Yeah, I think I am."

Avery returned his stick and they started down the new path.

Sweat ran down his neck and he wiped it away. Good thing he'd remembered to drop the sweatshirt from last night before they'd come on the search. Now if his headache would ease up.

As they followed the path, Luca took in the jungle around them. Trees draped over them in great, towering arcs. Huge white flowers blossomed from several trees, and a sweet smell drifted on the air. The path went on and on, but any sign of the missing girls was nonexistent.

The longer they walked, the more his dizziness seeped back. He took another drink of his water then glanced at the others.

Benny barreled through the overgrowth with his head down. He'd never find anyone like that.

June kept her gaze forward. Every few steps she'd stop and examine a bush. At least she was trying.

Avery looked around constantly. At first, he thought she was being extra vigilant about finding Gabby and Katelyn, but then he noticed her eyes. They bolted back and forth nonstop, like a criminal in a sea of cops. She hadn't stopped frowning since they'd started on this path, and he realized she wasn't looking at the flowers or looking for the missing girls. She was looking for something specific. He'd have to ask her about it later.

"Is this a turn in the path?" June's words jerked him back to their reason for being in the jungle in the first place.

He stepped forward and checked out the stomped-down growth, then he took in the rest of the area. "Good call, June. I think you're right." He stepped onto the new path and began walking, but Avery stopped him.

"That path takes us even deeper into the jungle. Are you sure it's safe?"

"It doesn't matter. We have to find Gabby and Katelyn," June said.

Avery bit her lip and looked to him.

Great. The girls disagreed and Avery wanted him to settle it. "We came out to find them." There shouldn't be an argument about it anyway. It was why they'd come into the jungle in the first place.

She glared. "Fine."

"What? Would you rather leave them behind?"

She huffed and rolled her eyes. "Of course not. I just think it would be wiser to let the others know before we go even deeper into this jungle. If we get lost, they'd never find us." Even with her brave words, though, her gaze continued to roam.

Something had spooked her. Too bad she wasn't sharing what it was.

"We don't have time to go back," Luca said. "It would take the rest of the daylight hours just to get back to the desert and bring someone else out here. I say we keep going."

She clenched her teeth but didn't speak.

He took that as compliance.

She huffed and pushed past him, taking the lead.

Luca held in his sigh. Who knew what had scared her? In this place, there was no telling. One thing he did know. He couldn't get out of here fast enough.

9

Avery

Avery blinked against the sweat dripping in her eyes. Every step she took toward the heart of the jungle made her head spin faster. Every thought was a chore. Her mind was a war zone.

She swallowed against the fear in her stomach. No matter what her eyes told her, small black creatures were not following them. The creatures didn't increase in number with every step they took.

This was a certainty because no one else seemed to notice the shiny black things crawling everywhere.

Not crazy.

Not crazy.

Not crazy.

"Do you suppose they just got mixed up?" June's words broke into Avery's thoughts. "We've been walking for hours. They had to have realized they were going in the wrong direction."

Luca shook his head and shrugged. "It's easy to do when the light gets dim."

Speaking of dim. The deeper they hiked, the darker it grew. Avery shuddered at the thought of spending a night in the jungle, especially with the imaginary black things. They looked like giant water beetles crawling up the trees, through the leaves, across the paths.

Except they didn't crawl anywhere because they weren't real.

"I'm hot and hungry," Benny said. "Can't we take a break?"

Luca slowed to a stop and pulled out a few water bottles. "Here. I figured we could find some fruit here in the jungle."

"More fruit?"

Avery tuned out Benny's whines as she tipped the water bottle toward her lips. It wasn't even cold anymore, but it was the sweetest thing she'd ever tasted.

For the first time she felt clear-headed. She took another long gulp. Maybe dehydration was to blame for her "sightings." She nearly laughed as relief washed over her. She wasn't crazy after all.

"Avery?" Luca nudged her with his knee, bringing her back to the present.

"Hmm?"

"Are you OK? I called you three times."

She shrugged it off. "Sorry. I was thinking."

"Do you want some fruit? Benny found pomegranates."

"Oh, yeah." She shook herself and took the fruit, even though she agreed with Benny. If they were here much longer, they would need to break into the food supplies.

The soft, wet fruit opened her senses even more, and the black beetles began crawling away. She quickly ate the rest of her fruit and asked for more.

Benny sat down on the grassy floor, and June joined him.

Luca sidled up to Avery again. "Hey, are you sure you're OK?" he asked quietly.

Avery took another bite and nodded. "I am now."

"You seemed upset earlier. Kept frowning."

She shrugged and continued eating. She wasn't about to admit what she'd seen. He might worry about her. Wonder about her. She could take everyone else's cold shoulder, but not Luca's. She couldn't stand it if he deserted her, too.

Kind of like she'd done to him?

She pushed away the guilty thought. "Yeah, I'm fine."

Luca watched her for another few seconds before giving up on the interrogation. They finished their fruit, and he stretched. "OK, let's keep moving."

June and Benny stood up and brushed off their pants, then they continued their trek.

Avery followed behind them, with Luca at the rear. Farther and farther they trudged, but Avery only focused on the next step. As long as she didn't look around, she wouldn't have to see anything that wasn't actually there.

"How much time do you think has passed?" June asked. She wiped at her forehead.

"A few hours maybe," Luca said.

Benny shoved a hand in his pocket and pulled out his phone. "It's two seventeen, Iraqi time, if you must know."

Luca's hand shot out and grabbed Benny's arm. "Wait, you mean your phone is getting signal?"

The rest of the group stopped and stared at Benny.

He shrugged and laughed nervously. "Of course it does. It's the *latest* model."

Luca growled and rolled his eyes. "Why haven't you called for help?" He punched Benny in the arm.

Avery winced. He shouldn't go off on Benny, not

here, and not now.

"Get with me when we get out of this blazing, hot jungle, will you?" Luca growled. He waved his hands forward and they re-started their march.

After a few steps in silence, June continued her questioning. "Do you think the rescue van arrived yet? Or maybe they got our van working."

"I hope so," Avery said. "I hope my dad is there."

"Your dad?" June glanced in Avery's direction and frowned.

"He's the group leader. He's in the other van."

"Oh, I remember him. I bet you miss him."

Avery smiled and shrugged. She did miss him. Didn't she? Truthfully, she wasn't used to him being around anyway.

He was always off searching the globe. And when he was home, he was dictating her every move—like where she'd go to college. What she would do for a living. Who she was not going to spend time with. Or he was making promises he never kept.

"Guys, look!" Benny said. The path veered to the left and there was a small, round section of grass and brush that had been beat down. "What do you think it means?"

"It looks like someone slept here," Luca said. He squatted beside the spot and put his hand out. "It looks big enough for two people."

Avery studied the space, thinking about Gabby and Katelyn sleeping out here for the night.

It might have been someone else sleeping here, though. What if it was Rae? She hadn't been dehydrated when she saw him.

Glancing around, she searched for anything that looked like a house. She even looked toward the trees for a tree house, but there was nothing. He'd said the girls were on their way back, but here was a place where it looked like they'd slept. Besides, they hadn't made it back yet.

She closed her eyes and shook her head. He hadn't been real, either. He'd been as imaginary as the black beetles. She needed to accept that. She opened her eyes and turned to Luca. "What do you think?" She needed to focus on the real. The here and now.

Luca sighed as he stood. "I don't know. Do you see any other trails leading out of here?"

Avery glanced around with the others. It looked like the trail stopped cold with this alcove. Refusing to give up, she stepped into the circle and looked for a way out of it. The move paid off. "Here," she said, pointing to a narrow but definite path.

Luca hurried toward her. "Good eyes. This looks like a single person made the path. Would they have walked single file?"

June shrugged. "Who knows? I think it's worth it to follow."

Luca nodded and looked at June. "You're right. Let's go."

He agreed with June a lot. Why did that bug Avery?

Again, she pushed the thought away and refocused on the search. They'd walked for hours and had seen nothing. No people, no houses, no sign of life in this jungle outside of normal jungle creatures. This path was their only hope. It seemed to take a fairly straight shot, and the group walked for an hour without saying a word. The confusion seeped back in as sweat pooled at the small of her back. She swallowed hard, noticing her mouth felt like cotton.

Why hadn't she grabbed a spare piece of fruit?

Her vision swam, and instead of seeing three companions she saw six. She blinked them away and gritted her teeth. "Luca, do we have any more water?"

He glanced at her, studying her. Hopefully he couldn't see her confusion. "Sure. Here you go."

She snatched it from his hand and quickly turned it toward her lips. The wet liquid rushed down her throat and she sighed. Much better. She closed the bottle and handed it back. After a few more steps, something began moving up ahead.

It definitely wasn't the girls, and no monkey stalked them that she could see.

Was it the tree branches? Or the air? Whatever it was, she was seeing the wind again. She turned away, trying to put the strangeness of the place out of her mind, but the movement held her eye.

Maybe it wasn't the air, after all. She squinted ahead and realized she wasn't seeing things. There was fruit on a few trees in front of them. "Look, guys!"

"Are those bananas?" June asked.

Benny grinned. "Score!" He jogged to the tree and began shimmying up.

"You can climb that?" Luca asked.

"Sure, my granddad used to take me hunting, and we climbed up without a stand."

Avery couldn't imagine giving Benny a gun, but she kept that to herself.

He tossed down a bunch of bananas.

Avery grabbed a few to distribute. The sweet fruit was better than any full course meal she'd ever eaten. "Should we take the rest back to the group?" she asked.

"Yeah, good idea," Luca replied.

June frowned and kicked at the dirt. "So, is the search over?"

Luca studied June, his eyebrows drawn tight. "We're not giving up, but this path seems to lead back to the desert. They may have beaten us to it."

Found their way back? That's exactly what Rae said would happen.

Still, June didn't seem to want to accept it.

Avery put her arm around June's shoulder. "It will be fine."

June smiled but it didn't reach her eyes.

"Let's get back to the group," Luca said. "We'll rest and see if they've made it back."

"And then what?" June pressed.

He shrugged. "We'll go from there. We're not giving up on them."

Why was Luca coddling her? The path was obviously leading back to the group. What more did June want?

Avery took a deep breath and tried to calm her nerves. She wasn't being fair. It was just this place. She grabbed the remainder of the bananas and continued her walk.

The others caught up.

"What's the hurry?" Luca asked, jogging to catch her.

She shrugged. "I just want to get out of here. I need to see the sun."

That appeased him. "We'll figure something out. We'll find them."

Let him think that's why she was upset. She sure wasn't going to tell him the missing girls had nothing to do with it, and she wasn't going to admit a huge, black beetle had just crawled across her feet.

10

Luca

The good news was pretty obvious as soon as they stepped into the light of the open desert. Dry heat hit Luca in the face. It was at least ten degrees hotter than the jungle, but without the humidity, it was bearable.

Everyone in the group gathered in a circle, talking over each other in loud, excited voices.

"They're here!" June sprinted through the sand. Her feet slipped and she almost nose-dived, but she righted herself and made it to the group. Pushing herself through, she threw herself at Gabby in a hug.

The girls laughed.

Luca smiled. "Can't believe we did all that and they made it back on their own."

Avery turned to look at him but winced. "I'm really sorry about your head."

The lump on his forehead felt bigger than it had before. He shrugged. "It's really no big deal."

"At least you have a great story to tell. You were attacked by a jungle monkey."

He laughed but it faded fast. "I think we all have a great story to tell. We've been stranded in the desert for days."

Her smile fell away, too, and worry lines replaced it. She wrapped her arms around her waist. "Can you believe this? Why hasn't anyone come looking for us?"

He fought the urge to hug her. To comfort her.

A rumbling in the distance caught his attention and he let a slow grin spread across his face. "Do you hear that? It sounds like they got our van running."

Her head snapped up, and she gazed across the sand toward the van. The guys gathered around it, laughing and high-fiving.

This was good. Better than good! They'd found the lost girls and fixed their van, and now they could get out of here for good. Just in time, too, because Benny wasn't the only one who was tired of fruit.

Luca could go for a double bacon cheeseburger and super fries right about now. He nudged Avery. "Come on. Let's check it out."

They walked side by side toward the missing girls.

"Do you want to say something to them?"

She shook her head and kept her gaze on the van. Seemed strange, but he didn't question her. Instead, he led her to the van.

"You did it." Luca shook hands with Bradley and Sam. "Do we have a plan to get out of here?"

"The tires are buried deeply in the sand," Sam said, "but we are working on a plan."

"Excellent."

Bradley wiped his hands on his shirt and stepped toward them. "Dude, did you hear those girls' story yet?" He cocked an eyebrow when Luca shook his head. "It's pretty crazy. You might want to go have a listen."

Luca turned to the girls who were still surrounded by the rest of the group. That didn't really sound like good news. He turned back to Bradley. "Thanks. And good work on the van."

An uneasy feeling settled in Luca's gut as he and

Avery stepped closer to the group gathered around Gabby and Katelyn. He moved close to them and waited for a break in the conversation. "So," he finally said. "Where have you been?"

Avery cleared her throat and stepped around him. "How are you? Were you hurt? We heard Katelyn has asthma."

Luca cringed. He should have started with that.

"I'm fine," Katelyn said. "We found water and fruit, and we got back as soon as we could find our way."

They did look OK—no cuts or bruises.

"How did you sleep in there?" Avery asked. She shuddered.

Gabby stepped forward. "We didn't sleep at all. We were only gone a couple of hours."

Luca's nerves went on high alert. "What do you mean?" He glanced at Avery and she frowned, her head cocked to the side.

"We only went in to use the bathroom. We didn't go more than a few steps in, but when we turned around, we realized we were lost. After about an hour of walking we found a creek, and later some fruit, then we found our way out."

So his original water path had definitely crossed with the girls' path, but their timeline was way off. "You guys have been gone since yesterday morning," he finally said.

Had they gone crazy?

Avery's face looked troubled, and she wrapped her arms more tightly around her waist. It was something she didn't do in the past. Must have become some kind of nervous habit.

Katelyn shook her head, bringing him out of his

thoughts. "Everyone keeps saying that, but we weren't there all night. It never even got dark."

Their story made no sense. The alcove had been beaten down by someone's body, and the pathway leading away from it came straight to the desert.

"So how did you find your way out?" Avery asked.

"We had a feeling," Katelyn said. "It happened to be right."

Gabby chuckled, and her tight black curls bounced around her face. "Yeah, that and your vision. Tell them about him."

"Vision?" Luca asked.

Bradley was right. This was getting weirder by the minute.

"She saw some guy dressed in white," Gabby said. "She said he pointed to the way we should go."

A cold, uneasy feeling crept up Luca's spine. He pushed out thoughts of the white flash he saw, and forced himself to be logical. "I don't understand."

Katelyn frowned and elbowed Gabby. "You promised you wouldn't tell."

"It's nothing to be ashamed of," Gabby said. "We were hot and hungry. People see things. You just happened to see something that got us out of there."

Avery choked and coughed. She pulled away from the group, covering her mouth.

Luca turned back to the girls. "So a guy in white told you how to get back."

"I guess so," Gabby said.

"Where did you see him?" Avery had stepped back to the group.

Luca kept cool about it, but her shaking was obvious.

Gabby and Katelyn glanced at each other, almost as if they were trying to remember.

"It was after we saw the fruit tree," Katelyn said. "Do you remember that?"

Gabby frowned but nodded. "I think so, but I didn't see him."

Katelyn blushed and shrugged. "I wish I didn't see him, either. I thought I was going crazy! But at least we made it back."

A guy dressed in white.

Luca swallowed hard. If Katelyn was hallucinating, it wasn't because she was hot and hungry, and she wasn't the only one.

11

Avery

Their words gave Avery goose bumps, but not in a bad way. Maybe she wasn't crazy after all—someone else had seen Rae.

Something irked her, though. He'd been a vision to Katelyn. A hallucination. He hadn't spoken to Katelyn or given his name.

Why had he talked to Avery? And more, what was he, if Avery could hear him and Katelyn couldn't?

She turned away from the group, trying to gather her thoughts.

The van purred behind them. The sound was sweeter than the water from the creek, but still.

She spun back to Luca. "Will we be leaving now?"

Luca paused mid-sentence.

Oops. She should have waited.

"I think the guys are working out a plan. We should get everything repacked, and maybe gather some fruit and water."

That's what she'd hoped. Water meant going back into the jungle, and going back in gave her a chance to get a few answers. When the plans were made and it was determined a couple teams would go back for water and fruit, Avery was first in line.

June tugged on Avery's elbow. "Come on. We'll go with you."

Benny stood at June's side, looking less than enthused about it all.

Avery managed a smile, even though she wished she could go in alone. "Thanks, June. I guess we should get some water bottles."

They moved toward the van where Luca had left the water supplies. Someone had cracked the windows, letting the air circulate. They would all appreciate that later.

Every bottle they'd filled that morning was already empty, so she stuffed them all into Luca's bag and hefted it onto her shoulder.

As she turned to go, a foot on the back seat caught her attention. She craned her neck and saw that Erin lay stretched out, her arm over her eyes.

Avery frowned. Whatever was bothering Erin was something she wasn't willing to talk about, but she was the youth leader, and their only authority figure for the time being. Avery glanced toward Luca, but he was still talking to the other guys. She climbed toward the back of the van. "Erin? Are you OK?"

Erin's chest rose and fell with each breath she took, but she didn't answer.

"The missing girls are back, and the van is running. We should be leaving soon. We'll get out of here and find my dad and Chad."

The arm came down and Erin stared at Avery with bloodshot eyes. "It's not going to work."

Avery paused. "Of course it is. We're almost ready to go." But inside, Erin's words made Avery shake. What if it was true? What if it didn't work and they were stuck forever? What if they never went home, and Avery never got to prove herself? Never got to win Daddy's approval. Never went to college, got married, or had kids.

She swallowed hard and said it again. "It will work."

"You'll see." Erin put her arm back over her eyes. "He'll be right. I can feel it."

Goose bumps were back. Avery climbed further into the van until she was leaning over Erin. "Who are you talking about? Who said that?"

"Never mind." Apparently, Erin wasn't talking anymore.

Avery glanced at her hands and realized they shook. Erin's eyes were closed, but Avery couldn't forget her words. It was time to get out of here.

She slipped out of the van without another word to Erin, and made her way back to Benny and June. "Let's make this quick. I'm ready to get out of here." Erin's warning gave her the creeps.

Maybe Avery and Katelyn weren't the only ones seeing people—or a person? Maybe Rae was only pretending to help while he was simultaneously torturing Erin.

A few others were heading into the jungle at the same time, going to look for fruit.

Avery glanced at the sun as they passed under the first few trees. It was making its way closer to the tree line, and soon it would be dark.

Everything looked normal as she walked. Tall trees, green leaves, thick brush. No giant black beetles or boys dressed in white. The gurgling creek came into view, and Avery handed Benny and June a few bottles each.

They all bent at the water and began filling.

The quiet was only broken by the running water and a few jungle sounds, but Avery's nerves were raw.

"So, June, how many kids from your group came on this trip?" She needed to talk about something. Anything.

"Besides me, Gabby, and Katelyn, the other van had two girls and a youth worker."

"No guys?"

She smiled and shook her head. "They were all too busy to go on a mission trip and help little kids."

"Yeah, I was surprised we had so many guys show up."

"Hey," Benny said. "I came, didn't I?"

June screwed the cap on the last bottle. She stood up. "Why did you come? Why not stay home?"

Benny paused. He glanced between them, then shifted from foot to foot. Finally, he smiled and forced a laugh. "I'd rather be just about anywhere than home."

Avery's heart squeezed. She'd seen his grandparents once or twice, and she had to admit, they didn't seem like the nicest people. Once, after church, she'd seen Benny's granddad smack him in the back of the head. She needed to be nicer to Benny from now on. It wasn't that she wasn't nice to him back home, but she'd grown used to no one talking to her and her talking to no one in return.

They stuffed the bottles back into her bag, and Avery waved her arm for them to lead the way back. Benny took front and she brought up the rear. Her gaze roamed from tree to tree as she tried to find anything out of place, particularly shifting air or a boy in white. The closest she came to something odd was a bright yellow lizard with neon blue spots.

Her blood pulsed through her body, her heart thundering louder with each step she took toward the desert. If they left, she would never know if this place was for real. She wanted to see Rae one last time. She wanted to find out if he was real. Did he live here like he said?

And had he talked to Erin?

That was her biggest question. Someone told Erin they wouldn't be able to leave. Someone had spooked her, and they must have done it as soon as the group had been stranded because Erin had acted strange ever since they'd arrived.

Avery frowned. Who else had been seeing things and keeping it to themselves?

She shuddered. It was best if they got out of here as fast as they could. Forget Rae. Something was definitely wrong with this place.

They marched back to the desert, and she took one last look at the inner jungle. Rae didn't appear, and she didn't see him hiding behind any trees. He was nowhere. He may not even be real. And now she would never know.

She stepped into the desert, ready to haul the bag of water back to the van.

The sun had already dipped behind the trees, and shadows danced across the sand. The food group had returned with fruit, and someone had repacked the luggage on top of the van.

A group of teens gathered around Luca at the hood of the van, and their voices carried in the late-afternoon air.

June frowned. "Do they sound angry to you?"

"I'm afraid so." Avery closed the distance between them and dropped the heavy backpack. "What's going on?"

"Your boy here thinks we should wait until

morning to get out of here. The rest of us want to go now." Bradley scowled at Luca.

Avery ignored Bradley's used of *your boy*. "If Luca thinks we should stay then there has to be a good reason." Even though she couldn't think of any.

"I've explained all of that," Luca said impatiently. His red ears gave away his frustration. "It's getting too dark. We'll never find the road before night fall. Even Sam admitted he doesn't know where we are."

Avery glanced at the van driver—whose name was obviously Sam. "What's the harm in waiting until first light? We can get a good night's rest and leave in the morning. I think the plan is solid."

Bradley didn't acknowledge that she'd spoken and she rolled her eyes.

"I'm not keeping us here to be a jerk," Luca said. "Can anyone even see the sun now? Because I can't. We won't make it a few miles in this sand before we won't have enough light to guide us. The headlights will only get us so far when there are miles and miles of sand in every direction. At least right now, we have food and water. What if we get stuck out there with nothing?"

Avery held her breath, but no one argued with him. He made legitimate points, and she hated to admit she was relieved. Something drew her to the jungle. It was almost as if they weren't supposed to leave, not yet.

"Maybe staying until morning is best," Tasha said. She, Mallory, and Brittany huddled together at the corner of the van. Her dark skin glistened with sweat, and she wore her ball cap pulled low over her face.

"You've got to be kidding me!" Bradley looked at every member of the group, but no one met his eyes.

No one except Avery. She wasn't afraid to tell him he was being a jerk. Not that he cared about her opinion all that much.

He held her gaze for a few moments and finally growled. Kicking at the sand as he spun on his heel, he stomped away—at least as well as he could stomp in shifting sand.

The others broke up and headed for the protection of the tree line.

Luca looked to her. "Got any water in there for me?"

She pulled a bottle from the pack on the ground and handed it to him. "Are you sure about this?"

"Are you doubting me, too?"

"Of course not. I just want to make sure we're not doing anything stupid. Right now, we're all together, and the van runs. We're not jinxing ourselves, are we?"

His face fell and he scowled. "Jinxing ourselves? Are you superstitious now?"

"Of course I don't believe in jinxing. It's just an expression." Apparently, he wasn't up to having his decision questioned. Not that it was really his decision to make.

Erin hadn't been in his little pow-wow. Maybe because she knew they weren't going to leave.

Uneasiness settled over Avery. It was almost as if Erin's warnings were coming true.

No, not Erin's warnings. *His* warnings.

Rae said he was trying to help them leave, but he'd also said he was waiting for her, and he'd given Avery the creeps. What if he was trying to keep them here instead of trying to help them leave?

The uneasiness turned to panic when she remembered what else he'd said. He'd implied that their leaving wouldn't be easy.

Part 2

Genesis 3:3-5
"But of the fruit of the tree which is in the midst of the garden, God hath said, Ye shall not eat of it, neither shall ye touch it, lest ye die. And the serpent said unto the woman, Ye shall not surely die: For God doth know that in the day ye eat thereof, then your eyes shall be opened, and ye shall be as gods."

12

Luca

Luca stomped toward the tree line, ignoring the others who stared at him. He had to get away—be alone—at least for a few minutes. Back home he'd gotten used to his solitude. His brothers knew to leave him be, and even Mom gave him whatever space he needed.

Here? It was never quiet, and there was never any down time.

He followed the natural wave of the growth until he was out of sight, then he punched a tree and let out a yell of frustration.

No one else had stepped up to take charge when they first got stranded. Nobody had thought about needing food or water, and no one else lined up to find Gabby and Katelyn when they went missing.

They sure wanted to be in charge now, though. Now that they didn't like his decision. Now that things seemed to be going good again.

Pain shot up his arm and blood seeped through a split on his knuckle. He wiped it on his shirt and took a deep breath. It didn't matter what they said. They'd be leaving in the morning, and after they finished the remainder of the mission, they'd be going home.

What a waste of time this trip had been. Signing up had been a mistake, period. He never would have volunteered if he'd known what was in his future.

Taking another deep breath, he started back toward camp. He kicked through the sand and looked across the wide, open desert. It was huge—easily the biggest thing he'd ever seen. It went on for miles and miles, and it made him feel like a blip. A tiny dot on the map. Totally unimportant.

How were they supposed to navigate their way out of an open desert? Finding a road in there would take a miracle.

He picked up a handful of sand and tossed it toward the nothingness in front of him.

"You are thinking what I am thinking." Sam stepped beside Luca. He looked at the desert. "We are very lost."

Luca studied Sam. "Do you think we're doing the right thing by staying overnight?" This guy knew the area like most guys back home knew their video games, but Sam had never seen this jungle before. Luca trusted his opinion.

Sam nodded slowly. His bare feet dug into the hot sand. "Yes. I believe so."

Luca choked back his relief. "Thanks."

Sam brushed sand from his pants. "We will leave in the morning. That will be good."

It couldn't come fast enough. This place creeped him out. Visions of white? Lost girls who didn't remember being gone?

Throw in a half-baked youth leader and you had yourself a regular circus.

Benny's face popped in front of Luca's as they reached camp. "How long between here and the village?"

Yep. Definitely a circus.

"I don't know, Benny. We don't know where we

are."

Benny's face scrunched up like a pit bull's. "This place sucks."

Luca barked out a laugh. "You're right about that."

Benny kicked at the sand and mumbled something as he walked away.

Everyone was ready to get out of here. This wasn't the way they'd planned on spending their summer, least of all Luca.

What if they never really got out of here?

Mom was completely on her own without him home to help. How was she supposed to keep the other four boys in line? The thought made him stop and laugh. Like she needed his help. They were all afraid of her—including Luca.

Still, she could use his help. Making him come on this trip was pointless. No amount of meddling from Mom was going to help him "heal." He was fine. Over it.

Yeah, he'd had a bad few months after Dad died. He was a bit angry.

Even Avery had let her dad convince her that Luca was no good, but what did Mr. Miles know? He was clueless when it came to his daughter. And his wife, for that matter.

If only Luca could get Avery to see he was fine. OK with Dad's death. "Healed." He sighed. That was enough of that. He joined the group in the shade and dug his heels into the sand. His mouth felt as dry as the desert air. He'd never complain about rain again.

Grabbing a bottle of water, Luca sat down on one of the logs someone had dragged from the jungle. At least someone around here could act without his instruction.

"We're going to sing," June said. "Want to join us?"

Her kind smile calmed him and he nodded. She turned to the group and started a slow song. It was a hymn, something he'd learned as a kid. At first, he couldn't remember all the words, but after a moment they came to him. He joined in, soft and low.

Avery took a seat near June. She watched him, but he tried to ignore her. If he stared back, it would only spook her and make her look away.

After a few songs, even Erin joined them. She didn't sing, but she passed around fruit so they'd all have something to eat.

It was good they were leaving in the morning. Luca would have hated to bust into the food supplies for the village.

Thoughts of the village stopped his singing for a minute. The people from the mission had to be wondering about their group. *Someone* had to be wondering. They'd been stuck here for two full days but no one had come. That was enough to make him think the other van hadn't made it to the village, either. Pushing tomorrow from his mind, he dove back into the music.

June smiled when he rejoined them. She was easy to please. That was refreshing.

The song ended and everyone headed to the van to get some sleep. Hopefully, it would be the last night they'd spend here.

He expected to stare at the van's ceiling while everyone slept, but once he'd gotten comfortable in his seat, his eyes slid shut and he couldn't get himself to reopen them. Sleep came fast.

Excitement buzzed in everyone's voices when Luca woke the next morning.

The girls hurried to refill their water bottles and wash up while the guys gathered fruit. They were back and ready to go within an hour.

Luca didn't have to instruct anyone to do anything—they were ready. The guys loaded into the back and the girls into the front. Luca sat in the passenger seat beside Sam, who looked to him and grinned.

His dark curly hair stuck to his forehead, and he wiped it away. "Are you ready?"

Luca smiled back. "Yep. Let's go."

The guys had worked the day before on unburying the tires and driving out of the rut, so now all they had to focus on was driving forward. Sam cranked the engine and put the van in gear.

Luca held his breath. This was the moment they had waited for—getting out of the desert.

The van lurched forward.

"We're moving!" Mallory laughed and a few others cheered.

Luca couldn't help smiling. He looked at Sam, and the driver gave him a thumbs up.

Sam drove slowly so the van wouldn't slip in the sand.

The jungle behind them began to get farther away. *Sayonara.*

Luca turned to take in the group. His eyes locked with Erin.

She didn't smile. She didn't even look happy to be leaving. A frown turned her mouth down in a way that put a bad feeling in Luca's gut.

He gulped and turned back to the front. "How are

we doing?"

Sam smiled and nodded, but it wasn't the same excited grin from before.

Luca's hope sprouted tiny wings and began preparing for takeoff. He closed his eyes and gritted his teeth. *Please let us get out of here.* It had been a few years since he'd bothered God with his life, but now seemed like a good time.

They were on a church mission trip and all.

They drove a few more yards, inching toward the open space and away from the oasis.

Erin's bad mood shouldn't affect anything.

They were fine.

The others laughed and carried on conversations behind him.

Even Avery seemed happy, except she kept glancing at Erin.

Avery felt it, he could tell.

Something was wrong.

Luca caught Sam's frown before Sam could hide it. "What's going on?" he asked quietly.

"We are low on gas. We were almost full yesterday. I am afraid there is a hole in the tank or lines."

"How?" It didn't make sense.

"I do not know."

"How long?" That was the big question. Could they make it to the village?

Sam's nostrils flared and he stared straight ahead. "Not long."

Hope's wings flapped harder and flew away. They weren't getting away. At least not today. "Should we turn around?"

Sam glanced at him, and then in the rearview

mirror. His face drooped and defeat made his shoulders sag. "We do not have enough gas to make it back."

Luca glanced in the side mirror and sighed. They were at least a mile away now.

The van sputtered and jerked.

The happy conversations behind Luca died down and everything went quiet.

"What's going on?" Avery leaned toward the front. "Are we breaking down?"

Luca gulped and angled himself toward the group. "It looks like we're running out of gas."

Bradley's expression exploded with anger. "What? We had a full tank!"

"The gauge has been dropping since we began," Sam explained. "There is a leak."

The van shuddered again and died.

Everyone moaned.

Tasha began to cry, and Luca glanced at June. Hopefully she wouldn't break down again.

She frowned but seemed to be in control of herself.

"We're farther out," Avery said. "Can we use the radio to call for help?"

Sam didn't look too confident with that plan, but he agreed to try.

"Driver one, can you read?"

Static.

"Can anyone hear me? We are stranded."

Nothing.

Sam sighed and tried one last time, this time speaking his own language, but no one answered.

Luca closed his eyes and lay his head back, but then he remembered something. He spun toward the group. "Benny, give me your smart phone."

Benny frowned but begrudgingly passed it up.

Luca powered it up and waited for everything to load. "There's no signal."

"I could have told you that," Benny said.

"When we were in the jungle you said you had signal." Luca worked to keep his impatience from showing.

"Yeah, in the jungle. There's no signal once I get in the sand."

The jungle. Great.

Luca met Avery's gaze, and he watched the excitement of getting away melt into defeat.

He pushed open his door and began to climb out. "It looks like we have to walk back."

13

Avery

The sun beat down on Avery's head as she walked. It was a relentless rhythm of *thump, thump, thump*. Her feet slid with every step, making her legs work extra hard to make it back to the jungle, and her thighs and lungs burned. She took a deep breath and let it out slowly through her mouth. She needed water. They all did. How could a mile take so long to walk?

It was a hundred times worse with Erin's predictions running through Avery's head. Who told Erin they wouldn't be leaving? And was this person keeping them trapped?

The driver had said the gas lines had a leak. It was almost like someone had sabotaged them, cutting the lines to keep them here.

Avery shuddered.

Luca walked ahead of her. He carried the bag with the bottled water, but she wouldn't ask him to stop and get her one, not until they got back.

"Where are we going to sleep?" Leave it to Benny to ask a question like that.

Avery looked around and had to admit it was a legitimate concern. Hiking back and forth to the van didn't sound very appealing, but neither did sleeping in the open. "I wonder if we could make shelters somehow."

"Out of what?" Bradley looked at her like she was just as crazy as Erin.

Avery shot him a look. "Sticks and leaves. Anything. We have all day and nothing to do."

Bradley shook his head. "I'm not sitting around here anymore."

The finality in his words hung in the air and no one spoke for a few minutes.

Finally Luca chimed in. "What do you mean?"

"I'm walking. I'll load up with water, then I'm going in search of the village. I'm good with directions. If I can't find anything after a couple of hours, I'll come back."

"You're going out there alone?" That sounded like the worse plan ever to Avery.

"We could go, too," Tasha said.

Bradley laughed. "No thanks. We don't need any girls to take care of."

"Hey!" Tasha's nostrils flared and she glared at him.

"No, he's right." It was the first time Erin had addressed them all day. "The girls don't need to go off with the boys alone. The girls will stay here."

No one argued with her, probably out of habit.

"It's better to go in groups of three," Luca said. "You need someone else."

Two of the others stepped forward, leaving Luca, Benny, and David with the girls.

"Let's get back to the tree line and load you up with some fruit and water," Luca said.

Excitement fluttered to life again. If they could find someone and bring help back then the group might still be rescued soon. They weren't totally hopeless.

In the meantime, Avery would have some time to look for Rae. He promised to help them. She wanted to see him again. To know whose side he was on. She wanted answers.

Everyone worked as a whole to gather fruit and water for Bradley's group. Once they'd loaded backpacks full of supplies, the entire group huddled together.

"The village is in the east," Sam said. "Keep the sun to your back. Look for any signs of civilization—roads, villages, huts. If you see a car, try to flag it down."

Bradley nodded. It was surprising that he was willing to take anyone's advice, but then Avery remembered they had worked on the van together.

Luca and Bradley both obviously respected Sam.

Avery would remember that.

The group stood together in the shade as the threesome made their way into the desert. Some of them sat in the sand to watch.

Avery had too much to do for waiting around. She turned to Luca. "We need to gather branches to make some kind of shelters. We also need our sunblock and sweaters from the van." They'd carried water and fruit, but staying overnight meant they'd need the rest of their supplies as well.

He studied her a moment, seeming surprised that she was taking charge again. She felt a blush coming on but instead of ducking, she chose to ignore it.

Luca grinned. "Yes ma'am."

She smiled and rolled her eyes. "Tell me what you need me to do."

He glanced at the jungle then back to her. "If you don't mind a hike across the sand again, you can help me bring back supplies from the van. Or you can wait here. Don't go in the jungle alone. I'll help you as soon as I get back."

"I can get some of the other girls to help me while you guys go to the van."

He looked like he wanted to argue, but after a second he snapped his mouth shut. "Sounds like a good plan."

Avery kept her smile to herself. Luca was trying to not boss her around like he was everyone else, but she could tell it wasn't easy.

Benny and David stood with Sam, arms crossed, as they watched Bradley's group grow smaller in the distance.

Luca made his way to them and spoke quietly for a moment, then the four of them headed toward the van.

"Where are they going?" June asked.

Avery watched them then turned away. "We need supplies and shelter. Want to help gather large branches and sticks?"

The other girls glanced at her, but no one offered to help.

Avery took a step closer to them. "Come on, guys. Do you want to walk back and forth to the van every morning and night?"

"We're not going to be here much longer, though, right?" Katelyn asked. "So it doesn't really matter."

June shook her head. "It's better than doing nothing."

Katelyn looked to Gabby for support, but Gabby was already standing to help Avery. Katelyn rolled her eyes and sighed. "Fine. I'll help."

"What about you guys?" Avery looked at Tasha,

Mallory, and Brittany. They didn't look happy about it, but they finally agreed to help, too.

Avery led them into the jungle and everyone went their own way, searching for giant leaves and fallen branches. "Don't go out of eyesight," Avery warned. "Stay where we can see each other."

Starting at the edge of the trees, they pulled large branches into the shady sand.

Avery scanned the jungle constantly, but there were no signs of Rae.

Sweat pooled on her forehead and began dripping down her temple. The humid air sucked the life right out of her, and the farther into the jungle they moved, the more she wished she'd gotten a bottle of water from Luca. She grabbed branch after branch and carried it to the tree line, then returned each time for more.

The other girls worked along with her, even though Tasha, Mallory, and Brittany took a few dozen breaks.

If it wasn't so hot, she could get more done. She could move faster. Gather more. Clear her head. Think. She blinked rapidly to clear the sweat from her eyes. Or maybe it was to stop the blurs in her vision. She closed her eyes and held them shut for a few seconds as she swallowed and calmed her nerves. Then, a thought hit her. Every time her vision blurred, something strange happened. Something appeared.

She peeled her eyes open slowly and focused on the area directly in front of her. Fruit hung two feet away, dangling from the tree like a life line. Was she making things appear by wishing for it?

The fruit was round and red, exactly like a red delicious apple. She plucked one from the branch and took a bite. Sweet, cool apple juice swirled in her mouth and she swallowed in pure satisfaction. This was the fourth time this had happened. Whatever it was, she was glad for it.

She glanced around but nothing else seemed out of place. No more visions. No mysterious guy. Only a fruit tree in the middle of the jungle, and a few other girls who didn't pay her any attention.

Avery finished the apple and tossed the core, then finished carrying her last few branches to the tree line.

June came close as they piled up their branches and she leaned in to speak to Avery. "I was thinking that everyone seems a little down."

Of course, everyone was down. No one wanted to be stuck here. Avery only smiled sadly and nodded.

"What if we did something fun?"

"Fun? Like what?" Avery couldn't imagine doing anything fun in this place.

"I have an idea, but I'm not sure how you guys do things at your church."

Avery frowned and wiped the sweat on her forehead. "What do you mean?"

"What if we turned a part of the creek into a swim hole?"

Swimming? Right now that sounded like heaven. "I think that would be perfect, and I'd bet everyone would go for it."

June's smile erupted into a full-scale grin. "Great. We can work on it when we're done with this."

The thought of swimming boosted Avery's spirits and she worked on the shelter with an extra spring in her step.

They finished separating the branches into piles by size just as the guys hauled a few suitcases toward them.

Sam and Luca carried a large box between them.

"What's that?" Avery asked.

"Food." Luca didn't look happy about it, but Avery remembered the conversation with Benny the day before. They had to eat. "At least they'll have medical supplies when we get to the village."

But going to the village didn't sound appealing at this point. By the time they got out of here—if they got out—the trip would be over. Besides, Avery wanted to go home.

Daddy's arguments against her coming here passed through her memory. Maybe he'd been right. Maybe she should have stayed home. Something in the back of her mind nagged at her, telling her he was always right. Right about her college future, right about this trip, right about Luca.

"Are you finished gathering branches?" Luca's words broke into her thoughts.

She turned to him and smiled when she realized, no, she didn't regret coming. She'd missed Luca's friendship. She'd missed him a lot, no matter what anyone said about him. "We have enough branches to build the shelter. And June has a really great idea about making a swimming hole at the creek."

Luca's eyebrows shot up. "Swimming? That sounds great."

"That's what I said."

The other girls moved to get what they wanted from their bags, and Avery noticed the sweatshirt she'd given to Luca was tied around his waist. Her heart squeezed. She never intended to give the sweatshirt back. She wore it to bed almost every night back home. Of course, she wouldn't tell him that.

"You want to see what's in here with me?"

Avery frowned and glanced away. She'd been staring at Luca. "What?"

"Do you want to look through the food with me?"

"Oh. Yeah, that sounds great."

He pulled a pocket knife from his pants—who knew where he'd gotten that from—and sliced through the tape on the box. The flaps lifted easily and the greatest treasure she'd ever seen sat before her. Boxes of noodles, jars of sauce, boxes of individually wrapped peanut butter bars, and more were stacked neatly to the top of the huge box.

She looked up at Luca and grinned. "I think we're going to have a feast tonight!"

He smiled back and nodded.

They tossed a few peanut butter bars around then put the box to the side to begin working on the shelter.

Luca, David, Avery, and Sam worked on figuring out structures for the walls, and the others worked on filling in the walls once the structures were built. By the end of it, they were all drenched in sweat.

"That swim-hole idea is sounding better and better," Luca said. He grinned at June and she blushed.

Avery tensed, hating herself for it. Instead of pouting she turned away. "Should we do that next?"

Erin didn't protest so they made a beeline for the creek in the jungle. The path was well worn by now. They chose a spot down creek from where they gathered their water in the mornings, and everyone pitched in to dig out a pit that was big enough for swimming.

Avery pulled brush away from the shoreline so they could make a clearer path, but her foot got stuck in the mud. She tugged at her leg, and her foot came loose with a sickly slurping sound. She tumbled toward the ground, fast.

The splash into the water was enough to get everyone's attention. She sat, blinking back the droplets that had sprayed into her eyes. At first, no one moved, but then Luca chuckled and shook his head. "You couldn't wait?"

Avery smiled and scooped an arc of water towards him.

He didn't need any more provocation. Jumping in, he made a splash big enough to drench anyone standing nearby.

Everyone followed his path then, and before long they were laughing and having fun. That was a first since they'd arrived.

Avery kept an eye on Luca while they goofed off, but he didn't seem to pay any more attention to June. He caught Avery looking, and she blushed and turned away. They used to have all kinds of fun together like this, but that was before their lives went down the tubes. Before Luca turned into a 'rabid dog', as Daddy called him.

But maybe the old Luca was still in there. Somewhere. Maybe he just needed help finding his way out.

By the time they finished, everyone was cooled off and happy. They marched back to the tree line, all dripping wet.

"It's a good thing you brought our luggage back from the van," Avery said.

Luca smiled. "Yeah. Too bad I don't have any."

"You can borrow some of Benny's. It might be a little tight."

He snorted and shook his head, then moved away

to talk to David. Luca was taller, but David's clothes would be a decent fit.

Avery looked around at their shelters and the box of food near a small fire pit they'd dug into the sand earlier. This wasn't so bad. They could last here another night or two. She glanced toward the desert and thought of Bradley's group. Where were they now? For their own sakes, Avery hoped they'd found the village.

14

The bite of the morning air was twice as bad when she was waking up to it without the shelter of the van. Avery groaned and rolled over. There was no use trying to sleep longer and stay warm if she had no blanket to cuddle.

A few others were already out of their rickety shelters, and Benny had started a fire.

Out of habit, Avery looked for Luca. He still slept in the boys' shelter. How could he sleep in when they were stuck in the desert? She smiled and turned away, but her heart pumped in confusion. They'd had fun last night swimming in the creek, and afterward, as everyone ate real food for the first time in days, she'd felt normal with him. She missed that feeling.

She and Luca had been best friends since they were little. Wherever Avery had been, Luca had been there too. All through elementary and middle school, and then through high school.

Things hadn't turned romantic until about a year ago, as they realized high school would be over soon, and they'd be moving into the big, bad world on their own.

Avery hadn't been able to imagine life without Luca.

At least until their dads had messed things up for them—hers by wanting to keep her out of public sight like he was embarrassed by her "episode," and Luca's by taking his own life.

Forcing the thoughts out of her mind, she moved to sit by the fire. She could revisit her decisions later, once they were home. For now, they needed to focus on staying safe and getting out of here. She grabbed a piece of the fruit they'd brought in from the night before.

They'd spent a few hours in the jungle and she hadn't gotten confused even once, so maybe she wasn't crazy.

She glanced at Erin who woke up and grabbed one of her water bottles from home. Last night, Erin had sat by while everyone else had fun. That was unlike her— at youth group she was always jumping in to whatever activity was on the agenda. Erin was obviously way more tormented by whatever it was that was making Avery feel off balance.

Avery finished her fruit and made her way to the youth leader. "How are you this morning?"

Erin finished a long drink and glanced up at Avery. "I feel my best in the morning, thanks."

Avery smiled and offered her a pear. "Can I ask you a question?"

Erin nodded so Avery squatted beside her in the sand. "You said that *he* warned you we wouldn't get out of here. Who were you talking about?"

Erin's face darkened so fast that Avery turned to see if something had happened behind her. The area was empty. She turned back to Erin, anxious to hear what she had to say.

Erin shook her head. "I don't want to talk about that."

"I'm sorry to bring it up. I only ask because…" she swallowed hard and looked down. Would Erin think she was crazy? Considering Avery's history, it was really hard to admit what she'd seen. She took a deep breath and plunged ahead. "I ask because I saw someone, too."

Erin's eyes widened. "What?"

"I saw him the day I got lost in the jungle. He said he'd helped Gabby and Katelyn, and he would try to help us leave. He made it sound like he wasn't sure he could do it. He said he lived here."

Erin's nostrils flared, and she shook her head. "That's not the same person I see."

Avery stilled. Even her heart seemed to stop beating. "The person you see? Do you see him often?"

The youth leader's eyes closed, and when she opened them, her face had gone as white as a wedding gown. "I see him almost every moment of every day."

Avery gasped. "What does he look like?"

Erin shook her head vehemently, her hair waving around her face. "I don't want to talk about it. He's not here now, and that's all I care about for the moment."

"Does he live here? Rae said he lives here."

"What are you talking about?" Luca demanded.

Avery spun around. She hadn't meant for him to hear about Rae. She quickly stood to face him. "There's something strange about this place. I was just talking to Erin about it."

"Who is Rae?" His eyes seemed too watchful, too suspicious. He was angry she'd kept this from him.

"I met him in the jungle the day I got lost. He said he lived here, and that he'd try to help us get out of here."

"No one lives in this jungle."

She put her hands on her hips and tried to keep her anger down. "Someone was in the jungle. Katelyn saw something, and Erin too. I'm not crazy." The last sentence came out a little too forcefully—and loud.

His haughty façade faded away and he shook his head. "I know you're not crazy."

Avery stood awkwardly, not sure how to respond. She glanced around and a few of the others stared at her.

June, Gabby, and Katelyn didn't know the significance of her statement, but the others in her youth group did. They looked away guiltily, and she looked at her feet, unwilling to meet Luca's eyes.

"I didn't say you were crazy, but I wish you had told me you saw someone. I saw something too."

Her head snapped up. "What?"

"The first day we were here I saw something at the tree line. It was a flash of white, but it looked like the form of a person."

Chill bumps raced up Avery's arms. "Rae said he lived here, but when I told him he had to come back and help us, he said he couldn't come with me. Do you think that's who Katelyn saw?"

"I don't know," Luca said. "She said that whoever she saw was all white. What was this guy wearing?"

She frowned and tried to think back, but everything was a blur. "I don't know."

Erin stood up behind Avery.

"You see it too?" Luca asked.

Erin shook her head, but she didn't speak.

Poor Erin.

"She said whoever she sees is different from what we've all described. She doesn't want to talk about it."

Luca didn't seem satisfied with that answer, but he let it drop.

"Do you think we should go look for him?" Avery

asked. It was what she had wanted for two days now. She hoped Luca would agree. "If he really does live here then he should be able to help us."

Luca frowned and stared at the jungle for long, torturous seconds. Finally, he sighed. "I don't know if it's the right thing or the wrong thing, but if there's someone who can help us then I think we should find him."

"It won't help."

They both turned to Erin. She stood in the sand staring past them, almost as if she was looking at someone behind them, but no one was there.

"He says it won't help. He says we need to go deeper. We'll find answers there."

Luca spun around, his nostrils flaring and his anger showing. "Leave her alone!" he shouted at the open air. "We don't take orders from you."

Erin chuckled and shook her head. "Don't worry about me. I think I'm beyond hope." She took the few steps back to her shelter and climbed inside.

Avery's heart clenched. There had to be something she could do to help. They had to find Rae. "When can we leave?"

Luca glanced around. "It's not like we have anything else to do. Let's see who wants to go with us." He led the way to the others and filled them in on the plan.

Benny volunteered right away.

Katelyn quickly stepped forward, too. "I want to see him again. He was really fascinating."

With Katelyn coming, Gabby signed right up.

June stepped forward, too. She stood near Avery and offered a small smile. "I'm not real thrilled about this, but if there's some dark force floating around Erin then I'd rather not hang out with her."

Avery hadn't thought about it like that. She glanced at Erin, worried about leaving her alone, but the youth leader seemed to be asleep again.

They started toward the jungle as a group, but Avery kept her head down as they walked. Everyone must have heard the conversation between her and Luca. Now they all knew she'd seen some random guy. What did they think of her? Especially the kids from her own youth group.

She chanced a glance at the others, but no one seemed to care about her one way or another. That eased some of her anxiety, but it felt like the day her mom left all over again.

Inside the jungle, even the morning air was hot, and sweat quickly pooled on her back, forehead, and neck. She took a deep breath and let it out slowly.

That was when she saw the first black bug. It skittered across the path in front of her, barely missing Luca's feet.

Avery shuddered and pushed ahead.

"What if we see another monkey?" Benny asked.

"Or another snake?" June wrapped her arms around her waist.

Luca shook his head. "We've done OK so far. I'm not worried about that."

Right now Avery felt she could deal with a snake or a monkey. What she was worried about was seeing another black beetle. She watched the others' faces as they hiked deeper into the jungle, waiting to see if anyone else saw the things she was seeing, but no one seemed to be freaked out like her.

After a half hour of walking, the group paused for a break and passed out the water bottles.

Avery took a long drink then glanced around the jungle to figure out where they were. She recognized the location immediately. "I think we should head that way," she said, nodding to the left. That was where she had seen him.

Luca frowned and looked toward the direction she pointed. "It doesn't look like there's a path that way."

"I've been there before," she said quickly.

He nodded. "OK. We can check it out."

They finished their water and turned to the left, beating out a path as they walked.

Excitement built with each step Avery took. Who was Rae? Did he live nearby? Could he tell them where they were and how to get out? Where to find help?

Who was sabotaging them?

Regardless, he might know where they could go to get out of here. Since none of their phones seemed to work, he might know of a place they could call for help.

The thought brought her up short. "Luca!"

The entourage stopped and everyone looked at her, waiting.

She couldn't keep the smile off her face. "We're in the jungle! When we got back yesterday, well, we all got caught up in building shelters. We never checked for signal on Benny's phone."

Luca's face lit up and he spun to Benny. "Did you bring it?"

Benny frowned but pulled the phone from his pocket. "Yeah, but the battery is just about dead. I'm not sure how much you'll be able to use it."

Luca grabbed the phone and Avery pushed in closer to see whatever he saw. He powered up the phone and waited for everything to load. One green bar indicated the tiniest of signals.

Avery glanced at Luca in excitement. "See if you can call my dad."

He shook his head. "What if your dad is lost, too? We would waste what battery we have left." As soon as he'd finished speaking, the phone chimed.

Plug into charger. 4% battery power remaining.

Luca typed in a different number—Avery recognized his home number—but when he hit the call button, a message flashed that there wasn't sufficient signal for the call to go through. Luca growled.

"Try the internet," Avery said.

"Here." Benny pushed past her. "I have a maps app." He touched the screen, and a new app opened.

Avery leaned in close. She was familiar with maps of the Middle East. Daddy had been digging there since she was a little girl, and she'd seen dozens of maps of the place. She recognized Baghdad right away, and a few other Iraqi cities. They were all very far away.

Odd, since the village they were going to was only a two-hour drive from the airport in Baghdad.

A small, blue dot blinked for their location, and they seemed to be in the middle of nowhere.

The phone chimed again.

Battery depleted. Powering down.

"Great," Luca said. "That didn't do us any good."

But it had done Avery some good, even though she chose to keep it to herself for now. They had been whisked hundreds of miles from the road where they were driving, and they really were lost in the middle of nowhere.

This jungle just got a whole lot weirder.

15

Luca

Luca pushed another branch out of the way and peered at the jungle. No white flash, no natives, no vision. Nothing. The phone idea hadn't done any good, and now Avery's directions were coming up short.

He wiped the sweat from his forehead and sighed. How much longer should they keep trying before heading back? They'd already stopped twice to eat fruit, but after eating real food for supper last night, his stomach was demanding more than the few pears he'd scarfed down.

"Anyone see anything?" he asked.

Everyone shook their heads.

Avery stared straight ahead as she walked, almost like she was determined to find whatever it was she was looking for.

But the others looked tired, the same way he felt. June's shoulders sagged and Benny kept falling farther behind. Katelyn and Gabby had walked most of the morning with linked arms, but even they had stepped apart and now trudged one behind the other.

"I wish we knew what time it was," he said. "I have no idea if we should head back."

"I don't know what time it is, but I do know I'm tired," Benny said.

No surprise there.

Avery stopped and frowned. "We haven't found anything. If there are people who live here and can help us, we need to try and find them."

"No one lives here," Katelyn said. "All I said was that I saw a vision."

Luca turned to Avery cautiously. He didn't want to upset her, but he was really tired. "And all I saw was a flash of white."

Her eyes narrowed, but she didn't accuse him of calling her crazy again. He would have to be more careful about his word choices from now on, especially if he was ever going to convince her that he wanted their friendship back.

"I know what I saw."

"And I believe you. All I'm saying is we may need to call it quits for today. We can try a different path tomorrow."

"Besides, maybe that Bradley guy will be back by tomorrow," Katelyn said.

"We can't wait on the hope that he's coming back," Avery said. "He may not find anyone."

Luca didn't like the tone of her words, or what they implied. She said it like it was already a done deal—Bradley's little excursion into the desert was pointless. He would have to ask her about that later.

"Why don't we go on for a little while longer, and we can come back tomorrow if we don't find anything soon?"

Avery frowned but nodded.

He kept in his sigh of relief. He hated fighting with her.

They walked for what felt like an hour or more when Avery stopped. She glanced around, her breathing quick. "I think we're close."

Luca stepped around everyone to stand close to her. "What makes you say that?"

She frowned and glanced around, then looked back at him. Studying his face for another few seconds, she almost seemed—nervous?

Finally, she gulped. "Because the bugs are gone."

Now it was his turn to frown. "What bugs?"

She sighed. "I see huge black bugs. I've seen them all through the jungle. But there aren't any here. I think we're close to him."

Luca kept so still he didn't even blink. Giant bugs? For real? He kept his breathing steady as he glanced around. Nothing stirred on the branches, not even a few small bugs.

But others had seen weird things.

Even he had seen them. It was hard to swallow, but the least he could do was take her seriously. "OK. So he's around. Can you call to him?"

She bit her lip and glanced across the jungle.

He followed her gaze. Nothing here indicated someone had come through recently, and it definitely didn't look like anyone lived here.

She cleared her throat. "Is anyone here?" Her voice barely made it to the canopy of trees above them, and it echoed weakly through the air. "R—Rae?"

Silence answered her, and the look on her face snapped his heart in two. The urge to squeeze her hand and show his support was so strong he had to clasp his hands behind his back.

"Hello?" she tried again.

They waited a few more moments and he was just about to turn the group around when a twig snapped nearby. He spun around, looking for anything that might have made the sound. For all he knew it could be another crazed monkey, or worse.

But they all stared in shock when a guy their own age stepped through the trees. His eyes didn't scan the group because they were stuck on Avery.

Luca frowned.

The guy stepped forward tentatively, coming closer and closer to Avery. "You found your friends, I see."

Avery stared at him with wide eyes. At first, she didn't reply, but then she seemed to shake herself. "Yes. Thank you."

"So, it was you!" Katelyn said. "You're the one I saw!"

He—Rae—glanced at Katelyn. "Yes. It was me. I am glad for your safety."

His gaze swung back to Avery. "Why are you here? I told you I would find you when the time was right."

"We need your help getting out of this place." Avery stepped closer to him, her voice pleading. "We tried to leave and it didn't work."

Rae frowned, and he looked around at all of them. "The time is not yet right."

That was enough of that. Luca pushed forward. "Where are we? If you can give us some idea then we'll be on our way."

Rae looked at him then, but he didn't give in to Luca's demand. "You sent others away."

Luca tensed thinking about Bradley and his group. "How do you know that?" Had this creep been watching them?

Rae backed off. "I know this jungle well. I move fast through it, and I see a lot of things. I believe you will find your way out."

Luca stepped close to Rae, his fists balled and his breaths coming too fast. "Tell us where we are!"

Rae's eyes softened as he stared at Luca.

After only a few moments, Luca wasn't mad anymore. Not anxious, or jealous. Whoever—or whatever—this Rae guy was, he had some sort of calming powers.

Luca frowned and stepped away, and Avery stepped forward. "Are you going to help us?" she asked. "You promised to help."

He nodded. "I am working on it, but it takes time."

"Who's in charge? Are there others besides you?" Luca asked.

"As I said, I am working on it. I will find you all when I have something for you."

That wasn't nearly good enough for Luca, but his desire to fight had all but vanished.

Rae took a few steps backwards, like he was ready to leave, but Avery stopped him.

"Wait! Are there others? Others who aren't as kind as you?"

Rae frowned deeply, his face cautious. "What do you mean?"

Avery shifted from foot to foot. She wrung her hands. "Our youth leader is seeing someone, but she said he's not like you, and none of us can see him."

Rae's face fell, and his nostrils flared. "I was not aware of this. I will try to take care of it."

"So there are others," Luca said. It came out louder and more angrily than he'd meant for it to, but he didn't care. If Rae was keeping things from them, they couldn't trust him.

Rae didn't acknowledge his statement. "I will find

you. Soon, hopefully." He retreated to the mass of trees behind him and was gone.

Everyone pressed closer together.

Luca couldn't blame them. He didn't know how to describe it except to say it actually felt less safe with Rae gone. Luca looked to Avery and she smiled.

"He's real," she said.

His heart softened a little. "Did you think he wasn't?"

She nodded and swallowed hard. "I worried."

He tried to smile but it came out more like a grimace. "I don't trust anything he said. Let's get out of here."

Benny spun toward the direction of camp and started walking. "You don't have to tell me twice."

The others followed him.

Luca tugged on Avery's arm, gently asking if she'd walk with him. She hung back until the others had gone a few steps ahead, then they began walking together. "Why didn't you tell me about him?" he asked softly.

She glanced at him. "You saw him too, but you didn't tell me."

He shook his head. "That was different. I saw a flash of something that could have been my imagination. You saw him and spoke to him."

"He could have been my imagination, too."

"Avery, you can't say things like that."

She stared forward stubbornly and didn't answer him.

Luca let it go. Her self-confidence had never been all that high, but in the last couple years, her dad had squashed what little she did have right out of her. Luca longed to see it built back up. She'd been amazing since being stranded, always stepping up and volunteering for whatever needed to be done. He wanted to help her see who she really was.

Luca sighed and moved on to something else. "You say there aren't any black beetles around when he's there?"

"That's right."

"What about out in the desert, when you're around Erin. Do you see anything then?"

She frowned and glanced at him. "I don't think so. It's only in the jungle. Why?"

"Whatever Erin is seeing is different than Rae. If the bugs don't come around him, I thought maybe they were coming from whatever's bothering Erin."

Her frown deepened and she hugged herself. "Would you agree that whatever is bothering her isn't human?"

He didn't like thinking of it that way, but...

"Yeah, I guess so."

She glanced at him, her worry written all over her face. "So what does that make Rae?"

16

Avery

Erin sat near the small fire when they returned. She poked it with a stick, keeping it from burning out. Not that they needed the heat during the day—it was sweltering—but at some point they would run out of matches, so they'd decided to keep a fire going at all times.

Benny had pointed out it might help with rescue, too, if a plane happened to fly overhead. Not that anyone had seen a plane.

Sam sat near Erin, whispering quietly. He seemed to be helping her.

She didn't look as upset as normal. She looked up as the group approached. "Did you find him?"

Avery nodded. "Rae said he would try to help us." He also said he would try to help Erin. She hoped he followed through with that.

"No sign of Bradley?" Luca asked.

Sam shook his head but Avery wasn't surprised. Of course, he wouldn't be back with help.

There weren't any villages or cities around for hundreds of miles, though no one else knew that.

She wanted to bring it to their attention, but at this point, something held her back. It was the same feeling she'd had earlier, the feeling of the jungle drawing her in. Maybe something had brought them here for a reason, even if she had no idea what the reason could be. It was almost as if she belonged. As if she were needed. The thought bugged her. "Can we eat?" she asked, ready to put those thoughts aside.

Erin nodded. "Some of the others went to get fruit and water."

Avery sat beside Erin and sighed. The jungle always took something out of her—it took something out of them all. Water sounded like heaven.

It wasn't long before she heard laughter coming from the trees, and a few moments later the others in their dwindling group stepped through the tree line.

David carried a bag of water bottles and the girls each carried a bundle of fruit in what looked like handmade baskets.

"How did you do that?" Avery asked. She fingered one of the delicately weaved contraptions. "That's awesome."

Mallory beamed. "My mom took a basket weaving class last summer." She rolled her eyes. "I was totally annoyed when she made me come, but I guess it came in handy."

Everyone gathered around the fire and passed out the fruit and water. They had agreed to only eat the boxed food once a day. It would last longer that way, just in case Bradley couldn't find help. No one talked about what would happen if Bradley never came back at all, or if no one ever came to their rescue.

Avery hated to admit it, but she was beginning to realize that without some serious intervention from God, they weren't getting out of here any time soon. She glanced at their group and considered what this meant for each of them. They had clothes, but how long would those last? A few years? A few decades?

She shuddered and looked at the group. No one else seemed all doom and gloom. In fact, the others seemed to be enjoying themselves.

Luca said something that made June throw back her head and laugh.

Avery frowned. That was something she didn't plan on watching.

The sun crept closer to the tree line and before long June and Luca started singing an upbeat song she recognized from church. How did Luca even know all these songs? He hadn't been to church in months.

She turned away from them so she wouldn't have to watch. If the van were here she'd close herself in, but the shelters were in plain view of everyone, and she'd still be able to hear them if she holed up inside one. For now, she was stuck listening, but she didn't like it. Music didn't soothe her like it used to, not like it did before Mom left and Daddy wrote her off.

The songs ended and the cool, desert air began stirring. The sun was gone now, and the desert was bathed in darkness.

Avery turned her face toward the sky. Stars stretched into infinity. It was the first time she'd looked up and noticed the stars since arriving, and the sight took her breath away. The others' chatter faded away as she stared into the heavens. The silence of space echoed in her head and for the first time, she realized it was silent in her mind. That was encouraging, at least. She could make it a few minutes without worrying. Without wondering.

A rustling noise sounded behind her and she turned.

Nothing.

She frowned and looked back at the group. No one

had heard—they were too busy having a get-together—but she'd definitely heard it.

Standing quietly, she stretched her arms and kept her eyes on the trees. The rustling sounded again and she stepped closer, but everything was silent and still. She waited another moment and let out a slow breath. She was too uptight. Turning back to the fire, she heard it again. "Snakes!" she screamed.

Chaos erupted around the fire. Everyone leaped to their feet, pushing into each other and screaming.

A dozen snakes poured from the jungle, rattling their tails like babies' toys. They spread out like lava, but these weren't like any snakes Avery had ever seen. Their scaly skin was a bright yellow with red and black rings circling their bodies.

Avery shivered. Running was pointless but she couldn't help it. She wasn't even sure where she was going. She scrambled on top of the box of food. It was the highest point she could see.

Luca lunged for his shelter and Avery frowned. Did he think that rickety shack would save him? He emerged a second later carrying the huge stick. It was the same one he'd carried in the jungle when they searched for Gabby and Katelyn.

David came from the trees a moment later, and he carried a stick, too.

They worked together at bashing the snakes.

Tasha, Mallory, and Brittany huddled together, crying. Two snakes coiled a few feet from them, hissing but not attacking.

Benny had passed out a few feet into the desert.

Avery glanced out further and gasped.

Gabby and Katelyn had made it away and bolted for the van.

The van! They needed to make it there for protection.

She waved her arms, trying to get Luca's attention, but he was too busy beheading the snakes. It almost looked like he was enjoying it.

And then the most disturbing part of all; Erin sat on her log, same as before. She stared straight ahead, not watching the chaos around her, and no snakes bothered her.

Chills raced up Avery's arm and made her shiver, chills that had nothing to do with the cold night air.

"Is that all of them?" Luca called out. He held his stick like some kind of ninja warrior, his eyes scanning the ground.

"I don't see anymore," David said.

Luca loosened up and dropped his stick. "Let's make sure everyone is OK."

Climbing off that box was the hardest thing Avery had ever done. She put one foot down, then the other, almost like the disturbance in the sand would alert the snakes and they'd come slithering back into camp.

Dead snakes lay scattered around the sand and she shivered again. So many all at once? That couldn't be normal. Then again, what about this place was normal?

"Gabby and Katelyn made it to the van," she managed to call out.

Everyone else seemed unharmed, but Benny still hadn't woken up from his fainting spell.

She turned to scan the others and gasped.

"June!" Avery slid in the sand as she made her way over. "June, are you OK?"

June lay in the sand, as if she'd fallen off her log.

Luca raced toward them and bent down to examine June. "Was she bitten?"

Avery's hands moved over June's body, searching for any sign of a bite. She rolled June's left leg and her stomach dropped. Two perfect dots of blood marked her calf.

"What do we do?" she asked. Panic erupted. "What do we do?"

Luca shook his head and gulped. "I don't know."

Avery glanced around like an answer would be floating in the night sky. Her gaze landed on the van and her heart soared. "The medical supplies! We have to open the box of supplies."

Luca frowned but stood, taking June in his arms. "Let's go."

"June's been bitten," she called out. "We're going to the van."

The others fell in line behind them, even Erin.

Avery guessed no one wanted to sleep near a snake-infested jungle. Avery reached the van before Luca.

Gabby and Katelyn sat inside, breathing hard.

Katelyn held her inhaler to her lips, taking a deep drag.

Avery didn't speak to them. She tore her fingernails trying to rip into the box of medical supplies. "Do you think we brought any anti-venom?" she called out. "I don't know what that looks like."

Benny jogged over and dug through the box. He had a knot on his head, but he seemed otherwise unharmed from his fainting spell. He pulled out a small container and handed it to her, then dug around some more until he found syringes.

She stared in shock.

Benny blushed and shrugged. "I watch a lot of TV."

She managed a smile just as Luca arrived with a lifeless June in his arms.

"Lay her in the van," Avery said.

Luca obeyed as Avery filled the syringe with whatever was in the vial. It was cold, and she realized it had been surrounded by ice packs. She stared at the needle and licked her lips. Needles didn't bother her, but she'd never given someone a shot before.

"Put it in a vein," Benny instructed. "In the bloodstream."

Avery took a deep, steadying breath and obeyed without question, plunging the needle into her thigh. June didn't move or even groan, but there was nothing else they could do.

Everyone piled into the van, huffing and puffing. They'd all just run a mile.

Avery's whole body ached. "What do we do now?" she asked.

Benny leaned forward excitedly. "Now we wait. She may have an allergic reaction. We'll have to wait and see."

"Will she wake up?"

Benny shrugged. "That's the waiting part."

Tasha burst into fresh tears and Avery swallowed hard. Things kept getting worse and worse, instead of better. When was Rae's help going to kick in?

She glanced at Luca, but he only had eyes for June. His nostrils flared and he stared at her, his arms crossed across his chest.

Avery looked back to June. She was one of the nicest people Avery had ever met.

This anti venom had to work. It had to. And when June woke up Avery was going to make sure she got to know her better. She would find out why she'd come on this trip, what her hopes and dreams were, and what she liked to do for fun back home. June had been a good friend to her, and it was time to repay the favor.

Everyone slept in the van that night.

June took up an entire seat, but without Bradley and his crew, there was still enough room.

Luca slept up front with Sam, like he'd been doing all along.

Avery overheard their conversation about the impossibility that they were actually attacked by snakes.

Sam claimed he'd never seen snakes like that.

Avery sat directly behind June's head. She propped her temple against the window so she could keep an eye on June's breathing, but keeping herself awake was nearly impossible. Her eyes drifted closed a few different times, and finally she wasn't able to jerk herself awake. Dreams played through her mind, one after another. She saw Mom. Rae. Snakes. Daddy. A hospital.

Everything swirled together in one chaotic dream, and when she woke up the next morning, her head ached and her muscles pinched. Taking a deep breath, she sat up and checked on June.

June slept peacefully, her breathing steady and sure.

Avery smiled in relief. *Thank you, God!* At least something had gone right.

The others began to stir.

A few minutes later, June woke up too. Her bright blue eyes shone in the morning light.

Everyone crowded around her as best they could in the small van.

She smiled and assured them she felt OK.

But something bothered Avery, something she was afraid to tell anyone.

June's eyes were supposed to be green.

17

Luca

The campsite at the tree line looked undisturbed since running away the night before. The dead snakes had shriveled some, and he quickly tossed the corpses into the jungle before picking up a few other things that had been knocked over, and relighting the fire. The others wouldn't want to sleep here tonight. He couldn't blame them, but the choices were pretty slim unless they could manage to put the van in neutral and push it back to the camp.

Now for the hard part. He glanced at the trees and took a deep breath. Raising his stick, he moved toward the bushes and branches nearest the camp. He rattled his stick through the brush, hoping to scare out anything they didn't want hanging around their camp. When nothing came slithering out, a pent-up sigh escaped his lips. He turned toward the van and waved the stick over his head.

David stood at the hood of the van in the distance and he waved back.

The line of kids from the van started toward him.

It would be a while before they got there, so he pulled food from the box and started cooking it over the fire. He sat on a log and watched them move his way.

What were they doing here? Would they ever get

home? There didn't seem to be any hope in sight.

Luca kicked at the sand and sighed. If there were a good way out of here, he didn't know what it was.

Rae—whatever he was—didn't seem to have a clear plan to help them. He may live here, but he didn't seem all that smart about the area. And by the way he watched Avery, it was almost as if he didn't want to help them leave.

That bugged Luca. A lot. Luca forced himself to relax when he realized he was clenching his teeth.

The group inched toward him.

Even June limped along with the others. She really did seem OK.

He'd never seen anyone with a snake bite, so he hadn't been sure what to expect. It looked like everything worked out OK—except for the fact they'd been attacked by strange snakes.

Maybe Rae would have an answer for that.

By the time everyone arrived, the food Luca had set over the fire was ready. They gathered around the fire and pulled out the water, fruit, and noodles he had cooked. The talk was mostly non-existent. Everyone looked around them continuously, glancing at the branches and listening hard.

They were anxious. Anxious about snakes. About rescue.

About non-rescue.

When they'd finally finished eating, and everyone had almost-relaxed, Luca moved to sit by June. "How are you feeling?"

She leaned close and smiled. "I'm OK. My leg's a little sore, but if that's the worst of my problems I guess it's not too bad."

"Good point. Take it easy today, though, OK? We

don't know how that anti venom stuff works."

"I'll do whatever you say, oh fearless leader." She grabbed his forearm and smiled again.

Luca forced out a smile and pulled his arm away. She must be loopy from whatever Benny had given her. "I'm going to check on the others."

He slipped away and moved toward the rest of the group. Erin seemed lucid this morning. That wasn't necessarily a good thing. She acted resolved to seeing strange dark creatures. Used to it.

No one should have to get used to that.

Avery talked with Benny about who knew what, and some of the other girls huddled together in the girls' shelter.

Luca headed for the other guys. "What do you think about trying to push the van back?"

Sam's eyebrows rose and David frowned.

"You would like us to push it for over a mile?" Sam asked.

"I know it's a lot of work, but no one is going to want to trek back and forth every morning and night."

"Wait," David said. "How much longer do you think we're going to be here?"

Luca shook his head. "I wish I could answer that, but I can't. None of us know where we are, and so far it doesn't look like anyone is looking for us."

David's frown deepened and he shifted in the sand. "Do you really think we can push it that far?"

Sam nodded. "It is possible, though many things may go wrong."

Luca looked to Sam, thankful for his stamp of approval. Having Mom thankful for his help was one thing—but she was his mom. She had to be thankful. Sam was different. Having approval from him meant that maybe Luca was doing OK after all.

Glancing around, he calculated who else could help. Benny might do some good, and Avery always jumped in with both feet.

"OK," he said. "It may take us half the morning, so let's get started." He quickly rounded up Avery then Benny—who complained about making the back and forth trip for a second time that morning—and they turned to head toward the van.

Something moved in the distance.

Luca frowned. He held out his arm. "Wait. Do you guys see that?"

The others squinted toward the rising sun and open desert. At first no one said anything, but then someone gasped.

"Is that Bradley?" Tasha said from behind them. "It's Bradley, and he brought a rescue group!"

The other girls ran forward, squealing and shouting their excitement. The feeling was contagious and Benny whooped while David and June grinned.

Tasha started crying—again—blubbering about being saved and getting home.

Luca watched the approaching group with restrained excitement. Bradley had definitely found someone, but something felt off. He glanced at Avery.

She frowned. "Are you thinking what I'm thinking?"

He looked back to the group and nodded. "They're all walking. If they were here to rescue us, wouldn't they have a van?"

"Exactly. He found someone, but it looks like he found someone else who was lost."

Defeat wrapped around him like the hot water in his shower back home. He hated to break it to everyone. They were going to be devastated when Bradley's large group made it to them.

And it was a large group. It looked almost as big as their own group.

That's when he realized who was coming.

Avery made the connection at the same moment and she gasped. "Daddy!"

He tried to keep her back—she'd collapse from heat stroke if she ran that far—but she was too fast. She slipped and slid through the sand as she made her way toward them. If she was going then Luca guessed he was too. Avery's dad had some questions to answer, and he probably had a few questions to ask of his own.

"Avery wait!" Luca said. "We can't run that far. Wait until they get closer!"

She slowed down, but barely.

They ran all the way to the van before they slowed to a stop.

Luca bent over, panting. Running was a dumb thing to do.

"I can't believe he found them." Avery sucked in deep breaths as sweat dripped down her temples. "There's no one around here for miles."

He frowned but didn't reply. What did she mean by that?

"They're coming from the direction they left," Luca said instead. "So did he find them in the middle of the desert?"

She shrugged. "It's almost like they walked in a straight line and back."

Luca gulped and looked toward the jungle. Where were they?

The group drew closer and Avery couldn't contain her excitement. "I can't believe they're here. I was afraid I'd never see him again."

He smiled, but inside he cringed. He'd never win Avery back with her dad hanging around. He didn't understand why she wanted to please him so badly.

Mr. Miles had no time for Avery, and he never had. Once, he'd promised to take her skiing for Christmas. He'd told her to have her bags packed on Christmas Eve morning. Then, when the big day arrived, he was gone. He'd left in the middle of the night after getting a tip on a big dig. He hadn't called to explain, or even apologized when he finally got home.

Then, after Avery's *episode* when her mom left, he'd practically stopped speaking to her—period. Instead of Avery getting angry, she'd tried harder to make him happy. When Mr. Miles was around, it felt like Avery barely had a brain.

He glanced at her again, and her smile melted his heart a little. No matter what had happened, he would always wish he'd been enough for Dad. Maybe he could understand Avery's motives after all.

Finally, the group drew close enough for Avery to reach and she raced out to greet them. She laughed and threw herself into her dad's arms. He wrapped her in a hug and whispered something into her ear, and Luca couldn't help but smile for her. A jerk or not, Avery loved him.

At least she still had her dad, which was more than he could say.

Luca took a deep breath and forced himself to unclench his fists. Breaking open his knuckles—again—on the side of the van wouldn't help anyone, especially in front of Mr. Miles.

He reached the group a few paces behind Avery

and clapped Bradley on the shoulder. "I'm taking it you didn't find a rescue group?"

Bradley's eyes showed his confusion, but he shook his head. "We walked straight out into the desert, but somehow we ended up on the other side of the jungle."

Luca winced, and confusion clung to his brain. How was that even possible? "This place doesn't make any sense."

"Where's Erin?" Chad stepped forward and Luca saw his face. Worry practically dripped from his shoulders.

Bradley must have told him how his wife had been acting.

"She's back at camp," Luca said. "She'll be glad to see you."

Chad didn't wait for anyone else as he jogged through the sand and toward the tree line.

Luca turned back to Bradley's group. "Have you guys eaten? Did you run out of water?"

"We found fruit and water on our side of the jungle," Mr. Miles said.

"What about your van?" Luca felt kind of absurd asking Mr. Miles these questions, as if they were equals when Luca knew full well they weren't. And he knew that Mr. Miles hated him.

Mr. Miles shook his head. "Won't crank. Bradley tells me you guys ran out of gas."

"That's right. But we have food and medical supplies from the back of the van, so let's get everyone back and we'll make sure everyone eats something more filling than fruit."

Mr. Miles smiled and clapped Luca's shoulder. "Well done, Luca."

That was a first.

Luca shook off his surprise and led the march back to the tree line. As they drew closer, they came upon Chad and Erin. Chad held Erin and cried. Erin rested her head on her husband's shoulder, but no emotion showed on her face. It was almost like she wasn't even happy to see him. It wasn't like her at all, but that wasn't unusual in this place.

A few girls from Mr. Miles' van broke free from the group and ran to meet Gabby, Katelyn, and June. They all hugged in a giant, girly love fest.

The rest of the group mingled with the kids from his own church.

It was good to be together again. Really good.

With more of them, they should be able to figure out a way home. There would be more brains working together, and Mr. Miles was sure to know something about their location—he knew everything about the Middle East.

A few of them moved to boil noodles for the newcomers, while the rest sat in the shade to rest from their long journey.

"Tell me what happened," Luca said as Bradley got comfortable near the fire.

Everyone gathered around him and he cleared his throat. "We started off heading toward the open desert, but by midday we knew something was off. We'd made a wrong turn somewhere along the line.

"The next thing we knew we were walking toward the jungle instead of away from it, but when we got closer we saw the van. We thought we'd made it back here, to our own camp, but I noticed the van was pointing toward the jungle instead of away from it, and that's when I saw Mr. Miles."

"We were blown to the other side of the jungle,"

Mr. Miles broke in. "We've been there for days now."

Avery frowned and shook her head. "Daddy, how is this possible? We were on the same road, but we ended up in two different places. Two entirely different places."

Mr. Miles didn't seem at all disturbed. He shrugged and shook his head. "Stranger things have happened."

Luca frowned. There was more to his answer that he wasn't sharing. And he wasn't even upset at being lost. Luca knew he'd never trusted that man.

Bradley continued his story and Luca turned to listen. "Once we'd rested for the night with Mr. Miles's group, we loaded up and headed back here. We stopped to sleep for the night, and we weren't even sure we were headed in the right direction, but first thing this morning we continued the trip." Bradley pointed at their van and laughed. "I never thought I'd be so happy to see that old clunker."

Luca smiled on the outside, and he was glad Bradley and the others had made it back, but his mind worked quickly.

Mr. Miles was hiding something, and whatever it was, it had to be big.

18

Avery

Based on Daddy's behavior, Avery was sure he knew something about their location. Or at least suspected something.

He acted relaxed and excited, instead of uptight and anxious to be rescued.

And worse, based on Luca's facial expression, he saw it too. Luca didn't think much of Daddy at all, and it killed Avery. Daddy could be kind—when he tried.

She swallowed hard and looked away. Sometimes she saw families who looked so happy. So normal. They didn't know how blessed they were.

The food was passed around and Avery took her small portion. Her stomach twisted when she looked at it, but she made herself eat it, nerves or not.

After everyone ate, she worked up the courage to talk to Daddy. He might shoot her down—he usually did—but she had to try.

He stepped away from the group and stared into the jungle, and Avery quickly followed him.

He spotted her and turned her way. "I missed you, Avery. I worried about you." He smiled and patted her shoulders.

She smiled and nodded, but she almost doubted his words. He'd never played the part of the worried father all that well, especially when he was excited about an upcoming dig. "I thought I'd never see you again," she admitted. "This place is really strange."

He glanced up at the massive jungle canopy over their heads. "Strange is too weak a word. This place is special."

"Daddy, what do you think about it? I've been trying to figure it out."

Something passed across his face. Surprise, or suspicion, maybe? But it was gone as quickly as it had come. He shrugged. "Too early to say, but we've stumbled onto something big. I've been trying to dig up some information from my side, but I had a whole group of teens to take care of."

Why did he have to sound annoyed over that? He had agreed to chaperone a mission trip, after all. He could put away work for a few days during *an emergency*.

She didn't say that to him. Never would.

"Now that we've found each other, I shouldn't have to play such a vital role in caring for the others. I'll be free to figure out what's going on."

"Daddy, you can't be going out in the jungle alone. It's dangerous. Last night we were attacked by—"

"I'm a grown man who's been on a lot of dangerous digs, Avery. You just keep doing your part in taking care of everyone here, and leave the discovery work to me." He patted her shoulder like he was comforting a dense child.

He was dismissing her—and what she wanted—just like he always had.

She stood awkwardly, not sure how to answer him, but there was no need to worry; he wouldn't listen to her anyway.

Daddy looked deeper into the jungle, practically

glowing with excitement. "I can hardly wait to get in there and learn this place's secrets!"

She could tell him a few secrets—magically appearing fruit, a state of confusion that permeated the jungle air, a dark force. And one couldn't forget the inhuman natives.

But she didn't tell him any of that. Rae had chosen to reveal himself to her, and *only* her. That is, until they'd gone tracking him down. Even then, though, he'd spoken to her during their exchange. If anyone could get the jungle's secrets from Rae, it was her. Not Daddy.

"Avery?" Luca's voice gave her an excuse to get out of there, but Daddy stopped her with a tug on her arm.

"I hope you haven't gotten involved with that boy again."

She frowned and pulled her arm away. "Of course not."

"Good. I see that he's really stepped in and taken care of everyone here, but that doesn't mean he's good for you."

Anger bubbled up her legs and spilled over into her stomach. "We've all taken care of each other here."

She stomped away before he could reply, and she hurried to find Luca.

He stood near the shelters, backpack in hand. "We're going to the water hole. With this many people we're going to need a lot. Want to come?" His relaxed, undemanding attitude calmed her down.

"Yeah," she said. "That sounds great."

They gathered two backpacks full of empty water bottles, then they hiked into the jungle with Benny and June. Avery frowned at June as she climbed over a fallen tree. "Shouldn't you be staying off that leg?"

June scowled at Avery. "I'm OK. It's not even sore anymore."

Avery's cheeks burned and she looked away. What was June's problem? She'd never said a mean word to anyone, and now she was mad at Avery?

Luca cleared his throat and glanced at her. "I tried to tell her, but she said we're the water group and she's not missing out."

Benny grumbled and marched ahead.

Avery decided to let June's rude remark pass. She turned and teased Benny. "You aren't trying to shirk your duties are you, Benny?"

He huffed and walked faster.

Avery frowned. He'd been more open and willing to help ever since they'd arrived, but now he seemed back to his usual pity-partying self. It seemed everyone was grumpy since the other group had arrived.

They reached the creek and everyone bent to fill the empty bottles.

"I almost didn't ask you to come," Luca said. He squatted beside her. "I thought you might want to stay with your dad."

Avery worked to keep her face neutral. "Yeah, well, he seems less excited at seeing me than I was at seeing him." Telling Luca these things was safe. It was nothing he didn't know already. She wanted Luca and Daddy to get along, but maybe she wanted a sounding board more.

"What do you think of all this? Of everything Bradley told us?"

She screwed the lid on a bottle and grabbed another. "I don't know. I'm working on it."

His eyebrows rose. "You got a theory?"

Did she? Finally, she shook her head. "Not really, but there are a few things I can't shake. I'll let you know when I figure it all out." She ended with a grin and he smiled back.

He believed her. Believed *in* her. He was the only one who had, or at least the only one who had in a while.

Guilt pinged at the edge of her mind, guilt that he believed in her more than she had believed in him. And when he'd needed her most, she'd followed Daddy's order to stay away. It was a wonder he even spoke to her.

Still, this felt good. Renewing their friendship couldn't hurt anything, and she needed a person she could be herself with. Someone who wouldn't stare at her or ignore her.

A thought occurred to her and she paused. In the last few days, there hadn't been any stares. No one had left her out of anything. She tucked the information away for later and kept working.

They finished filling all the bottles, and Avery pulled a pack onto her back. Luca took the other and they started back.

"Do you guys care if I stay here for a while?"

Everyone turned to June, surprised by her question. "You want to stay here alone?" Avery asked.

June's eyes still sparkled a startling blue. Avery hadn't brought it up to anyone, especially since it was just another reason everyone might think she'd lost her marbles.

June glanced at the guys and blushed. "I wanted to swim for a while. You know. Wash up."

Washing sounded really good. Better than good, it sounded great. "Why don't we get some shampoo and stuff from our bags? We can come back with all the girls."

"Actually, I wanted to do it alone."

It was so unlike June, Avery wasn't sure what to say. She looked to Luca.

Leaving someone alone in the jungle was a definite breach in the rules everyone had agreed to.

"What if I stay but the guys go?" she asked. "I won't go in with you. I'll stay at this end of the creek, and I won't look."

June frowned but didn't argue.

Benny took the pack of water from Avery's shoulders and put it on his own back. Luca grabbed her elbow. "Are you sure about this?"

"What other choice do we have?" she whispered.

He nodded, his frown deep. "OK. We're coming back for you, though. Stay put until we get back."

She agreed and glanced at June.

The blonde girl smiled shyly at Luca then moved toward the swim hole as the guys moved away.

Great. She was alone in the dark, creepy jungle with a girl whose eyes had changed color and who was seriously acting weird.

Finding a big rock, she slid to a seat and folded her legs Indian style. The soft sounds of splashing drifted upstream from where June washed a few feet away. Shampoo sounded heavenly, even if June didn't think so. When they got back, she would have to get all the girls together and return to the creek. She sighed and lay back on the rock then stared at the trees above her. No matter how small he made her feel, Daddy's presence in their camp was good.

He brought a feeling of security to everyone. Of leadership. A plan.

But how had Daddy's van ended up on the other side of the jungle? And where, exactly, was this jungle? She focused her mind on maps she'd seen in Daddy's study over the years. He'd been almost obsessed with Iraq, and he'd made many archeological discoveries throughout the Middle East since Avery's childhood. Was he after another one on this trip? Was that why he'd come?

Anger. Betrayal. Disbelief and yet total belief.

Feelings ransacked her heart until reason pushed them out.

He couldn't have known about this place. No one could have predicted a sand storm that would blow them halfway across the country and deposit them in an uninhabited oasis. Whether he was prepared or not, though, he seemed excited to be here. He suspected a few things about their location, and remembering the maps on his desk, Avery suspected a few things as well.

She closed her eyes and let her mind drift, and she almost didn't notice when the sounds of the water faded away. June must have finished.

Avery opened her eyes. That was when she saw the first bug. It scampered over her rock and disappeared into the water. Avery gasped and pushed herself to the edge, looking over to make sure there weren't more.

A second bug darted along the creek bed, and a third sat in the middle of the path back to the desert.

"June?" she called. "Are you OK?" She hated the way her voice shook.

No one answered and Avery frowned. She did not want to get off this rock with that giant, nasty bug sitting on the path, but it didn't look like she had a choice. "June, I'm coming over there. I need you to answer me."

The only sounds echoing in the air were the jungle sounds of bugs and leaves rustling. Avery shivered when another black beetle crawled up the tree in front of her. Panic crept up her arms and she picked up her speed. "June?"

The swim hole was empty of June, but also of black bugs.

"June!" she screamed.

No one answered her.

Perfect. She stood at the edge of the water and searched for any sign of where June had come out of the water. A muddy path across the creek led into the jungle. They'd never trekked that way, and it was obvious this side led to the path. How had June gotten turned around?

Unless she hadn't gotten turned around at all. Something was different about June since she'd gotten bit. Something more than her eyes.

Avery gnawed her lip, unsure of what to do. If she went after June she might miss Luca when he returned, but if she didn't go after her, June could be in trouble.

She glanced into the denser part of the jungle and paused. Maybe she had one other choice. Maybe.

She closed her eyes and prayed a silent prayer that she wasn't crazy, then she turned and hiked toward the path she'd used to find Rae.

Luca wouldn't be returning for a while. He wouldn't want to chance coming back before June finished, and then there was the time it would take to hike back and forth.

Black bugs followed as she walked, but once she'd gone further, she stopped and swallowed hard. This probably wouldn't work at all. "Rae?" she called out. "Rae, if you can hear me then I need your help."

The black beetles scurried off the path.

Avery swallowed hard and tried again. "Rae?"

More beetles raced up the tree trunks and out of view.

She took a shaky breath and tried one last time. "Rae?"

Leaves rustled and the sound of someone approaching echoed through the thick, jungle air. Avery held her breath.

Something moved up ahead. Leaves rustled. The air vibrated.

Avery squinted. It almost looked like a building. A temple or something? She glanced around, but the beetles were gone. Gulping, she turned back to the temple. She was really seeing this, wasn't she? She stepped toward the stone structure cautiously. She still knew where she was—which meant next to nothing in this place—but hopefully she could find her way back.

The stones of the building were stacked in neat rows, and moss and other vegetation covered them. It was old but well cared for. And it had appeared out of thin air.

Avery moved to the door, an old wooden thing that seemed in as good a shape as she would expect. "Hello?" she called out, knocking on the wood. It was rough under her fingers, but definitely there. Real.

She laughed to herself. It was a nervous-type laugh. Maybe she was crazy after all, if she was knocking on doors of what might be an imaginary temple in the middle of a magical jungle. Taking a deep breath, she pushed through the door and looked around.

The temple had one open room. The middle of the room held some kind of podium or pulpit. The rest of the room was empty from what she could see, so she moved closer to the middle.

The podium was made of stones, and the closer she got the more she could see. It wasn't a podium at all. It was more like an altar. Avery swallowed hard and ran her fingers along the cold stones. Had something been sacrificed here? Animals?

People?

Icy fear crept up her back and she shivered. Suddenly, she had the worst feeling that the black beetles were crawling across her skin. She cried out and jumped away, brushing at her arms and shuddering.

"Are you well?"

The voice made her cry out again, and she spun around. "What are you doing here?" It came out as a shout, and she clamped her lips closed and took a deep breath through her nose.

Rae's face was guarded, and he stepped back. "You called me, did you not?"

"And then an old church appeared out of thin air." Her words still held an angry clip, and she forced herself to calm down. "Sorry. I called you because I hoped you could tell me more about this place. Like what's on the other side of the creek, and why can't you tell me more than what you have?"

It wasn't why she'd come at all. She'd wanted to find June. Find out about the change in June, and the snakes. But now all of her questions came bubbling to the surface. "We were separated from the rest of our group, but now we've found them. Where did they come from?"

Rae opened his mouth like he would answer, but instead he shook his head. "You have to leave this place. I'll help you."

"You keep saying that, but it's not doing any good."

"You can help, as well," he said. He glanced behind him, toward the door, and his face became more nervous than before. "You can help."

If she wasn't crazy, Rae definitely was. "You're not making any sense."

He nodded toward the altar then stepped away. "Hurry. You do not have much time."

Then, he stepped out the door and was gone.

"Rae? Rae!" Avery rushed to the door, but the area was deserted. She growled out her frustration and turned back to the altar. He'd said to hurry. Hurry and what?

A book sat on top the altar. The altar that had definitely been empty when she first came in. Taking another deep breath, she stepped toward it.

The book cover opened easily, and the pages fluttered with the effort. She licked her lips and searched the book. She expected the words to be in Arabic, or at least Latin, but they weren't. It was more like Middle English. Not that she knew much about Middle English. She couldn't even master basic Spanish, but call her crazy, some of it seemed to make sense.

She scanned the words, trying to understand them.

For they are the spirits of devils, working miracles, which go forth unto the kings of the earth and of the whole world, to gather them to the battle of that great day of God Almighty.

What did that even mean?

A voice called in the distance, and Avery spun toward the door. Would anyone else see this temple? Dread filled her, and she remembered Rae's words. She could help. She was meant to see this temple and read this book. She knew she'd felt a pull to the jungle like no one else had.

Making a final decision, she slammed the book closed and hurried out the door, back into the jungle.

June burst through the trees several feet away. "Avery? What's wrong? I heard you yelling and thought you were hurt."

Avery spun to see if the temple was still there, but only jungle greeted her. She deflated. She wasn't sure what was bigger—her relief at seeing June or her disappointment at not seeing the temple. Finally, she turned back to June. "Where were you? You scared me half to death!"

June shrugged, her cheeks turning red. "I had to go to the bathroom."

Heat crept up Avery's neck and ears. She hadn't thought of that. "Oh. Sorry. I just got worried." At least her overreaction had led her to Rae. To the temple.

"It's OK. I'm actually ready to go back now, if you're ready."

Avery nodded and they began walking back to the path when Avery stopped.

June turned and frowned. "What is it?"

Avery watched June for only a second before shaking her head and moving forward, but she shivered.

June's eyes were green again.

As they reached the path near the creek, Luca made his way toward them.

"Wow, that was perfect timing," June said with a smile.

Luca smiled back. "Excellent. Let's get back, shall we?"

Shall we? Since when did he talk like the words from a Middle English book of prophecy?

Avery caught one last smile between June and Luca, and her stomach twisted in knots.

She frowned and dropped to the end of the group as they marched back to camp. June was OK, and that was fine and dandy, but Avery didn't want her and Luca to become best buds.

The pettiness of her jealousy hit her full on. She'd just read words from an ancient book, in a disappearing temple in the middle of a mysterious jungle. High school drama wasn't worth her time.

Avery glanced behind her one last time as they exited the jungle. She knew she wasn't crazy when a flash of white dashed behind a tree.

19

Luca

Avery and the other girls had been gone to the swim hole for almost an hour. Everyone except June, who seemed happy to sit alone in the girls' shelter.

Luca turned back to the guys sitting around the small fire. "We're going to need more shelters," he said. "We have twice the people now. What do you say we bring the van back? It's what we'd originally planned for today."

Bradley leaned forward. "You want us to push that thing through the desert?"

"Why not? There are a dozen of us. It should be easy, and we need the shelter."

"It's a good idea." Mr. Miles nodded slowly, looking at the nothingness of the desert. "You should get started right away."

Which meant he wouldn't be pitching in, obviously.

Sam stood. "I will help."

Luca stood, as well, and several of the others joined him, including the other van's driver. Bradley huffed and rolled his eyes, but he stood, too.

Luca ignored the bad attitude, for now, but he couldn't help thinking that a smack down would knock the problems out of him once and for all. "Once we get everything situated we can start looking for another way out of here."

"I say we find a way out of here now and forget about getting things situated."

Luca bit back his reply to Bradley. They had tried getting out of there, taking many different avenues, and so far, it hadn't worked. Now their only hope of being rescued had shown up at their door. For now, they needed to concentrate on staying safe and alive.

They reached the van and Sam put it in neutral.

"You think you can steer this thing?" Luca asked Benny.

"Of course I can." Benny hopped in to the driver's seat.

The rest of the guys began pushing it backward toward the jungle. Even with so many of them working together, moving a heavy, metal vehicle through the sand wasn't easy. Luca's feet slipped and slid constantly.

At one point, Bradley lost his grip and slid face first into the sand. He jumped up, sputtering and glaring at everyone, but he put his hands back on the van and kept pushing.

By the time they reached the camp, the girls were back.

Avery met them with the bag of water bottles and quickly handed them out while the other girls sat around the fire, laughing and talking.

A moment later, June joined Avery.

"Mind telling me what's going on?" Avery asked.

"We needed more shelter with all of these people. I thought this was easier than building more rickety structures."

She smiled. "You think of everything. But the girls get the van, right?"

He would give her anything she wanted, but he kept that to himself and just laughed. "Yeah, I guess that could work."

They made their way back to the fire and sat down, and Avery glanced around and frowned. "Where's my dad?"

"Your dad?" Luca looked around, too, but Mr. Miles wasn't around. "I don't know. He didn't come with us."

A frown wrinkled the middle of her forehead as she bit her lip. "You think he's OK?"

"I'm sure he's fine. He's a grown man."

She nodded, but the worry wrinkle didn't disappear.

A few of the others approached and surrounded the guys who had pushed the van.

Tasha stepped closer and honed in on Bradley. "What was it like on the other side of the jungle?"

"It looked the same as here. We had to find fruit and water before we came back, and we slept in the other van."

Bradley *could* be a decent guy. Luca didn't understand why he chose not to be, and now, why he was acting like he deserved respect even when he didn't give it.

"How far into the jungle did you go?" Avery leaned toward Bradley casually—too casually—and Luca knew she was after something with her question. She wanted to know if the other group had experienced the weird things their own group had faced. She was going at it all wrong though, since Bradley hadn't ever had to go too far into the jungle on the other side.

One of the other boys, Jeffrey, shook his head and

spoke up. "I couldn't say. It didn't take us long to find food and water, though. There were fruit trees all over the place, and a spring ran right through the tree line."

So they probably hadn't gone in far at all.

"And everyone's been OK?" Avery pressed him for more information. "No one's been sick or feeling strange?"

Jeffrey frowned. "No. Why? Have you guys been sick?"

"Only Erin," Benny said around a mouthful of fruit. "Oh yeah, and Katelyn sees things. And I guess Avery too." He stopped and frowned. "Am I missing anyone? Oh. The snakes. We were attacked by snakes, and a rabid monkey."

A few from the other group frowned and started asking questions.

"Benny," Luca growled. "That's enough." He glanced at Avery, and her cheeks flamed. Probably because Jeffrey took a step back when Benny mentioned Avery seeing things.

Benny held out his hands. "What? He asked what had been going on here so I told him."

"I don't understand," Jeffrey said. "What do you mean you've been seeing things? What's wrong with you guys?"

Erin and Chad sat together in one of the shelters, but they could obviously hear the entire conversation. Erin strode toward them now. "You don't want to know what I see, but some of you won't be so blessed." She turned to Bradley. "And you may as well give up on getting out of here."

Chad hurried to the group, a giant frown on his face. "Erin, there's no need to scare everyone. We're going to find a way to leave. Greater is He that is in us than he that is in the world."

Erin didn't look convinced.

The couple went back to the shelter but no one else in the group spoke.

Luca recognized what Chad had spoken. It was a Bible verse he'd learned as a kid, and it referred to God's power versus Satan's.

Why had Chad brought it up? Luca didn't like the implications. Was Erin seeing something satanic? Like a demon or something?

A loud rustling moved through the woods and everyone from Luca's group jumped up defensively. Luca grabbed a stick, ready to cut some heads off snakes if he needed to, but only Mr. Miles came bursting through the overgrowth.

He grinned and waved at them all excitedly. "Waiting for me?"

"No, Daddy," Avery said, her breath rushing out. "You scared us all half to death."

His excitement didn't waver. "Why? Oh, I see you got the van over. Perfect." He cruised past them all and climbed into the van, pulling his backpack from his back and slamming the door behind him.

"What's he doing?" someone asked.

"I don't know," Avery muttered. She watched the van long after everyone else had lost interest.

"Thank you."

Luca turned to June who stood behind him. "What?"

"Thank you, you know, for taking care of everyone. I don't think we would have made it without you." She stepped close to him.

He managed a smile, but he shuffled back a step or two. "You're welcome, but you don't owe me any gratitude. We've all worked together. Look at you. You even got a snake bite."

She smiled and shook her head. "Yeah, but who carried me to the van for anti-venom?"

"You're welcome. Really."

She moved away, and Luca took a deep breath. This place was mind-numbingly confusing at times. Hopefully, June wasn't getting any weird ideas about their relationship. He pushed the thought aside and tracked down Bradley instead of joining the group around the fire. "What did you see while you walked?"

Bradley glared at him. "Why should I help you?"

"Help me? Dude, we're all trying to get out of here."

Bradley paused, but when he didn't have anything to fire back, he shrugged. "Nothing. We walked toward the sun as it rose, and away from the sun as it set behind us. We were clearly walking away from the jungle. The next thing I knew it was right in front of us."

"Maybe it was a different jungle."

Bradley shook his head. "I don't think so."

Luca frowned and looked away. "It doesn't make any sense."

"Tell me about it."

"What about when you came back?" Luca asked. "Did you do the same thing? Or did you follow the line of the trees?"

Bradley shook his head. "That's the weirdest part. We followed the tree line around, and it took us longer to get here. By nightfall, we hadn't reached the camp, so we stopped for the night to sleep. The next morning it took us another couple hours to get here."

Luca turned to study the jungle. It was almost as if

they weren't allowed to leave. "Whatever this place is, it's messed up."

Bradley nodded but didn't offer any more opinions.

Luca stood and headed back toward the group. Avery waited near the van's side door.

"What's up?"

She frowned and looked toward the van window. The windows were tinted, but that didn't stop her from looking. "I don't know what he's up to. He's excited about something, but I have a feeling that whatever it is, it's not going to get us out of here."

"Yeah, I got that impression, too. What do you think it is?"

"I haven't figured it out yet, but I think it has to do with this place. He thinks he's found something here."

"How would he find anything if Jeffrey said they never went into the jungle?"

She shook her head. "I don't know. And who knows if he went in or not, you know? No one would think his behavior was odd. They probably wouldn't pay attention. I wish he'd talk to me, but he's so artificial with everyone."

Luca rolled her words around in his mind. It gave him an idea. "I wonder if Chad would answer our questions."

Chad was more concerned with helping his wife at this point than he was in taking care of them, but he might answer a few questions.

Avery's gaze trailed toward their youth leader. She shrugged. "He might. Do you think Erin even wants to be rescued?"

"Why would she want to stay?"

Avery shook her head. "I don't know. Maybe

because she's not herself."

"That's for sure."

They trekked through the sand and Luca stooped outside the girls' shelter. Now that he was here, he wasn't sure what to say.

Chad and Erin stared at him expectantly.

Finally, Chad cleared his throat. "You guys need something?" The sun had definitely done a number on Chad and his group. Blistered skin showed under his eyes and on his nose. They must not have thought of hats or sunblock.

"Yeah, we were just wondering if you could tell us what all Mr. Miles has been doing since you guys got stranded." It sounded stupid, even to him. He glanced at Avery for help.

"He says he's looking for something," Avery said. "I just wonder what it is."

Chad frowned and shook his head. "He stayed with the group at all times that I can remember. The only time anyone went into the jungle alone was for— well, personal reasons."

"He didn't seem to be acting strange to you?" Luca asked.

"Sorry, no."

"They say someone will find it," Erin said. She rubbed her forehead like she had a headache. "A devil, or demon. I don't know the word for sure. It's probably your dad."

Chad turned to her, his eyes showing how upset her words made him. "Who said that, Erin? You can't listen to them."

"It doesn't matter, Chad. I hear them whether I listen or not."

"They said that?" Avery looked away then spoke

like she was talking to herself. "So they want something to be found. Maybe they're keeping us here to find it?"

Luca frowned and tugged her back. "Let's leave Erin to rest. Thanks for your help, Chad."

Avery frowned at him as they walked away. "Why did you pull me away? She was giving us good information."

"Yeah, but Chad is here now. He won't appreciate his wife being badgered to solve a mystery."

"I wasn't badgering her."

"No, but he's trying to help her overcome whatever it is she's seeing. If that were you, I wouldn't want anyone bugging you, either." He'd heard people talking about putting their foot in their mouth. If ever he'd wanted to take something back, it was now.

She would think he thought they were getting back together. She would put him in his place. Distance herself.

He watched her, gauging her reaction, but she didn't huff and stomp away.

She didn't frown or remind him they'd broken up months ago. She just nodded.

Maybe he hadn't messed up, at least not this time.

"If she's right," Avery went on, "then Daddy is listening to whatever those things are. He's being led by—I don't know—something. We need to get out of here. It isn't right."

He took a deep breath, remembering what Chad had said about God being greater than the devil. "Yeah, I agree with you, there."

She gave him a crooked grin. "When do you disagree with me?"

There was one area, for sure, but he didn't want to

push his luck in bringing up the way her dad dumbed her down. Instead he smiled. "Good point."

She stared at him with her mesmerizing blue eyes and it took his breath away. He should ask if she wanted to talk, not about getting stranded or her dad. Just talk.

She smiled and her hair blew slightly with the breeze.

He opened his mouth to ask her.

"Luca! Luca, come quick!"

Benny's frantic call brought him out of his bad idea, and he spun around. "What's going on?"

Benny slid to a stop in front of them, panting. "It's June. She's having a seizure or something."

20

Watching June's body jerk around in the sand turned his stomach. He swallowed hard and pushed the feeling away as he marched toward her. "What happened?"

"We were sitting here, and she just started shaking." Katelyn wiped tears from her face, but it looked like she'd stopped crying for now, thank goodness. "We didn't know what to do, then she fell sideways and kept shaking in the sand."

Erin pushed through them and knelt beside June.

Luca moved out of the way to let her examine the girl. He almost felt guilty for not calling her in the first place, but he'd forgotten about Erin being an authority figure, especially since she'd been practically useless since they got here.

But crazy or not, Erin's instincts seemed to have kicked in and she quickly went to work. June had stopped shaking and Erin called to her softly as she checked her pulse and lifted her eyelids.

June moaned and turned her head.

Avery jogged over and handed Erin a bottle of water. Erin took the bottle and held it to June's lips. "Can you drink this?"'

June lifted her head slightly and took a sip before laying back. "What happened?"

"You had a seizure," Erin said. "Do you have a history of seizures?"

"No, I don't think so."

"Could it have been caused by the snake bite?" Luca asked.

Erin nodded. "Definitely. You need to lay back and relax for the rest of the night. No more hiking through the jungle."

June gave them all a weak smile. "You got it."

She blinked up at Luca hovering over her and smiled a little brighter, but she turned away before he knew what to make of it.

Something tugged at his mind, something about her eyes. He wasn't sure he liked the thought so he pushed it to the back of his brain before he had to figure out what it really meant. His stomach growled loudly and it gave him the perfect excuse to step away and find something to eat.

A basket of fruit sat in the shade but all he found were pears. That was the last thing he wanted. His gaze moved to the jungle, and he studied the trees and shadows inside. He could go in alone. The thought simmered for a moment, and he glanced around to see if anyone watched him. Sure, he didn't want anyone else doing it, but he needed to be by himself. Being surrounded by so many people all the time was exhausting.

Glancing around one last time, he stepped into the jungle and hiked toward the banana tree they'd seen a few days ago. Farther and farther he trekked, until sweat pooled on his back and ran down his temples. He pulled off his shirt and slung it over his shoulder as he continued deeper into the jungle. His eyes moved back and forth constantly, scanning for snakes or monkeys or weird native people.

Nothing stirred the trees though, and after a while,

he spotted yellow ahead. Luca grinned. He'd remembered the banana tree's exact location. Excellent directional skills; just another perk of hunting and tracking. The reminder tensed him up as he remembered the uncertainty waiting for him back home.

In the winter months, he helped his uncle at the family taxidermy shop. His dad and his uncle worked there together for years, stuffing animals and preserving experiences. They also ran a meat processor, but when Luca's dad died a few months ago, his uncle couldn't handle both sides of the business.

Luca had begged Uncle Jimbo to keep the processor so he could run it when he graduated from high school, but Uncle Jim said he had no choice.

Now Luca was nearing graduation and had nothing to fall back on. Uncle Jim didn't need a partner, and the new meat processor wasn't looking to sell the business back. What would he do when he got back home?

He stood at the base of the tree and peered up, trying to figure out how to get the bunch down from the tree. He sighed and placed his foot against the peeling bark. Going up was the best way he could figure. He hefted himself up the first few paces before it started to get hard, and at the top he pulled out the small pocketknife he'd found in the van a few days ago.

The knife was dull and the stalk was thick, but the bunch finally broke free and fell to the ground with a thud.

"Watch it!" someone called up.

Luca sucked in a fast breath and stumbled on the

tree branch. He grabbed onto the closest branch he could to steady himself before looking down.

A guy his own age stood on the ground below. His dark hair stood in spikes around his head, and his dark skin reminded Luca of Sam, the van driver. This guy definitely was not from their mission trip.

"Who are you?" Luca needed to get out of the tree, and fast. Standing up there made him feel like a coward, but climbing down put him in a vulnerable position, and that was something he didn't much like.

"Rafa," the newcomer said. "And you are?"

Luca frowned. This guy—this Rafa—acted as if they were meeting at the skate park instead of the middle of an abandoned desert oasis.

"I'm Luca. Watch out. I'm climbing down." Luca kept his gaze on Rafa as best he could as he slid down the tree trunk. The thick bark sliced into his arm at one point, but he kept his gasp in so Rafa wouldn't notice. At the bottom, he slipped into his shirt and wiped the blood from his arm on his shorts. His other hand palmed the knife, just in case. "Where did you come from?" Luca demanded. "We've been here for days and haven't seen anyone."

Rafa's eyebrows rose. "I thought you met Rae. He said he'd spoken to the group of abandons."

Rae.

Luca tried to relax, but he found himself tensing instead. "You know Rae?"

"Yeah dude. We both live here."

They lived here. In this jungle. "We haven't seen any housing. We haven't seen anything that hints at people living here."

Rafa smirked. "You think you have seen the entire jungle? This is a big place."

The guy made a good point.

Luca took a deep breath and forced himself to relax. "Sorry. That's true. Can you help us? We want to get out of here."

"Of course we can help you. Anything you need."

Just like that? After Rae's hemming and hawing, Luca hadn't expected immediate compliance. "Really? Because we could use a phone or computer, or a working van to get out of here."

"You left another van on the other side of the jungle, didn't you?"

Chills pricked Luca's arm. Did these guys see the group's every move? That wasn't right. Something wasn't right.

He smoothed out his face and worked to look cool. "That's right. We had two vans, and the other group moved to stay with our group. They had to leave their van behind because it wouldn't start."

"Couldn't you take the gas from the non-working van and use it in the other van?"

Luca shifted uncomfortably. "Yeah, I guess that could work."

Rafa grinned. "Glad I could help. Listen, we're around if you need us. We don't go hanging out in the open because, hey, that's not our thing. But if you need us, just come looking. Really."

The muscles in Luca's shoulders relaxed a little more, and he nodded. "Thanks, man. I appreciate it."

Rafa nodded then stepped into the shadows and out of sight.

Luca grabbed the bananas and slung them over his back, heaving a grunt with their weight. It was stupid they hadn't thought of it earlier. All they had to do was patch the hole in the gas lines of their own van while someone else made the trip to the other van and drained the gas out.

Now they just needed a gas container, but there had to be something lying around they could use.

He had worked up a full-blown sweat by the time he reached camp, and it was only as he set down the bananas and Avery glared at him from the girls' shelter—she must have noticed he'd gone alone—that he realized something. Two somethings, to be exact.

How did Rafa know they had a gas leak in their van?

And if he lived in this jungle—and had for a while—why did he speak in non-accented English?

Part 3

Genesis 3:24

"So he drove out the man; and he placed at the east...Cherubim, and a flaming sword which turned every way, to keep the way of the tree of life."

21

Rae

Fire seethed through Rae's body, his mind, his blood.

Rafa had spoken to one of them. He had implied he and Rae were friends. He had promised to help them. Rafa had no intention of helping them do anything, least of all leave the jungle.

Rae stormed through the trees, not caring when the branches snagged his clothes or skin.

Rafa needed to answer for what he had done. He did not have permission to speak to the outsiders, and now he was going to explain himself.

The air grew thicker. Heavier. More damp. The foliage curved around Rae's body like a blanket, bending and moving with his every step. What little sunlight filtered through the trees dimmed. Rae stopped and watched as a night flower bloomed before his eyes. It was midday, at latest, and these flowers only bloomed in the dark. "Rafa," he called.

Silence answered.

"Rafa!" His nostrils flared, and he barely contained his anger. "I know you are here."

Rafa stepped from the burrow in a huge tree trunk. He smirked at Rae, his face full of ego and amusement. His dark hair stood on end, and his clothes were a crumpled and dirty mess. "What could you possibly want with me? Unless you're willing to accept my offer, that is."

"You spoke to one of them. That is against the commandments."

"You spoke to them, too, don't forget. More than once, and more than one of them. You are a watcher, so you have commandments to follow. I broke no supposed law."

Rae worked to control his breathing. He had not allowed himself to consider the facts Rafa presented, but the fallen angel's words rang true.

"I was trying to help them," Rae spit out. "And you are not."

The air fluctuated and Rafa stood directly in front of Rae in the blink of an eye. "I can help you, though. Would you like to be human? Live like the humans? Have the freedom they have?"

Every muscle in Rae's body coiled like a snake ready to strike. Rafa's offers were ridiculous.

"I see your mind working behind those eyes." Rafa circled Rae. "You follow the elders' rules so easily. 'Don't speak to them,'" he mimicked. "'Don't help them. Don't intervene. They will find their way out.'"

"And they would," Rae interrupted. "If you would leave them alone."

Rafa stopped and grinned. "Perhaps you are right about that. But I have other events in mind."

Rae knew all of that. It was exactly what Rafa had said when he'd tried to get Rae to join his cause the first time around.

Rae could help him, Rafa had said. *Rae could have whatever he wanted in return*, he had promised.

Rae clenched his fists. "I will never help you."

"Then you will have to work hard against me," Rafa said. "Because I won't stop trying. And I'm through playing nicely."

Rafa slinked back to the hole he crawled from and Rae worked to calm his nerves. He did not succeed. Instead, he shot through the trees at the speed of the jungle cats. His feet barely touched the ground.

The elders had to be notified. Someone had to do something to stop Rafa. His goals were wholly unacceptable, and Rae would do all he could to put a stop to it. When he had reached the entry to the inner jungle—his home—he paused. Closing his eyes, he sniffed the air. He stood perfectly still and let the air vibrations bounce off his skin.

Finally, he let out a relieved breath. For today, at least, Rafa had not won. Their home was undisturbed.

"You have done foolishly."

The voice of the highest watcher spun Rae around. "Jacob. You scared me."

Jacob stood patiently, so Rae went on.

"I have come to warn you. Rafa is working to keep the outsiders stranded. He hopes to bring them here, to the inner jungle. I felt I had to intervene in order to help them find a way out."

"They don't need your help to leave." Jacob towered over him. He was almost big enough to frighten Rae, but Rae had seen enough of Jacob to know he was not to be feared. They had been working together for years.

"You forget your place," Jacob said. "Your job is to keep them out. Whatever else they do is not your concern." He stepped closer to Rae, almost nose to nose. "That includes whether or not they find food or water. Stop intervening."

Guilt seeped through every pore of his body. Jacob knew everything Rae had done—the times he had shown them how to find food, water, paths back to their camp. But Rae felt the love of the Father in them. He pitied them—loved them, even.

He bowed his head. "Forgive me, Jacob."

"You do not need my forgiveness."

Rae glanced up and Jacob smiled at him. "Do not worry over Rafa. He is a fallen angel who is doomed for eternity. Unlike others I know."

Rae stood a little taller and nodded. Jacob had been the keeper of the jungle since the beginning. The fact that he thought Rea sufficient enough to help him and the other elders spoke volumes.

Jacob slipped inside the inner jungle and left Rae to stand alone. Rae would not fail the elders, but what about Avery and her group? If he left Rafa alone, he would get to her.

Rae had already almost failed once. The other girls, Gabby and Katelyn, had come way too close once before. If he had been guarding his post as he should have been, instead of following Avery and her group around, the girls never would have gotten near the place.

At least Jacob had not reminded him about that.

Rae clenched his teeth and thought of Jacob's words one last time. He had orders. He had a job. A mission.

He had to forget about Avery's group and protect his home.

22

Avery

How could Luca? Tromping off through the jungle alone? Bringing back a huge bunch of bananas? He must be losing his mind along with everyone else.

Either that or he hadn't changed at all, not since he'd impulsively punched out a window in his downstairs living room in a fit of blind rage. Not since he'd let his anger take over his personality, and she'd had to stay away from him.

He set the bananas down and a few others flocked to him.

"Do we have enough water to boil the noodles for tonight's meal?" Tasha asked.

Avery pulled her attention away from Luca—who now stood with a few other guys, speaking with serious faces—and pointed to one of the baskets in the shade. "All of our water is being stored in there, but I think we've got plenty."

Tasha smiled and grabbed a few bottles, then moved back to the logs around the fire.

Now it was time to find out what was going on with Luca. Avery marched toward the guys.

"You should stay with Erin," Luca was saying to Chad.

"No. I need to get her out of here. I was at the other camp, and I know how to get there and back. I'm going."

Luca's lips pressed into a thin line but he didn't argue.

"What's going on?" Avery asked.

"We're sending a few guys to get the gas from the other van, while I stay and fix the busted gas lines on our own van." Bradley puffed out his chest like he was the homecoming king and had just scored the winning touchdown at the big game.

Avery turned to Luca. "This just came to you, or what?"

He frowned and turned away, and a tiny seed of guilt wafted through her. OK, so she shouldn't have been so snappy, especially not in front of the others, but he shouldn't have gone into the jungle alone.

The guys talked for a few more minutes and Avery had to admit, it wasn't a bad plan. It would be dangerous to send others around the jungle for a second time—who knew if or when they'd come back—but it was worth the risk. What other choice did they have?

They finished making their plans and agreed that Chad and a few other guys from his van would leave first thing in the morning.

Avery peered around their broad shoulders at Erin, who lay in the girls' old shelter. It was what she seemed to do most of the time, lately. She claimed sleep was the only way to ignore the things she saw and heard.

The other guys moved away but Avery stayed put, staring a hole through Luca so he would know, without a doubt, she wanted to talk to him.

Finally, he sighed and turned to her. "It's the best way to get out of here, Avery. You have to see that."

"I do see it, but why did you have to be alone to figure that out?"

His eyebrows rose and she could almost see his anger beginning to boil. "Are you serious? It's constant girl chatter around here. A guy needs some alone time."

Alone time. It was something he'd always needed, so she couldn't really fault him for it. "You could have at least let someone know so we could come looking if you weren't back after a while."

He studied her for a few moments. His eyes clouded over, and she gulped. He was going to let her have it. But he only nodded. "You're right. Sorry."

She stared for a second but shook herself. "Apology accepted."

He chuckled. "You're such a dork. Anyway, I actually have something I wanted to tell you." He glanced around then pulled her farther from the group. "I didn't come up with that idea myself, and I wasn't actually alone in the jungle. Not the whole time, anyway."

Avery frowned. She hated herself for it, but she glanced for the briefest second at June. Shame on her for thinking it, even for a second. Luca wouldn't take June into the jungle alone. He wasn't like that. "What do you mean?"

"I saw someone while I was out there. He called himself Rafa, and he's one of that Rae guy's friends. Said he lives here, just like Rae told you."

"What?" She moved closer to him. "He told you about the gas?"

"Yeah. It kind of creeped me out that he knew what our mechanical issues were."

"How did he know?"

"I don't know and I don't care. We're going to fix the van and get out of here."

Avery nodded. No wonder he'd let the anger thing go. "I'm all for that." She wrapped her arms around her waist and looked at the camp.

Erin slept quietly in the shelter, and June sat with Tasha near the fire.

Avery shivered. "This place gets weirder and weirder every minute."

"What do you mean?"

Avery paused. Should she bring up June? No. It would make her look like the jealous ex-girlfriend. Which she was not. She shook her head instead. "Just too many weird things. I want to go home, and I am never coming back here again."

"No more dreams of breaking free?" he asked.

He had remembered that was why she wanted to come in the first place?

Before she could answer, the van door banged closed and they both turned to see Daddy strolling away from it. Obviously, whatever he'd been doing holed up in there had ended.

"I want to talk to him. I'll talk to you later. And don't go back in there without telling anyone, please?"

He nodded. "Promise."

Avery hurried toward Daddy, almost needing to be near him. She'd seen him so rarely over the last couple years since Mom left. Most of the time by his choice. Now that they were together, he continued to ignore her. She would never be good enough. Unless she helped him solve this mystery. She paused mid-step. Was that what she was trying to do? No. She wanted out of here, whether he solved his mystery or not.

As she drew closer, a flap of paper blew out of the stack he shoved into his pocket.

She darted for it. It took a few lunges, but she finally caught it. Her big toe pinned it down while she bent for it.

It was Daddy's handwriting. So this was what he'd been doing in the van.

Avery squinted at the small handwriting. She could hardly make it out, but the drawing was clear. It was a map. She gasped. It was a map of the jungle!

Daddy had drawn a detailed map of the places he'd seen, including the trek around the desert to this side of the jungle. There were alcoves outlined, including alcoves on the opposite side. He'd snaked a line through the middle of it all, and by the location, it must be the creek. Another part he'd labeled "fruit orchard."

A shaded out area drew her attention. It must be the area he hadn't yet explored, which meant it was where he was heading the next chance he got.

She scanned the rest of the map, but there was nothing about the mysterious temple, and definitely no indication he'd found any type of housing. Avery looked up and glanced around. Had anyone seen her?

Everyone went about their business.

Even Daddy talked and laughed with a few others from the group.

No one had seen her. They didn't know what she held, or its importance.

But Daddy believed this place held something special.

Shoving the map into her pocket, she strode back to the rest of the camp. Should she tell anyone? Her gaze moved of its own accord to Luca. He'd trusted her with the knowledge of the new guy, Rafa. She should trust him with this map.

He bent over the hood of the van with Sam and Bradley.

At the same moment, Erin groaned from her shelter, and Avery looked her way.

Luca could wait.

Avery moved to Erin and knelt over her. "Do you need something?"

Erin swallowed hard. "I'm really thirsty. I don't feel so great."

Avery placed her hand on Erin's forehead. "You're burning up. Do you think there are any thermometers in those medical supplies?"

Erin shrugged. "Ask Benny. He's the one who found the anti-venom. And can you bring me some water? I finally used up all my bottles." Erin was the only one who hadn't been drinking water from the creek.

Avery had forgotten about her huge case of water she'd brought from home. "Sure, I'll be right back." Avery hurried to the basket of bottled water and grabbed one. She dropped it off with Erin before going after Benny.

He sat alone, as he had since the other group arrived.

She'd been so busy she'd forgotten to ask him what the deal was. He'd gone from being suddenly confident and full of ideas, to reclusive and sulky.

"What are you up to?" she asked.

He glanced at her and shrugged. "Being bored. How about you?"

"I'm actually looking for a thermometer. Erin's not feeling well. Did you happen to see one in the medical supplies?"

His eyes lit up and he practically flew off the log where he sat. "I think so. Come on and I'll find it."

She followed him to the back of the van.

Benny peeled back the flaps of the cardboard box and dug through the contents.

Avery watched him patiently. For some reason she knew that if a thermometer was available, Benny would find it.

Benny was typically alone at every youth activity. He sat alone at church. He hung out by himself at school. There were times when she wondered why he even bothered showing up at church at all, since he didn't have any friends.

But after his statement a few days ago about anything being better than home, she guessed she had her answer. Guilt nagged at the edges of her mind. She hadn't done a very good job of being friendlier to him since then. In fact, she'd practically ignored him. "Hey, thanks for helping out around here. You've really been a big asset."

He shrugged and kept digging, but she was pretty sure he stood a little straighter. "Got it!" A long, white stick came out of the box. "Digital and everything."

She took the cheap medical instrument from him. "Thanks Benny. Don't close this up. If Erin's really sick, we may need more of these medicines."

"You got it." He followed her across the sand and knelt behind her outside of Erin's shelter.

They waited in silence until the minute passed and the thermometer beeped. Erin pulled it from her mouth and sighed. "One hundred point one. No wonder I feel so terrible."

Avery took the thermometer back and frowned.

"What can we get for you? That van is full of medicine."

Erin sighed and lay back against her makeshift pillow. "I don't know. There's no way to tell what this is. Bacterial? Viral? Fungal?"

"What's your best bet?" Avery pushed. "We have to try something."

"There are no other symptoms. Clean water and rest is all I need, for now."

Avery huffed. "Come on, Erin. Don't you want some aspirin or something?"

Erin paused. Finally, she offered a small grin. "OK, I guess aspirin wouldn't hurt."

"You got it." Benny bolted for the van and disappeared behind the opened door.

"He's quite the willing helper, isn't he?" Erin said. "He's surprised me on this trip."

"Yeah, I was thinking that too."

Erin sighed and closed her eyes. They sat quietly for a moment before she spoke. "I saw you looking at a piece of paper earlier. Your dad dropped it. Care to share?"

Avery's eyes widened. "What?"

"I saw you. No reason to deny it."

Nerves tightened her stomach. What could she say? Erin was always full of understanding and encouragement, but she'd probably say Avery was being rebellious against her father or something like that.

Erin reached out and squeezed Avery's knee. "You're doing OK, Avery. Don't worry about that."

Avery's gaze flew to Erin's face. How could Erin know exactly what she'd been thinking? She swallowed hard. Maybe Daddy's behavior over the years hadn't gone totally unnoticed by everyone else.

Benny jogged over to them and thrust the bottle toward Avery. "Here, and there's more where that came from."

Avoiding eye contact, Avery passed the pills to Erin. Once the youth leader had swallowed them, Avery stood and brushed the sand from her shorts. "Get some rest, Erin. I'll check on you later, OK?" But she couldn't bear to just leave her that way. It felt— disrespectful. She cast a final, pleading glance Erin's way.

Erin smiled wearily and waved her away. "I'll see you in a bit."

Avery sighed in relief and hurried away, but Benny stayed on her heels.

"I saw a bunch of antibiotics in there, too. You think she needs them?"

She wanted to brush him off, get rid of him, find Luca. But she couldn't do that. It would be wrong. "I don't know. It may come to that. Thanks for your help, Benny. I really mean it."

He smiled and nodded. "I'm always willing to help. Anytime you need something. I'm your guy. I was thinking we could even build bigger shelters. We need to figure out a way to keep cooler. The heat could be adding to Erin's sickness, too." He rambled on and on.

Avery bit her tongue. No wonder they didn't hang out back home. She let him finish his spiel and she smiled. "You have a lot of great ideas. We'll have to talk about them more when everyone's around to discuss them."

"Great. Just let me know."

"I will."

He shoved his hands in his pockets and shuffled back and forth. OK. So he wasn't leaving.

She hated to do it. Really hated it. "Excuse me, Benny. I'll talk to you later."

His face fell a fraction but he covered it nicely.

It killed her just a tiny bit. She watched him slink back to the logs and take his lonesome place among the others.

Tasha and the rest of the girls worked on cooking their supper—because boiling noodles was a joint effort, obviously. Later tonight, some of them would be heading to the creek to scrub clothes. Now that *was* a joint effort.

Avery had never appreciated modern appliances more. What she wouldn't give for a microwave to make hot chocolate, especially once the sun went down and the night air turned chilly. She paused at the thought. Would she go home just for a microwave and a washing machine? Would she give up the friendship she'd found here? The acceptance?

The people here had talked to her more in the last week than in the last two years. Since Mom had left. Since Avery had sort of flipped out. Or maybe completely flipped out.

Luca's voice pulled her back to the here and now, and she smiled. Everyone had pulled away from her back then, except Luca. He'd always been there, every step of the way, even when Daddy hadn't bothered coming home when his wife left him and his daughter ended up in the hospital.

Luca stood back from the van now. Bradley and Sam had crawled under it and were bickering about some line that ran along the frame.

Luca caught her looking and smiled. He loped

over to her. "Hey. What's up now?"

"Erin's got a fever, but we gave her some aspirin." Avery fingered the paper in her pocket. "But actually, I wanted to talk to you about something else. Got a second?" It was a stupid thing to say, especially since they had nothing but time around here, but he nodded immediately.

"Sure. What is it?"

"I found this. Daddy dropped it."

He took the paper and looked it over. A crease formed over his eyes as he read it. "Why does he need a map?"

"I don't know, but I'm guessing he's going to try exploring this shaded area next. Do you think he's been sneaking away in the dark? How does he know this much about our side of the jungle?"

Luca's frown deepened. "What does he expect to find?" His eyes met hers over the paper and she looked away.

What did he expect to find? She had no idea. She didn't, did she? Of course, she did know something. She knew June was acting strange since the snake bite. She knew she'd seen Rae again, and he'd said she could help. But how to say all that? Her ideas and suspicions were just that—suspicions. Still, an idea was forming in her head. She might need to get something out of her luggage soon. Finally, she sighed. "I don't know, but Daddy wouldn't be going to all this trouble if he didn't suspect something big."

She wasn't sure why she wasn't telling Luca the whole truth. He'd proved himself here. Proved Daddy had been wrong about him. Proved he'd only gone through a really bad time, and Avery had let him down. Still, this felt like something she needed to figure out for herself. It felt like a way to prove herself.

Luca's gaze drifted back to the map. He studied it a few more minutes before handing it back to her. "So, what's your plan?"

Her mouth dropped open and she fumbled to shove the paper into her pocket. "My plan?"

"I assume that's why you're showing this to me. Are you wanting to follow the map? See what's out there?"

Yes.

No.

How did he know her so well when she hadn't even considered it herself?

"Do you think we should?"

"I think we need to keep your dad as safe as we need to keep everyone else. With everything that's been going on in there," he nodded toward the jungle, "we can't take any chances. Let's be honest, Aves. He's almost as unstable as Erin at this point."

Her heart wilted, but Luca was right.

"How should we do it?"

He took a deep breath and shook his head. "I don't know. If we take others, they'll want to know why."

"Benny's been a big help. He told me he was willing to do whatever we needed done." Except maybe he knew nothing about what he'd be getting himself into.

"Benny? Are you serious?"

"He's misunderstood, Luca."

Luca chuckled and shook his head. "If you say so."

She tried to hold in her smile but he was right, she did sound sort of ridiculous. She let a tiny laugh out before she forced herself to stop. "He's been OK. You've got to admit it."

"Yeah, OK. Who else? June?"

Of all the people, why did he have to request her? Avery forced a smile and nodded. "Sure, if she's up to it. When do we leave?"

His gaze moved somewhere behind her and she turned to see Daddy searching his pockets frantically. After a few minutes, he scurried back to the van and slammed the door behind him.

"Guess you've got what he's looking for."

Avery cringed. "Let's go first thing in the morning."

"Agreed."

She turned to go but he tugged on her arm. Heat climbed up her neck, but she ignored it.

"Thanks for telling me."

She managed a smile and a shrug. "You told me about Rafa. I figured if you could trust me than I could trust you." *Liar!* Screeched through her mind but she pushed it aside.

He smiled and rolled his eyes. "Whatever. Talk to you later."

"Later."

He turned back to the guys working under the van where Sam and Bradley still argued.

Avery bit her lip and turned away. She should have told him about the temple. Needed to tell him. She would definitely tell him. As soon as she had more answers.

23

Luca

Luca searched Chad's face, hoping for some crack in his determination to make the trek to the other side of the jungle. "Are you sure you want to go? Someone else can take your place. Erin needs you."

The morning air gave him goose bumps and he hoped that one last plea would do the trick. In truth, he wanted to keep Chad around for himself. It almost felt like he didn't have so much responsibility with Chad here—someone else was making the decisions. Luca was just a guy again. He could do what he needed to do, without worrying about everyone else in the group.

"Buddy, we've got to have a serious talk about who the authority figure is in this relationship, but it can wait until we're home." Chad smacked him on the shoulder and nodded. "Yes, I'm going. Hopefully we can make good timing and be back by tomorrow."

He glanced behind Luca and Luca turned to follow his gaze.

Erin rested as she always did lately. Her eyes were closed, but she didn't seem to be asleep.

"Make her take some antibiotics, will you?" Chad said. "She won't listen to me."

Luca chuckled. "Yes, sir."

The rest of the group gathered to send Chad and

his group off. They'd found a few containers in the food box and luggage that could be used to carry the gas, and Chad would tear off a hose from the old van to use for syphoning.

Luca and the rest of them waited until Chad's group was several yards into the desert before they broke up to their own tasks.

Bradley and Sam moved to the van and continued their work in finding the leak in the gas line. Today they would work on plugging it up, then they would get everything repacked for tomorrow in hopes Chad would return by nightfall.

"Should we go?" Avery's soft voice pulled his gaze away from the van. She was a much more welcomed sight. He needed to tell her that, maybe soon.

"We've got to talk to Benny and June. Have you seen your dad?"

"He's in the van again. What if we run into him in the jungle? Do you think he'll be mad?"

Luca put his hands on her shoulders. "Don't worry about that, Avery. Why would he be mad? We're in the jungle, looking around same as him."

She nodded, but the worry lines around her eyes didn't disappear. "OK."

"Do you want to talk to June? I'll ask Benny to come along," she asked.

"Yeah, that sounds good."

She moved around him and headed for Benny who sat near the fire.

Luca turned and scanned the camp for June. She sat alone near the trees, and he made his way through the sand toward her.

When he got close, she looked up at him and

smiled. "Hi."

He smiled back and nodded toward the sand beside her. "Care if I sit?"

She shook her head so he slid to the ground. "We're going into the jungle to do some exploring. Feel up to coming?"

"Exploring? What for?" She fidgeted with her shirt hem.

He paused, frowning. June wasn't what he would call coy, so he wasn't sure about the sudden shyness. But he let it go. "There are parts of the jungle we haven't seen yet, and we'd like to check it out. See what's out there." That was mostly true, and there wasn't any need to include Mr. Miles's name in this.

"Sure, I'll come. Who else is going?"

Did he imagine she leaned into him?

"Um, Avery. And Benny, I think."

"Great. When do we leave?"

Luca glanced around for Avery. She and Benny strode toward him, so he stood. "Now, if you're up for it."

June moved to her feet. "Absolutely."

"You guys are nuts," Benny said. He turned to Avery. "No offense. But this is crazy. Haven't we seen enough of this place?"

"I think it's a good idea," June said. "This place could hold all kinds of treasures. I can't wait to look around!"

Luca caught Avery's look at June's odd words. "I didn't know you were so interested," he said quickly. June couldn't know about Mr. Miles's activities.

June shrugged. "I've had lots of time to let my mind wander."

Avery seemed to relax, so Luca shrugged. "Yeah, I

guess that's true. Should we go?"

Avery didn't reply, just turned and started walking. She seemed to know which way she was going. She must have memorized the map, which was good because they definitely didn't want to pull it out for the others to see.

"What do you think we'll find in here?" June asked. "Any suspicions?"

"I heard a few kids from the other group talking about a fruit orchard," Avery said. The words rolled right off her tongue like she'd been practicing how to respond to the question. Knowing Avery, she probably had.

"We have fruit," June said. "And hopefully we'll get out of here soon so it won't matter."

Avery turned and frowned as she walked. "I thought you wanted to come."

"I do. I just don't see what's so great about a fruit orchard. Maybe we can look around more than that."

Luca watched her, holding in his frown, but curious. It almost felt like she was fishing for answers. Maybe a specific answer.

Luca cleared his throat. "We've been stuck here for days. We just want to see what else is out there." No need to have a fight right here in the jungle. And what had gotten into June, anyway?

Truthfully he'd rather be doing this than sitting around the desert, watching Bradley and Sam work on the van while he fiddled his thumbs, useless. Something hit him, though, that almost had him turning around. "We forgot about Erin."

"I gave her more aspirin just before we left. I even got her to take some amoxicillin."

Everyone looked to Benny.

Luca stared in shock.

"You did that?" Avery asked.

Benny frowned. "Sure I did. I'm not totally useless, you know."

"I know you're not, Benny. I told you before you've been a huge help on this trip. If you can call it a trip."

"Yeah. Thanks." Benny stormed ahead of them.

"Benny, wait!" Avery dashed forward to catch him. "You don't know where you're going."

"Going home will be nice, don't you think?" June strolled beside him as they brought up the rear. A thin sheen of sweat glowed on her skin.

"Definitely," Luca said. "But we'll have to get you to the hospital right away. You need to have that bite checked out."

"It's no big deal. I'm fine."

"Still. You got bit by a snake."

She smiled and nodded. "Right. I'll get it checked out."

They walked a few minutes in silence.

Up ahead, Avery had caught Benny and they walked together now. Avery spoke, but Luca couldn't make out what she said.

"So you and Avery used to date?"

She seemed genuinely interested, but he definitely didn't want to discuss it with her. "Yeah, a while back."

"It's too bad it didn't work out."

"I guess so. We should probably catch up to them." He picked up the speed and June jogged to follow his long strides.

Benny's sour face had relaxed, and Avery patted his back. Whatever Benny's issue was had been worked out now. Thank goodness.

Luca had enough girl drama; he didn't feel like dealing with guy drama, too. "Do you think we're getting close?" he asked Avery.

She met his eye and nodded. "We're on the right track. It will be a while before we get there, though."

Luca wracked his brain for a clear image of the map. The fruit orchard was beside the shaded area. It had been a long way into the jungle; definitely closer to the other group's camp. If he'd been so close, why hadn't Mr. Miles explored that area before they left their side of the jungle? It didn't make any sense.

They walked a mile or two in silence, and when sweat began pouring down his back, Luca pulled out the water bottles and passed them around. The water sailed down his throat. It was seriously the best water he'd ever drank. If someone could bottle it and ship it out, they'd make a fortune.

"Let's take a break," Avery said. "I want to sit for a minute." She didn't wait for anyone to agree, just sat on a boulder at the end of a rock wall. Her eyes scanned the area constantly, maybe looking for signs of the orchard.

But then Luca remembered the beetles. Was she seeing them now?

"Thank goodness for breaks." June's words pulled him away from staring at Avery. June leaned against the natural rock wall. "Walking in this humidity is exhausting."

"Are you sure you're OK?" Luca asked. "Is your leg sore?"

"I'm fine. More water, please."

He managed a laugh and handed over a bottle.

She took one, long swig and sighed. "This water is

so good."

Luca frowned. Her eyes looked different. Green now? He shook his head. They'd always been green, hadn't they? Forget it. He shouldn't be noticing her eyes anyway.

After resting for a few minutes, they restarted their hike.

"We've got to be getting close by now," Luca said.

"Yeah, I think so," Avery agreed. Her eyes continued their constant scan.

After a few minutes, he picked up a pattern.

She kept looking to the left—their group was veering right. What did she see?

"I've got to go to the bathroom." Avery paused. "Can you guys give me a minute?"

"Sorry, no bathroom out here," Benny said.

They all paused. Was he serious? But he grinned.

Benny trying to joke? That was new.

Luca laughed. "Very funny, dude."

Avery scurried to the left and disappeared behind the trees.

Luca frowned. It was the area she'd been watching, and something about that didn't sit well. Not that he could exactly follow her, but still. If she didn't come back quickly—drastic times called for drastic measures.

Or whatever.

24

Avery

Avery stepped lightly across the jungle floor, trying her best not to attract any attention from the others. The air had been wavering and twisting for the past half hour and she finally decided it was time to figure out what was happening.

Glancing behind her one last time to make sure she wasn't being followed, Avery barreled ahead.

A moment later, the temple appeared.

She sucked in a deep breath and slowed to a stop. She pressed her hand against the cool stone walls. Was she really meant to find whatever she would learn inside?

There was only one way to find out.

She pushed her way inside, then drank in the interior. The room was enormous and empty, all except the altar. Avery moved toward it but the book was gone. She huffed and ran her hand over the smooth stones. Why had the temple appeared, if there was nothing to see?

She spun around, searching for anything she might have missed. A single window rose toward the ceiling at the far end of the temple. There was no glass, only bars. Avery moved toward it and peeked into the jungle. Nothing looked familiar and Avery's stomach dropped. What if she ended up like Katelyn and

Gabby, lost for two days?

But then she turned and saw the front door, and she remembered the way she'd come.

Closing her eyes, Avery took a deep breath. She was being ridiculous. This was ridiculous.

"Why did you bring me here?" she said out loud.

Rae must have brought her to the temple for a reason.

"Where are you?" The words came out too loud and echoed around the cold, dim room. She sighed and turned back to the altar, and there on the stones lay the book. Avery gasped again and rushed forward. She opened the book and the pages fell to where she'd left off.

For they are the spirits of devils, working miracles, which go forth unto the kings of the earth and of the whole world, to gather them to the battle of that great day of God Almighty.

She studied the words and considered their meaning. There was a devil here—it was something that didn't surprise her because of all the crazy things happening. But a battle with God Almighty?

She scanned the rest of the page, but most of the words sounded like gibberish. She read to the bottom when one last phrase stood out to her.

Life cometh to those who ofercom, but death cometh to those who are ofercom.

Avery swallowed hard then gently closed the book. None of this made sense. Why her? She couldn't do anything to overcome anyone, certainly not in some battle to the death in a war with the almighty God.

"You must stop him."

Avery spun to the door where Rae stood. He didn't come into the temple, only stood in the doorway, and he kept one foot out like he was ready to run. "Who? I don't understand any of this."

Rae frowned and glanced behind him.

"Stop who?" Her frustration was growing.

"He will bring down the Almighty's wrath. The time is vanishing quickly." A twig snapped somewhere nearby, and Rae vanished.

Avery raced to the door and glanced out, but he was gone.

Could he fly? What was he?

She growled in frustration again and moved back to the book. She was brought here for a reason, to stop *him*. Him? Maybe *he* was the one plaguing Erin.

But the second sentence called out to her. If she was overcome, it would mean death. Her stomach twisted into a tight knot, and she swallowed hard.

By now, Luca and the others were probably searching for her. She needed to get out of the temple and back to them quickly. And she needed to tell Luca the truth. He might be able to make more sense of it than she could.

She closed the book and hurried out of the temple. She'd only gone a few steps when the mirage faded and disappeared. Avery shuddered again and hurried back to where she left her friends.

25

Luca

Avery returned a moment later and Luca frowned. "Did you forget something?"

She froze and shook her head, her eyes looking panicked and totally guilty. "Of course not. Why would you say that?"

OK. "Well, you weren't even gone a minute."

Her eyebrows shot up and she glanced between him and the others. Finally, she shook her head again. "No, I was gone longer than that."

"You literally just stepped away, Aves." But when he saw her face, he knew it wasn't true. The jungle was playing tricks on them again. He sighed. "Never mind. Let's keep moving."

They started off, heading toward something. Who knew what?

Avery used the walking stick he'd picked up a few days ago to beat a clear path, but he noticed that with every swing, her effort lessened. The heat was getting to her.

He stepped forward. "Why don't you let someone else take a turn with that? You'll be sore tomorrow."

She paused but gave up the stick without a fight. "I forget you've done this a million times in the woods."

"Well, I wouldn't say a million."

She smiled and fell into step behind him. "Enough times, though. It's probably not even hard for you."

They walked a few paces in silence.

"I need to tell you about something."

The words were spoken so quietly he barely heard her. Glancing at the others to make sure they weren't listening, he stepped closer to her. "Is that why you've been acting so weird?"

She threw a frown his way but swept her gaze back to the front. "I guess, but it's pretty weird in itself."

More weird was exactly what they didn't need. "We'll figure out a way for you to tell me."

She nodded and fell silent.

"So, do you guys all go to school together?" June's voice pulled him away from Avery and it took him a minute to adjust. School? That seemed way too normal a conversation for this place.

"Yep," Benny said.

"And you graduated this year?" she kept on.

"That's right," Avery said. "What about you?"

"I've been homeschooled for a long time." Her words were spoken softly, almost like she was holding something back. "I came on this trip to spread my wings. I think I mentioned I've never been out on my own before." Yeah, she mentioned it the first day they got here, right in the middle of her crying breakdown.

"Me, too," Avery said. "I wanted to prove that I could do something worthwhile. It's not turning out too well, is it?"

The girls smiled at each other and they kept walking, but Avery's words played in his mind. In his opinion she had done exactly what she came to do—proved she was worthwhile.

They all fell silent again, and after a few moments, Avery stepped closer to him. He thought she would tell him her big secret, but she didn't. "Have you figured out what you're going to do after graduation, Luca?"

Her words threw him. He didn't want to talk about this, not now or ever. What was it with girls? "I don't know. I should be home right now, looking for a job."

"You'll find one."

"Right." He didn't mean for it to sound so final. He turned and offered a smile. "It'll work out. What about you? Ready for next fall?"

Avery would be moving across country to go to some fancy college Mr. Miles had insisted she attend, but she'd never wanted to go there. She wanted to go to a local Bible college and study to be a school teacher, or a missionary, or something where she could help people.

Mr. Miles was never for any of that, but Avery was too scared to stand up to him. She always had been.

"I don't know. I guess." Her words were almost whispered.

Luca wouldn't push her. No use as long as they were stuck in this place.

"Well, in case anyone is wondering," Benny broke in, "I'm not going to college. I'm not doing squat."

Avery turned to him. "You'll do something Benny, even if it's not college."

"Yeah. I'll work in my grandma's beauty shop, buying her supplies and sweeping up other peoples' hair."

OK, maybe Benny had it worse than him. Luca would give him that.

"Think bigger," June said. Her soft voice was a fresh perspective. "You don't have to do that, Benny. You can start somewhere else and move forward. Baby steps."

"Like what?" Benny asked. His voice showed how enthused he was about her suggestion—meaning not enthused at all.

"Get a job somewhere else. A grocery store. A hardware store. The city dump. The point is, you have to try."

Her words struck something in Luca's gut. He had to try. Take baby steps. Would it work in a relationship?

He glanced at Avery to see if she was thinking the same things he was thinking, but she wasn't looking at him. Her eyes seemed focused on something beyond him, something ahead.

Frowning, he opened his mouth to ask her what was up, but he never got the chance.

His feet slipped out from under him just as Avery screamed, "Luca, watch out!"

26

Avery

Luca's arms went up in the air like a cartoon character as his body plummeted into the sand. It covered him up to his chest, but at least the fall had left him with his arms free.

"Is that quick sand?" Benny's panicked voice reminded her of why everyone avoided him back home.

"We have to get him out of there," Avery said. "Luca, give me your stick."

He held it in his hands still, which was a huge plus. His eyes had widened. Swallowing hard, he reached the stick toward her. He reminded her of one of the deer he was always hunting—trapped.

"We're going to help you," she said way more confidently than she felt. Her heart thundered as she moved into position. "You guys, grab on to the stick behind me." She stepped as close to the sand as she dared, giving them room to line up behind her and take hold.

Benny stepped up and put his hands on the stick, but June was looking around, frowning. "I see fruit trees over there," she said, pointing to their far left. "Why are we going this way?"

"Is this really the time?" Avery snapped. "We have to get Luca out!"

June spun back to them and grabbed the stick. "I'm ready."

"OK. On three. Hold on, Luca. One-two-three!"

Avery pulled with every ounce of strength she could muster.

Luca slid up two inches. Maybe.

Panic threatened at the edge of her mind. Getting Luca out was priority. "Harder!" The thick branch cut into her skin and she gritted her teeth against the pain.

They pulled again, and he slipped up another inch.

Her arms went limp and she panted. "OK, break."

"He saw this." Luca's voice came out weak, like he was fighting for air.

Which she guessed he was with tons of sand pressing against him.

"That's why he hadn't gone further."

It was as if he read her thoughts. Of course Daddy saw it. He'd taught her to recognize dangers in the wild when she was just a little girl. He'd probably spotted it a mile back.

She, on the other hand, had spotted it just before Luca stepped in. Another fail on her part, and one that might cost Luca his life. Just when she thought she was getting the hang of this place, it laughed in her face.

"What are you talking about?" Benny asked. He wiped sweat from his head.

"Nothing." Avery stood and took hold of the stick again. "We have to keep trying."

"He barely budged," Benny said.

"So you think we should leave him here?" She didn't mean to snap at him, but really, what other choice did they have? She wasn't leaving Luca to die. They would never make it to the camp for help and get back in enough time.

"Fine," Benny grumbled.

They stepped back to the stick and everyone tightened their grips on it. "Ready? Pull!" She heaved with everything in her. More than everything in her, apparently, because Luca moved out to his waist.

"Whoa, good pull!" Benny said.

Luca's face was pure white, like the rare snows in Alabama, but he managed a smile. "That was good, guys. Maybe I'm not going to die today."

"Of course you're not going to die," June said.

"Let's go again." Who knew what had come over her a moment ago, but she hoped it happened again. They lined up and she gave the signal, then they all tugged.

Strong arms wrapped around her waist and she leaned into whatever force was aiding her.

Luca moved up to his shins.

"Can you move your feet?" June asked. "Maybe you can help yourself get free."

"If he moves around he'll sink farther," Avery said. She shouldn't gloat about besting June, but she kind of did. "He has to stand still."

"How do you know so much about this stuff?" Benny asked. They stepped to the walking stick again.

"My dad's been working in the area my entire life. I know a lot of stuff."

They pulled again, and this time Luca broke free of the sand and fell face forward.

Avery quickly latched on to him and helped him scratch his way to the safety of solid ground.

He fell on top of her with a thud.

They heaved together, tangled up on the jungle floor.

"Get a room," Benny muttered.

Avery's cheeks burned, embarrassed by Benny's annoying words. She wiggled away and stood to get her bearings. Whatever had helped her get Luca out, she was grateful.

"If you know so much, then where are we?" Benny asked. "You saw that map on my phone. Do you recognize where we are?"

She hadn't expected anyone to ask her that. Glancing around, she saw that all eyes were on her. Great.

"I noticed a few things, yes, but I'm no expert."

June frowned and stepped forward. "What do you mean? You noticed enough to make an educated guess? That doesn't sound good. It sounds more like we aren't where we're supposed to be."

Not good at all.

Avery unscrewed the lid on her water bottle and took a long drink. Finally, she sighed. "I noticed we were a little, well, a lot off course. That's all."

Luca frowned at her now.

He was going to stop trusting her altogether. "What do you mean, Avery? Where are we?"

"I don't know. I promise you that. I know we're nowhere near where we started. That's all I could say for sure."

"So something really did pick us up and move us off the road." Luca's statement felt like concrete in her heart, weighing her down. It confirmed what she'd been feeling for days; that something was seriously off. And they were in big trouble.

"Why didn't you mention this before?" Luca said quietly.

She shook her head. "I don't know." But then she

paused. "Or maybe I do know. I wanted to figure things out on my own. Prove myself, remember? I'm tired of everyone looking at me like I'm the plague." There, she'd said it. She didn't want to go crazy again. She hated the way people treated her, and she also hated that she let it hinder her.

Benny huffed and slid to the ground across the path from her. "Well, at least you went crazy for a good reason. My family doesn't have one. I've got a granny who likes to throw glasses at my head and call me names. So what if you're crazy, at least your dad still looks at you."

Benny didn't know Daddy very well.

"No one thinks you're crazy, anyway, Aves." Luca took her hand and squeezed, his face still white with fear.

Warmth erupted inside her.

"You're one of the most level headed people we all know."

Even June offered her an understanding smile.

Tiny slivers of glass began to crack around her heart. They didn't judge her? Didn't care that she'd been hospitalized for losing her mind after Mom left and Daddy didn't even come home from his dig to check on his daughter? No one minded?

She swallowed hard. "Thanks, guys."

Luca smiled at her and let go of her hand as he stood up.

When no one spoke for a few seconds, June turned to them. "So you guys never wanted to find the orchard at all, I take it? Why not just tell us?"

Avery heaved herself up and brushed off her shorts. "I'm sorry. We should have. My dad is coming this way, and we wanted to know why. But since the fruit orchard is over there, why don't we take a look?" It sounded like a good idea, especially since she was starving.

Everyone agreed, so Luca stepped to the front and began beating a path toward the fruit trees. They drew closer and Avery studied the trees. Each one was different, and none of them were recognizable.

"What is this place?" she asked, stepping around the trees. They grew in no particular pattern, except that they seemed to form a circular grove. The overgrowth was less here, like it was used regularly. "Do you think it's where Rae and his people get their food?"

"Rae and his people?" Benny asked. "You mean there are more of him?"

"You think one guy can live in the jungle alone? How would he get here?" Luca asked. He plucked an odd-shaped purple fruit from a tree and studied it.

"How did we get here, genius?" Benny said. "Who knows?"

Avery chuckled and grinned at Luca. "Benny has a point."

When they'd each picked their fruit, they gravitated together to compare their odd choices. Who would be the first to try it?

"We should just do it," Avery said. "Everyone at the same time."

"Why? So we can all die?" Benny said. "No way. You go first. I'm waiting for everyone else."

She managed a light laugh, but it was obvious he wasn't trying to be funny.

Fine. She would do it. Raising the fruit to her lips, she took a tiny, tentative bite. The sweet fruit washed through her mouth and she gasped. "This is delicious!"

She took another bite, not caring what anyone else did.

The others didn't wait long, and soon they'd all devoured a few pieces of fruit from various trees.

"This place is really amazing," June said. "I'm almost going to miss it. It's like an adventure."

Avery turned to June then froze. She stepped closer, frowning. "June, what color are your eyes?"

June's eyebrows rose. "They're green. Why?"

"This is going to sound crazy—sorry, it's where my mind goes automatically—but they are blue. They were green when I first met you. Bright green. But they're blue now. I promise you."

"She's right," Luca said. "I noticed, too. They're blue now."

Luca had noticed June's eyes? Avery was glad she faced away from Luca and he couldn't notice how much that hurt. Taking a deep breath, she pushed the thought away.

June frowned and took a step back. "I don't know what you're talking about. I don't know. Don't people's eyes look different in different light?"

"Not like this," Luca said. He glanced around, a deep frown on his lips. "This place isn't right. It's no adventure. We need to get home as fast as possible."

The realization that this place was messing with them put a somber blanket over the festive mood in the fruit orchard. "What do you say we head back?" Avery asked.

Everyone agreed, and they split up to take care of personal stuff.

But Avery grabbed Luca's arm. "I need to talk to you."

"More secrets?" His voice was soft, but definitely hurt.

"I'm telling you now, aren't I?"

He sighed. "Fine. What is it?"

"Earlier, when I went to use the bathroom, I was gone for a long time."

He frowned and swallowed hard. "Yeah, you said that. I believe you."

"You don't understand. I was gone for so long that for a while I was afraid I'd be lost."

He took a deep breath and rubbed his hand over his face. "Man, I really dislike this place."

She put her hand on his arm and shook her head. "It gets worse. When I was walking, I found a temple. An honest to goodness temple. And inside there was a book. It said a devil was here, and a battle was coming. Rae was there, and he kept saying I had to stop *him*, but he didn't say who. Then he vanished."

"What?" Luca's eyebrows shot up. "Are you sure about this?"

Avery huffed and turned away from him. "Never mind." This was exactly why she didn't want to mention it. He thought she was nuts. Wacko. Crazy. Loons.

This time he grabbed her arm, gently. "I'm sorry. It does sound nuts, but so does everything else in this place. Please, tell me."

She tried wiping the frown off her face, but it wouldn't budge. "I don't know what he was talking about, but he was in a hurry, almost like someone was following him. A twig snapped in the jungle just before he disappeared."

"Can you show me where this temple is?"

Avery glanced down and began picking at a tear in her tank top. "It disappeared, too."

He was quiet and she finally peeked up at him. A

frown stretched his mouth down, but he did seem like he was buying it.

June and Benny returned, and together they moved to follow the path back to camp. They walked a few minutes in silence, but then Avery asked the burning question in her mind. "Do you think Daddy has found another way into that part of the jungle?"

"Could be," Luca said. He seemed relieved to think about something concrete. "Maybe that's why he's making maps and all. He's getting ready to head back in."

"Should we try to find it?"

Luca shook his head. "After all that? No way. Maybe you should talk to him, Aves."

She gnawed on her lip as she walked. "Daddy won't listen to me. He never has."

The realization wasn't a nice one. He didn't care what was best for anyone except himself, not even when it came to his own daughter. He wanted her going away, finding her own life, and he'd pay good money for it. If she stuck close to home, he'd feel responsible for her. She might expect things of him.

The truth hurt.

By the time they got back to camp, no one was speaking. The heat in the jungle had drained every ounce of their energy.

Avery took a bottle and poured the cool water over her skin, washing away the sweat and grime, then she moved to check on Erin.

The youth leader sat up in her shelter, drinking water from the creek and laughing quietly with the other girls. This was the Erin Avery knew and loved.

She couldn't help smiling as she reached them. "Feeling better?"

"Much. I almost feel normal."

"Do you think you're fighting a bacterial infection? Maybe the antibiotics are working."

Erin shrugged. "Must be. I'm glad no one is giving up on me."

Relief burst through Avery. All hope for Erin wasn't lost. She leaned forward and wrapped Erin in a hug. "I'm glad you're OK. I've missed you."

Erin smiled, and Avery moved to find Daddy. She just needed to see him. To make sure he was OK. To make sure he wasn't gone.

"Hey, they fixed the van." Luca waved her over and she smiled at a beaming Bradley.

"As soon as Chad gets back, we'll be able to get out of here," he said. "We got it all patched up."

More good news. Forget about overcoming some demon in the jungle, Avery was going home. "I'm glad. Really glad, you have no idea."

Even Sam seemed to glow as he climbed back under the van for something. He was a really nice guy, she could tell, even though she hadn't actually talked to him.

She scanned the area for Daddy, but he wasn't within sight. She turned back to the van. "Hey, have you guys seen my dad?"

Bradley frowned and looked around. "No, sorry. I guess I've been too busy to notice."

"That's OK. I'll ask the others."

"Mr. Miles?" Sam peeked out from under the van. "Yes, he went into the jungle about an hour ago. He said he wanted to wash up."

"You let him go in alone?" Avery asked.

Sam's eyebrows raised. "You wanted me to stop him?"

Her shoulders sagged and she sighed. "No, of course not. Thanks for letting me know. Sorry for snapping at you."

He offered a small smile, paused, then climbed out from his spot in the sand. "You are troubled?"

Avery glanced around then back to Sam. They hadn't actually spoken, unless she counted the day they arrived in the airplane and he'd offered to take her bags. She swallowed hard and nodded. "He has a habit of disappearing on me."

Sam nodded solemnly. "I am sorry for this. Is there anything you need that I could help you with?"

She hesitated again. People being nice to her wasn't exactly an everyday occurrence. But then a thought popped into her mind—a reminder about something she'd wanted from her luggage. "Actually, I need something from my bag. Do you think you could help me unload it?"

"I can most certainly help with that." He vaulted onto the bumper and untied the luggage.

A moment later she pulled out her Bible. "Thank you, Sam."

He smiled and replaced her luggage. "It has been my pleasure, Avery. And if I may say something else?"

She waited, but realized he was waiting for her to give him permission. She nodded quickly.

"You are doing a fine job here. You and Luca make an excellent team."

Her eyes widened. If she'd expected him to say anything, it wasn't that. She cleared her throat. "Thank you."

She darted away, suddenly uncomfortable, and sat alone on an abandoned log. Now that she had her Bible, she might be able to find a few of the answers she was looking for. And hopefully, Daddy would actually come back.

27

Rae

Jacob would not be happy with Rae, especially when he found out about this latest breech in obedience.

Helping Avery. Again.

It should not matter to him if Avery's friend got sucked into the sand. As a watcher, it was his job to guard the garden and keep humans out. But the concern remained, and helping her group went toward his ultimate goal of making certain the inner jungle stayed protected.

"Dodo bird at ten o'clock."

Rafa's voice spun Rae around. Rae glared at him. "What do you want?"

Rafa nodded to the left. "Like I said, dodo bird at ten o'clock."

Avery's father trekked alone through the trees, right toward the inner jungle.

Rae sprang to action, moving soundlessly through the trees to put a roadblock in his way.

"You don't have to stop him you know."

Rae glared at Rafa. "You are holding me up. Go away." He maneuvered himself several yards in front of Avery's father and quickly moved the brush to block his path. If the other girls—Gabby and Katelyn—had not gotten lost here in the first place, there would be no path for him to follow.

Again, Rae's fault.

"You could have his freedom. Don't stop him. Let them stay a while."

Rae's body hesitated just a moment too long. The man breezed past, never knowing Rae and Rafa stood behind the overgrown trees.

Rae ground his teeth and growled at Rafa. "You distract me for your own purposes. Keeping them here will do us no good."

"You don't believe that or you wouldn't have hesitated." The air shifted, and Rafa was gone.

Mr. Miles's gasp echoed through the damp air and Rae spun toward him.

Mr. Miles turned, his eyes wide, and ran.

Rae moved to where the man had been, curious over what spooked him. A bright yellow snake slithered across the path. Black and red rings wrapped around its body. The snake morphed into a person. Rafa.

Rae frowned.

Rafa changing into a snake was no surprise—Rae had seen the chaos Rafa caused by the snake attack at the humans' camp. He'd done it for nothing more than thrills; he wanted to torture the helpless humans. He'd also been hanging around their group leader, Erin, Rae had discovered.

But it was something else that bothered him. "Why did you help me turn Miles around?"

"You were considering my offer, I could see it. I can wait for you to come around to my way of thinking, so I stopped him. No matter what you think, I am your friend."

No matter what Rafa said, Rae would never

believe his lies.

"No, Rafa, you are not my friend." He turned away and left Rafa standing on the abandoned path.

28

Luca

Quicksand. Really? After everything else they'd been through, now they had to worry about this as well.

But it wasn't really the new threat that had Luca worried. It was more the question of why. They hadn't seen any quicksand in any other part of the jungle. So why there?

Luca sat alone on a log, facing the desert and running dry sand through his fingers. Something—the quicksand—was keeping them out of that part of the jungle, and it was doing it on purpose. No wonder Mr. Miles was bent on getting inside the secret lair. Something lay behind the sand. Something big.

The sun moved closer to the trees. It made a long shadow. Normally he'd be thankful for the shade, but he was still shaken up after falling into the quicksand. His hands shook, sending the tiny granules of sand through the air. He sighed and tossed it away.

Yeah, sun definitely sounded better than shade, hands down. Standing up, he glanced around.

Avery stood at the edge of the trees, obviously upset. She glanced inside the jungle every few minutes.

Mr. Miles had disappeared again.

They'd known it was what he planned, so Luca wasn't sure why it upset Avery so much. Maybe just because she cared, even if her dad didn't deserve it. Erin sat with the others, looking much better.

June sat on a log and stared into the measly fire. She frowned like she'd just been given the worst news ever—maybe she'd been turned down for college or told she was going to have to spend the rest of her life working at a fast food restaurant. Or maybe it was her eyes. Had to be.

Would he be upset if he found out his eyes were changing colors? Probably not, but he was a guy. Girls were jittery. June probably thought it meant something. Maybe it did, but Luca didn't know what. He watched her another moment then turned back to Avery.

Avery had seemed weird around June all day, and now that he thought about it, June had been acting different—braver—since her snake bite. Maybe whatever had gotten into her was turning her into something Avery was picking up on. Something not good.

Luca didn't like the thought of that. He moved toward the desert, toward the sunshine. The hot air chased his chills away, chills he didn't want to admit to anyone. For a minute after he'd fallen into the sand, all he'd been able to think about was Mom. What would she do if he never came home? How would she survive? The whole family needed the money he would bring home.

He took a deep breath and closed his eyes, shaking off the bad feelings. He hadn't died. Somehow, the others had managed to pull him out. No idea how that had happened, but he didn't really care. He was alive, and he was going to find a way home.

Still. The protected part of the jungle pulled at

him. Would he leave right now if he had the chance? Would he leave without finding out what the secret was?

His gaze roamed back to the jungle. He could almost see beyond the tree line, straight to the heart of the jungle. Right to the quicksand. But he didn't care about the sand. He wanted to focus on what was beyond the sand. If he was going to almost die somewhere, he wanted to know why.

Would he leave right now if he could? Probably. But would he ever give up on what was in that jungle? Maybe not.

The farther he walked into the desert, the bigger the jungle looked. It stretched across the open space like an ocean of green. How many days had it been since they were stranded here? He wasn't even sure. Had it been a week? Ten days? Everything was so confusing. He stopped and rubbed his eyes. It was like cobwebs had invaded his brain.

Sighing, he turned back toward the jungle.

Chad's group had headed around the left side of the jungle. They really hadn't been sure if that was the way they'd come. Especially since when they'd left the first time, they'd followed the tree line but ended up coming straight from the desert.

What if Luca went the other direction? What would he find? He stared that way as he considered it. Avery would go with him, and probably Benny and June, too. They could be back in a day or two. They might be able to get into the protected part of the jungle from a different direction.

A movement at the tree line caught his eye.

The other kids were laughing and goofing off.

He couldn't leave them for a day or two.

Especially not with Chad and Mr. Miles gone, not that Avery's dad was doing much to take care of anyone.

It was probably better this way. He didn't need to learn something about this place that made him want to stay. He forced himself to walk back toward camp. Should he tell Avery what he'd realized about the quicksand in the inner jungle?

He laughed at the thought. She probably already knew it, anyway. She hadn't fooled him earlier when she'd said she wasn't sure where they were. She knew as much about maps of Iraq as Mr. Miles did.

Maybe she already knew what was inside the jungle. And maybe she did realize how well she'd been doing since they got stranded. If she didn't have such a big heart to help people, she'd be a great archeologist. It was in her blood.

He reached camp and slid to a seat beside June. "Hey, you OK?"

She gasped. "Oh. You scared me."

"Sorry."

She shook her head. "I don't know if I'm OK. I've been feeling weird, but then other times I feel OK. Maybe my eyes change with my mood."

Luca sighed. "There are a lot of maybes floating around today."

She frowned but didn't question him.

"Hey, do you know how long we've been here?"

Her eyebrows shot up and she turned toward the fire, thinking. Finally, she shrugged. "I don't know. I guess I lost count."

"Yeah, me too."

They sat quietly for a few minutes when she turned back to him. "Do you think our families even know we're missing? Is anyone even looking for us?"

"I'm sure the mission called when we didn't arrive." But did he really believe that?

"I'm worried about my grandparents. I live with them, and they're pretty old," she said. Then she added softly, "My parents died when I was a little girl."

"My dad died a few months ago," he said. "I'm sorry."

She shrugged, and he tensed, sure she was going to ask what had happened. But she didn't. "I don't remember them. It's no big deal, but I worry about my grandparents. I've been sick for a long time, and they were always there for me. If I never come home, though, I'm not sure they could handle it." Her gaze moved to Erin who sat at the edge of her shelter. "Now I'm thinking I should have just stayed home."

Luca studied her for a minute. She looked healthy enough to him. "Are you better now?"

She shrugged. "I had cancer, but it's over now. I was tired of being coddled. My grandparents didn't want me to come, but I insisted."

"Wow. I'm glad you came. Right now I'm thinking we all wish we had stayed home."

She studied him, her eyes full of questions. "You wish you hadn't come?"

Her question bugged him. Annoyed him down to the bottom of his gut. Did he wish he'd stayed home? He told himself he'd come because Mom made him. But truthfully, it probably had more to do with Avery, and now their friendship was on the mend. Something he wasn't going to talk about with June. "I don't know."

She smiled and nudged him. "Don't worry. You'll figure it out."

He forced a smile. "Yeah, I know." But he didn't know, not for sure. He'd been taking care of Mom so steadily since Dad died that his only goal had been putting food on the table and making sure the boys obeyed her. But Avery was always in the back of his mind. He wanted a life with her. That hadn't changed, no matter how much Mr. Miles hated him.

Of course, Mr. Miles wasn't totally off his rocker when it came to his opinion about Luca.

But his rage had been a one-time thing. Was he still angry? Definitely. Was he taking that anger out on people, places, and things anymore? No.

Suddenly it hit him how close he sat to June. Their arms almost brushed, and their shoes touched sole to sole. What was he doing here with her? He practically bolted out of his seat.

She frowned up at him, concerned. "Is everything OK?"

"Yeah. I'm thirsty. Want a drink?"

"No, I'm OK. Good talk."

He forced another smile. "Yeah. Good talk."

Spending time with June might not be the best thing he could be doing, but spending time with Avery right now wasn't too appealing, either. He needed to figure things out.

Instead, he made his way to the guys. They gathered around the van, and their loud voices carried in the dry air. Everyone smiled and laughed—they were excited. Thought they'd be getting out of here soon. Hopefully they were right.

"What are we going to do when we leave?" Benny asked.

Bradley scoffed. "What are you talking about, dork? We're going home."

Benny looked down and drew back.

Luca frowned. Yeah, Benny was really annoying, but he'd been a big help on this trip. "Kind of harsh, don't you think?" Luca asked. "And it's not that cut and dry. Benny's got a point. The mission is expecting us, and our tickets home aren't good for at least a few more days."

"Dude, I don't care what the tickets say. When we leave this jungle, I'm going home. My parents will shell out the money."

But Bradley didn't know what Avery had told them; they weren't near the village, and who knew where the closest airport was located.

"Whatever," Luca said. "I just hope we get out of here."

Someone else started in and Luca turned away.

Benny had melted away to sit alone, which wasn't so abnormal for the kid.

Luca wanted to say it was just that they were all so tired of being together. They were hungry and dirty, and bored out of their minds.

But none of it was true. They were mean to Benny, plain and simple—including him. Things had been worse since the other group joined them. All the guys treated him badly. Maybe that needed to stop.

Luca took a seat next to Benny.

Neither of them spoke, but the silence was comfortable. If something was going to change, it might as well start now.

29

Avery

Daddy had to come back soon.

If he didn't, Avery was going back in. It shouldn't be hard to figure out which path he took, since Luca knew all about tracking.

She paced in front of the tree line. Who cared if everyone thought she was crazy at this point? If it was their dad in there, they'd do the same thing.

The map Daddy had drawn crinkled in her pocket and she pulled it out to study it. The fruit orchard stood out, as well as the shaded area, but she squinted when she noticed something else. A small "x" was scribbled in the midst of a few trees. At least, it looked like an x. She studied the area, which had a line running through it—the creek. On the other side of the line he had drawn a path.

Avery gasped.

She and Luca had gone in near the grove, but on the opposite end was the creek and swim hole where they went for water. That was near the place Katelyn and Gabby's path had met with theirs. They hadn't found the girls at the creek that day, but what if that was because the girls had crossed the water?

Avery froze, searching her brain for some tidbit that seemed just out of reach. Last night, when Daddy had come out of the van, he'd sat with Katelyn and

Gabby. It had seemed odd since he didn't know them, but Daddy was used to being around strangers so she'd blown it off. What if he wasn't sitting next to them to be kind? What if he was drilling them for information?

Katelyn and Gabby had experienced something stranger than everyone else up to this point—well, except maybe June's eyes changing color and Avery seeing a disappearing temple. But Katelyn and Gabby had lost an entire day of their lives. They did, however, have recollections of what went on that day. They'd seen a vision that pointed them back to camp, a vision that was most likely their mysterious pal, Rae.

Rae lived in the heart of the jungle?

He must, and not only that, but he wanted to keep people out of it. It was the only explanation for the sand.

Now that she had a clue about what had prompted Daddy to head back in, she wracked her brain for more information.

Katelyn and Gabby had said something about the fruit tree. Had they been in the fruit orchard? No, that was the opposite side of the jungle. But a fruit tree wasn't all that significant. Weren't there fruit trees all over? Still, if what she'd read in her Bible last night were any indication, a fruit tree might be very significant—if it were the right fruit tree.

She gave up on waiting for Daddy and moved to sit with June's church mates. They smiled at her when she sat, but kept up their conversation. They were planning the rest of their summer like none of this had ever happened, like none of this was happening right now. How could they be so nonchalant about it all?

Her irritation seeped out and she interrupted

them. "Did you guys talk to my dad?"

They turned to her, surprise written all over their faces.

Finally, Gabby nodded. "Yeah, he asked us about where we'd gotten lost."

"What did you tell him?"

Gabby frowned. She didn't seem to like Avery's demanding questions, but Avery didn't care.

Would she have acted this way a month ago? No way. But after a week—or something like that—in the jungle, fending for herself and making hard choices, she didn't much care if these girls liked her questions or not.

"We told him exactly what we told everyone else. We wandered around for a few hours, and then something Katelyn saw pointed us back to camp."

"I found the path you used," Avery said. She'd almost forgotten about the day she got lost. "There was an alcove, and the path out led straight to camp."

"No," Gabby said. "We crossed the creek and took the path back that you guys use for water."

So she'd been right about the way Daddy would get in. But what had him wanting *in* to begin with? If he suspected the same things she did, they needed to know. "Thanks," she said. "I'm just worried about him. I hope he gets back soon."

Gabby's scrunched up face relaxed. She seemed to get that. "It's OK. I'm sure he'll be back before dark."

Avery smiled and nodded, but she wasn't so sure. Once, last summer, he'd gone on a dig in south Israel. He'd said it would take a week, but after a month, she finally broke down and called some of his coworkers.

They'd said he'd gone exploring in the area and hadn't returned.

Avery had freaked, but they assured her that for Mr. Miles, it was perfectly normal. Sure enough, he'd shown back up at the dig two days later. He never explained where he'd been or what he'd found.

She shivered. He wouldn't do that this time, would he? An entire mission group was depending on him. They were stranded, and they needed to get out ASAP.

Benny and Luca sat on a log a few feet away.

Neither of them spoke, but Avery didn't need empty words right now anyway. She slid into the spot next to Luca. He glanced at her and smiled. She smiled back as she picked up a handful of sand and began running it through her fingers. Things would be OK. And if he wasn't back soon, the three of them would resume their search.

June plopped onto to the log beside Avery and smiled. Her eyes were green again.

Avery smiled back and amended her resolve.

They would go back in, the four of them. Whatever was wrong with June's eyes, she had still been willing to help. That counted for something.

The sun finally dipped below the tree line, and the desert was bathed in shadow.

Everyone moved closer to sit around the fire, and Luca grabbed a few chunks of wood to give more light and heat. Sweaters were pulled out, food was passed around, and chatter rose.

Avery wasn't interested in any of it. Where was Daddy? Her feet itched to bolt, to get away from the singing and find him. Forcing herself to stay put, she endured the music. The first song ended, and they started right in on another.

By the third song about Christ and the angels,

Avery had relaxed a bit. It wasn't so bad, really, and their voices did blend well. She scanned the tree line for any movement, but the night was still. Her gaze fell on Erin, who for the first time in days had joined the group instead of sleeping supper away in the shelter. Something had loosened up with her. Maybe it was because she'd seen Chad, or maybe the voices that tormented her had eased up. But why?

Avery froze when she realized she was humming along to their song. She put a stop to that, but she didn't leave.

They sat together for another four songs, and disappointment washed over her when the group broke up for the night.

Daddy wasn't coming back, at least not right now.

Her legs felt like they weighed a million pounds each as she dragged them to the van. She let everyone else climb in before she joined them, and she scanned the trees one last time before closing the door with a thud.

The others closed their eyes and fell asleep within minutes, but Avery stared out the window long into the night.

30

Avery was the first one up the next morning. She pushed her way out of the van and into the cool morning air. Sunlight glared from a million miles out in space, but it wasn't enough to heat the desert just yet.

Shivering, she moved toward the fire to stir up the embers. A few guys moved inside the shelters when she dropped a chunk of wood into the fire and it popped, but she didn't wake anyone. Being alone was a rarity here. It was almost peaceful sitting in the open space by herself.

No wonder Luca had tried to sneak away.

Memories of his solitary hike came back to her. He'd met someone else, someone named Rafa.

Chills broke out across her arms, and she shivered and pulled her sweater tighter. Who else lived here? Watched them? And what were they doing here? She had her theories, but she could be wrong.

She stood and moved to the trees. The air grew warmer and moister the closer she stepped. It felt like a sauna after being in the cold desert air.

They were low on water and they'd have to go in today to resupply. If they were going to be at the creek anyway, there was no reason they couldn't cross over and check it out. Daddy was missing, after all.

Something moved in the trees, and Avery froze. Straining her eyes, she peered into the jungle. Daddy didn't burst through. In fact, nothing seemed to move besides the leaves.

The chills were back.

She scrambled over to the logs and climbed on top, remembering the snakes from a few nights ago. Had it only been three nights? Or had it been two?

Time didn't seem to move in order in this place.

No snakes slithered into the opening, though. Nothing came out.

"What's up?"

Avery screamed and fell off the log. Luca's arms caught her before she could smack into the side of the next log. They stood like that, his arms wrapped around her, and she swallowed hard.

He didn't move, only looked into her eyes. She couldn't lie to herself any more—she didn't only miss his friendship.

A twig snapped, and she scrambled out of his grip and backed away. "You scared me half to death, Luca!"

He put his hands up defensively. "Sorry. I just saw you standing up there and wanted to make sure everything was OK."

"Everything is not OK. Daddy didn't come back, and no one even questioned it." She didn't mean to sound so hateful, and she worked to calm her racing heartbeat.

"We questioned it, Aves. We went in to see what was up, but we didn't run into him."

Avery took a deep breath. He was absolutely right. She glanced around to make sure they were alone. "I think I know why we didn't run into him. I think I know which way he went."

"What?" He lowered his voice to match hers and pulled her farther from the guys' shelter. "What are you thinking?"

"I saw him talking to Gabby and Katelyn the other night, and so I talked to them myself to see what he'd said. They told me they crossed the creek."

"We can't trust what they said. They think they were gone a few hours."

"I don't know," she said with a shrug. She pulled out the map and showed him the "x". "I think he took what they said seriously. I'm sure he crossed the creek. I thought we could check it out when we go to get water later today."

His gaze moved to the trees and he scanned the area around them. "OK. There's no reason not to try."

Hope burst through her chest. This was good. Trying was good.

The van door squeaked open and a few girls piled out. The guys stirred, too, and soon the camp came alive. They ate together then broke into groups to gather more fruit, wood, and water.

Avery, Luca, June, and Benny stuffed empty bottles into backpacks to take on their hike.

"We'll leave in the morning if Chad gets back tonight, right?" Benny asked as they started into the jungle.

"That's the plan," Luca said.

Avery froze. She grabbed Luca's arm, shaking her head. "No, Luca. We can't leave if Daddy's still missing."

"We're going to find him, Avery. Don't worry. Of course we won't leave him."

She nodded and dropped her hand from his arm. June and Benny stared at her, but she shook off the bad feelings their strange looks brought. She pushed past them and restarted their hike.

"Chad might not get back until tomorrow anyway," Luca said. "That's how long it took Bradley's group to make it back the last time. If that's the case then it will be another day before we leave."

That made her feel slightly better.

They reached the creek and worked silently at filling the bottles. When the last bottle was capped, Avery stood and looked to Luca. "Should we just leave the packs here while we go deeper?"

"Whoa, deeper?" Benny stepped forward. "What are you talking about?"

"We wanted to check out another place Avery's dad might have gone."

"When were you going to tell us this?" Benny said. "Because I'm tired of getting yanked around. First yesterday and now today? No way. If you want my help you've got to start treating me like I matter."

The hurt on his face outdid the anger. He was right. They were still treating him as bad as they'd always treated him, only in a different way.

Luca opened his mouth but Avery stepped forward. "I'm sorry, Benny. You're right. I should have mentioned it, I was just so anxious to find him I wasn't thinking."

"You had time to tell him." Benny nodded to Luca. "And you could have mentioned it during our entire hike here. You kept it to yourself."

"Let's just remember to keep everyone in the loop from now on," June said. "Deal? We're all friends here. We're in this together."

Avery glanced at June and offered a smile of thanks, but paused. Today, June's eyes were blue.

Perfect.

"OK. I think he went over the creek and tried to

get into the secret area from the backside. I want to see if we can pick up a path."

"You want us to go over there?" June asked. "I'm not sure I like that idea."

"Why not?" Avery asked. "You went across the other day when you and I stayed here alone."

"That was different. I was in and out, not tramping through a side of the jungle none of us had explored yet."

"That side of the jungle looks exactly like this side," Luca said. "If you don't want to come along, you don't have to. But if you're in, we're heading over."

Avery sighed in relief. "Let's go."

She and Luca started through the water, their footsteps splashing with every stride. After a moment, another set of splashes sounded behind them, and then another. They reached the other side and started up the bank.

"There." Luca pointed out a trail to their left. A definite path had been trampled down in the grass. "The grass isn't dead yet. This path was made in the last day or two."

They fell into step behind him as they made their way to the inner jungle.

"What do you think he's looking for?" Benny asked.

Avery wanted to blow off his question, but his rant from earlier made her stop.

"He's an archeologist. The Middle East has been his playground since I was a little girl."

"Do you think he knows where we are?" June asked. "If he knows the area so well?"

Did he know it? It didn't matter if he did, she had to stop him. They had to get out of there before any big battle started.

Her ideas and suspicions about their location grew with every passing moment, but she hadn't even told Luca everything she was thinking, everything she'd heard Daddy say about this area of Iraq. Mainly because she could be way off.

She shook her head to get rid of the thoughts. "I don't know, but he must have some suspicions about something out here. I just want to find him before Chad gets back. Then we can all get out of here."

They walked a few more steps in silence before Benny started again. "Erin looks good, don't you think? The antibiotics must have started working."

Avery didn't mention that whatever had been bothering Erin had nothing to do with her illness. Surely, everyone realized that. Benny had seen Rae himself. How could he forget that weirder things were going on here?

No one spoke for a few paces, and Avery worked at calming her annoyance. It wasn't right to snap at everyone, especially if she needed their help. It was this jungle. This air. It was like the whole place was cursed.

They took a few more steps before coming to a fork in the path. One side went deeper into the jungle to the right, and the other veered left and back toward the creek.

Avery stopped and frowned. "He couldn't have gone both ways."

"The paths are fresh. He might have gone one way and realized he was on the wrong path. Then he turned around and tried the other direction." Luca bent to the ground to look more closely at the grass.

"So which way do we try?" Avery asked with a

sigh.

Luca stretched back to his full height. "I don't know. Eeny meeny miny moe?"

"Ha ha."

He grinned. "Glad I could help."

"What if we split up?" June asked. "We could count out our steps. No one goes more than two hundred paces before turning back this way. We'll meet back right here."

"No way," Luca said. "We're not splitting up out here. We can try the left first, then the right, if that doesn't pan out."

Avery didn't mind June's idea all that much, except she didn't want to split up from Luca and she didn't trust Benny and June to be able to find their way back.

No one complained and they fell back into step behind Luca. He led them down the path on the left before they came to a shallow slope.

"I'll go first." Luca started down and a moment later Avery followed. The mud was slicker than she realized, and she slid into Luca at the bottom.

"Sorry," she muttered.

He caught her eye and shook his head slightly. "What for?"

She shrugged and gave him a small smile.

They walked a few more minutes before the sounds of the creek babbled on their left. Avery looked through the trees and spotted the water rushing in its bed. "We chose wrong."

"No, look." Benny pointed to the path that clearly moved away from the creek and to the right.

Luca laughed and slapped Benny on the shoulder. "You're picking up on this tracking thing, huh?"

Benny grinned and Avery's heart squeezed. How long had it been since someone complimented him?

They followed the path for a few more yards before the trail went cold. Luca dropped to the ground and searched the grass. "It stops here. He turned around and went back."

Avery scanned the area. "Why? There's nothing here that says he was on the wrong track."

It didn't make sense. Why hike this far into the jungle then turn around and go back?

She sighed. Since when did Daddy do anything that made sense?

"Let's turn around then," she said.

Luca nodded and they turned back toward the fork in the path. They hiked for ten, fifteen, twenty minutes in hot, steamy silence. Avery's breath became steadily shallower until finally she grabbed Luca's arm. "I'm thirsty. I need a drink."

Luca nodded and pulled two bottles from his pockets. They each took turns drinking from them, and Avery closed her eyes and sighed as the cool water rushed through her.

"So you guys all know each other?" June asked. She leaned against a tree and took another drink. "Like, for a long time?"

Avery frowned. June's eyes were green again, which might not bother her except they'd sort of had this same conversation the day before when June's eyes were blue.

She stepped forward. "June, when was the last time you drank anything?"

June frowned. "What?"

"Your eyes changed again. From blue to green. It happened when you took a long drink of water."

"I don't know. That sounds really weird to me."

"I don't understand it either," Avery said. "I just know what I saw."

"I drank a few sips at breakfast this morning."

"But then we came into the jungle," Avery said.

"Yeah, so?"

June was right. So what? Avery hadn't figured it all out yet, but she was going to.

A loud crack sounded down the path and everyone jumped.

"What was that?" Benny asked, his voice panicked.

"Probably just a branch falling." Luca's face pulled together in worry.

"Must have been a big branch," Avery said. "We better keep going."

They packed up the water and went back to walking. They had just rounded a corner when Luca stopped short. Avery ran into his back, and June ran into hers.

"Luca, what's wrong?" Avery peered around him and then she saw exactly what was wrong.

It hadn't been a branch falling that made the loud crack.

It had been an entire line of trees engulfed in flames. The blast of heat that hit her in the face nearly knocked her backwards.

"What on earth?" June asked.

Luca snapped out of his shock. "I have no idea, but we're not getting through that."

"Um, I'm thinking we should run now, right?" Benny asked. "Fire in the middle of a bunch of trees is no good."

A blast of flames flared near them. It caught the

next set of trees on fire.

Avery and the others stumbled backwards. "Benny, I think you're absolutely right."

So they ran.

31

Luca

The heat from the fire singed the hair on the back of Luca's neck as he turned and ran. He practically shoved Avery into motion, and the others rushed behind her.

"What started that fire?" Avery shouted as they ran. "This air is way too wet for a spark."

"I don't know." His lungs already burned, and the sharp jungle brush had sliced his legs in several places.

They reached the fork in the path in record time, but Avery pulled up short. "Which way?"

Luca studied the path. His mind spun and he tried to remember which way they'd come from, but nothing looked the same. Finally he shook his head. "I don't know."

Benny looked behind them. "I'd rather not stand around discussing it. The fire is nowhere in sight, but who knows how long it will take."

Luca sucked in air like a dying man as he studied the path they'd just come from. Benny was right; the fire hadn't caught up to them.

"When we took this path we veered to the right, so I think from here we need to turn left." It was the best he could come up with, since his head still spun. He shook it like that would get rid of the fog.

"Sounds good to me." Avery turned left and they

started that way. Without the fire biting their heels, no one felt the need to bolt like they had before. The slower pace helped slow the confusion.

"What if Daddy's in there?" Avery asked. "What if he got caught in the fire?"

"What if he started the fire?" Benny said. "He shouldn't have gone in there at all."

Luca wasn't about to say it, but Benny was right. For all they knew, it was something Mr. Miles had done that caught the jungle on fire in the first place.

They reached the creek and crossed quickly. The cool water washed the blood and grime from his legs but suddenly his throat felt like the jungle—on fire. "Let's get a drink."

No one argued and they filled up the bottles they'd taken deeper into the jungle.

Luca's confusion vanished as he gulped.

"Where are our other packs?" June asked. She hadn't spoken during their entire run through the jungle, but her hair stood out like it'd been caught by a branch more than once, and she had a bloody scrape on her cheek.

"Are you OK?" He stepped closer and pointed to her cheek. "You've been cut."

She touched her cheek and winced. "Ow. I hadn't even noticed it."

"Wash it in the creek. The cool water will feel good."

She bent and cupped her hands before dipping them in the water.

When she stood, she glanced around. "Didn't we leave the packs of water here? What happened to them?"

Luca looked around. She was right. They'd left the

packs just off the path, but they were gone now. "Maybe someone from camp came looking for us. They probably took the water back with them."

"Maybe Chad's back," Benny said. "Maybe we're about to get out of here."

Luca glanced at Avery. She bit her lip and frowned, but she didn't argue this time.

He swallowed hard. He knew that look. It was determination. Avery wasn't leaving this jungle without her dad, even if it meant everyone else left without her. Luca touched her shoulder. "We'll find him," he said quietly.

She glanced at him and gave a small nod.

"Let's get back and see what's up," he said.

They trekked back to camp in silence, but Luca's mind wasn't on Chad or even finding Mr. Miles.

Fire? Seriously?

First quicksand, now fire. An odd thought occurred to him. What if no one had set that fire?

Now he sounded as crazy as Avery felt, but an idea formed in his mind. More of a theory than an idea, but he would tell Avery about it later.

They pushed through the trees and into the sunlight. Dry heat hit him, and Luca felt like he'd just come home.

Erin sat on a log with the other girls. Bradley, Sam, and the other guys fiddled with the van. No Chad. No Mr. Miles. No water.

"Dude, so glad you're back," Bradley said. "We're dying of thirst."

Luca ground his teeth. What was he supposed to say to that?

"You mean you don't have the water?" June asked. "Someone took our packs. We assumed it was one of you."

"Why would we take your packs? You were going to get water."

Now was not the time to explain where they'd been.

"Lay off," Benny said. "The jungle's on fire. We had to run."

"What?" Bradley's eyebrows shot up and he puffed up his chest like some kind of stupid rooster. "How'd that happen?"

"We don't know," Luca cut in before Benny or June could say anything else. "We were doing some exploring on the other side of the creek, and we left the packs of water just off the path. We saw the fire, ran, looked for the packs, and they were gone. We thought maybe one of you guys had found them."

By now, everyone gathered around to listen. Bradley glanced at the group. "Anyone get the water and forget to tell us?"

Silence.

"What about this fire?" Erin asked. She seemed recovered from her crazy spell, for whatever reason.

"I don't know," Luca said. "We were following a path and as we turned a corner, a huge wall of flames blasted us backwards. We ran and didn't look back."

"There's no smoke."

Everyone turned to Avery. She'd walked several paces into the desert and stared at the sky above the trees. She pointed. "The jungle's on fire. How is there no smoke?"

The group moved toward her and everyone looked up. She was right.

"I don't know," Luca said. "But we saw it."

They'd all seen it—Benny, June, Avery, and him.

His theory solidified in his mind.

"Let's not worry about that now," Erin said. "We'll keep an eye out for flames, but right now we need water." She acted like they were making it up. She knew they weren't, though, right? She'd been the one speaking to dark, invisible creatures.

Luca closed his eyes and took a deep breath. He was being way too sensitive. It was this place. It was cursed or something. Maybe they were all cursed along with it.

He took a deep breath through his nose and forced himself to calm down. "Does anyone else have any empty bottles? We took everything we could find this morning."

"I have one," Mallory said.

"Me too," Gabby offered.

A few others handed their bottles over.

"OK, we'll fill them up and be right back," Luca said.

Bradley glared at him. "Maybe someone else should go."

"You don't even know your way," Luca argued. "You've barely set foot in this jungle."

"Maybe because I've been slaving away at getting the van running, genius." Bradley's nostrils flared and he stepped forward.

Luca held in his laugh. Bradley couldn't beat him even if Luca promised not to fight back.

"Why don't we all go?" Erin said. "Swimming sounds kind of nice."

"What if Chad gets back?" Luca asked. "They won't know where everyone went."

Erin paused. "So a few can stay back. Any volunteers?"

"I'll stay," Avery said.

Luca's gaze swung around to her. If anything, he figured she'd be the first to get back in the jungle. She was up to something, and that meant he was sticking by her side. "I'll stay, too."

Avery gave him a small smile, and Benny and June offered to stay with them, too. Apparently they'd all had enough jungle time today.

After the rest of the group had disappeared into the massive greenery, Avery turned to them. "That was real, wasn't it? I really saw the flames."

"I felt the heat," June said.

"Me, too." Benny sat on a log by himself, kicking at the sand.

Luca took a deep breath. Should he say what he was thinking? Might as well. "What if whatever makes us see the visions, or hear the voices, or—," he stopped and glanced at June, "makes someone's eyes change color, what if it made all of us see something at the same time? Maybe it wasn't there at all."

Silence fell over them.

Avery frowned and squirmed in her seat.

No one liked the idea that something else could control them that way, but what other answer was there?

"I just want to go home." June sniffled and tears started slipping down her cheeks.

Luca held in his sigh. Putting up with her tears didn't seem so impossible anymore. She'd proven she was strong, and she deserved the outlet. He half expected Avery to move in to comfort June, but Avery stared absently into the desert. It didn't look like she'd even noticed the crying.

"It'll be OK," Luca finally said. It felt weird, not

hugging her or offering a shoulder to cry on, but he wasn't about to do that this time. Things between them had gone from OK to weird at some point.

June nodded and tried to smile, but her face was still scrunched up.

Avery shifted on the log, and her eyes changed. They sharpened. Focused. Like when a deer noticed something was off in the forest.

"What are you thinking?" he asked.

She turned to him. Deep frown lines ran across her forehead, and her eyebrows pulled low over her eyes.

"I think Chad's coming."

32

Avery

Luca spun around and scanned the direction where Chad and his group had left, but they weren't coming from that way. Avery nodded straight out in the desert, where she'd seen the mirage. "Look."

June's tears dried up and she gazed toward the ocean of sand, and Benny sat straighter on his log as he studied the distance.

Within a few moments, the other group came into view. The whole lot of them—Chad, the other driver, and the two boys who had gone with him.

Avery almost smiled. She was getting better at tuning into her senses in this place. At determining what was happening, why, and when. In fact, they were all getting better. Adjusting.

She fit in better here than she ever had at home, and the realization reminded her of what Sam had said the day before—she was doing OK here.

The thought vanished as quickly as it had come, but Avery didn't write it off completely. She fit in here, and the others knew it.

"Why are they coming from the middle of the desert?" June asked.

"Why does anything happen around here?" Luca stood. "I'm going out to meet them."

Avery followed him across the sand, thankful for

the tennis shoes she'd brought.

After a few moments, she realized Benny and June followed them, too. They reached the other group in about ten minutes. Avery wiped the sweat from her head as Luca stepped forward.

"You made it back early."

Chad frowned. "Early? You're mistaken, my friend. We're later than we hoped."

"You left yesterday morning," Luca said. "We weren't expecting you until at least tonight, but probably tomorrow."

Chad's frown deepened and he shook his head. "We left four days ago, Luca."

Avery's gaze flew to Luca. He looked to her then glanced at Benny and June. "I think we're all mixed up. Either way, did you get the gas?"

Each of them held up a container and they nodded.

"Good."

They made their way back to camp together.

"Where is everyone?" Chad asked.

"Swimming," Luca said. "We volunteered to stay back and keep an eye on camp."

Chad's face turned somber. "And Erin?"

"She's fine." Avery smiled at him. "Doing much better." She hadn't mentioned it, but she had a theory about Erin. Just like the creek water had pushed away whatever forces changed June's eye color, now that Erin was drinking creek water instead of her own case from home, her dark forces were being chased off.

Chad's face relaxed and he smiled, too. "Good to hear."

They reached camp and the guys moved to the van. "Did they get it patched up?"

"Yep," Luca said. "Good to go."

"Great. We'll leave as soon as everyone gets back. Why don't we get the camp packed up?"

Avery bit her lip. She glared at Luca, hoping he got the telepathic messages she was shooting at him.

"It's kind of late to set out today," Luca said. "What if we wait until the morning?"

Avery held her breath.

Chad laughed. "Buddy, I already told you we need to have a serious talk about who the authority figure is in this relationship, but that sounds fine. First thing in the morning it is."

Avery sighed in relief, but that didn't give her much time. She had to get back into that jungle, and soon. If the fire wasn't real, could she get through it? Hadn't she felt the heat, though? Would it still burn her? Maybe it was all in her head. If that were the case, it couldn't hurt her.

She sighed and gritted her teeth. Why couldn't Daddy just show up? For once in her life, she'd like to feel like she wasn't an afterthought.

Luca caught her eye and nodded.

Relief washed over her. He knew what she was thinking, and he was with her. She wouldn't have to go searching in the jungle alone. And maybe she wasn't *always* an afterthought.

Luca helped Chad pour the gasoline into the tank, and they all worked at packing up whatever supplies they could. "Should we stock up on fruit and water again?" June asked.

Avery could hug her. It was the perfect excuse for going back into the jungle.

"We don't have any water bottles," Benny pointed out.

Avery stepped forward. "The others are getting water. We can go after the fruit."

Chad nodded and Avery, Luca, Benny, and June quickly grabbed the baskets. Avery's heartbeat picked up with every step.

Once they were in the jungle, Avery set her basket aside and turned to the others. "How are we going to get across the creek without being seen by the others?"

"The creek flows through the entire jungle. We can find another spot to cross," Luca said.

June and Benny looked at each other and nodded. "We're in," Benny said.

Avery couldn't stop her smile. It had been so long since she'd had friends, she had almost forgotten how good it felt. "Thanks."

They made their way toward the creek, steering clear of being seen by the others. The sounds of splashing and laughing carried in the thick air as they drew closer, though, and just as they broke through the brush a few of the guys came down the path.

"Chad's back," Avery said quickly, thinking fast. "We're packing everything up to leave."

Bradley's eyes lit up. He turned and cupped his mouth. "Yo! Chad's back!"

Everyone cheered and climbed out.

"Don't forget to bring back water and fruit," Luca said.

"Fruit? Dude, we're getting the water. You get the fruit."

Avery rolled her eyes and balled her fists. She stepped forward and shoved a finger in his chest. "Listen, Bradley. I'm looking for my dad. I don't care if the entire van of you leaves me behind, but I'm looking for him. You want fruit? Get it yourself."

She stepped around him, not caring who stared at her, or hated her, or thought she was nuts. She would find her dad, figure out what was going on in this crazy place, and get back to camp in time to get out. That was all that mattered.

The trampling of brush behind her let her know Luca, Benny, and June hadn't given up on her. They splashed across the creek and headed back to the fork in the path. The sounds of the rest of the group climbing from the water echoed through the air but grew dimmer the farther they walked.

They reached the fork and Avery moved to make the turn right when Luca's arm shot out. He took hold of her.

"We need a plan, first, Aves. What if the fire is still burning? What if it burns us?"

She swallowed hard. "I thought of that. I don't care. If it's just a vision, then can it really hurt us?"

"I don't know, but what if it *does* hurt?" Luca asked. "Are you going to keep going?"

"Yes." She didn't even hesitate.

Luca turned to the others. "What about you? Are you in or out?"

Benny frowned and shifted from foot to foot. "I'm not getting singed. Sorry."

"I don't know." June swallowed hard. "I'll figure it out when we get there."

Avery almost felt sorry for her. This place was really creepy, but finding Daddy was more important to her than June's feelings right now. She couldn't bring herself to give up on finding him, not for June or anyone else's sake.

She stepped forward and led the way to the fire. It was a long, hot hike through the smoldering air, but just like they'd noticed from the desert staring toward the trees, no smoke filled the path as they drew closer. The air was clear, even if the crackling of the fire traveled in the air waves.

"It's not real," Luca said. "Can't be. We should be safe."

Avery nodded. "It's just around this corner."

They took turns drinking from the one water bottle they'd managed to bring along. It hadn't necessarily been the best of plans, but they were here now. What were they going to find once they got inside? Surely, Daddy wouldn't be sitting in a big chair just waiting for her to find him. In fact, if he'd gotten through the fire he would be long gone.

"Let's do it," Luca said.

They stepped around the bend, and the wall of flames burned just as brightly as before. But it hadn't spread farther into the jungle.

Avery swallowed hard. A real fire wouldn't stay contained. Right?

"Remember it's not real!" Luca shouted, confirming her thoughts. The roar of the fire rumbled in her ears, but how could they trust their ears when their eyes and skin were betraying them?

"It's too hot!" Benny shouted. "I'm not going in there."

"You can do it!" Avery said. "Just don't think about it."

He glanced at her sideways, his eyebrows pulled low. Now he probably really did think she was crazy, but it had nothing to do with her history.

"I'll go first," Luca said.

The thought of him burned to a crisp sent a wave a fear through her. She hurried ahead of him and put her hand on his chest. She had to shout to be heard. "I'll go first. He's my dad, and it's my responsibility to find him. If something happens to me, then you can all go back."

Luca barked out a laugh. "You can't be serious. I would never leave you behind."

Something broke inside of her. A dam that sent gushing torrents of water through her heart. He was hers, and she was his. Just like it'd always been.

She nodded. "I know you wouldn't. Together, then?"

"Together."

He reached for her. She hesitated at first, staring at his hand. Should she take it? Could she take it?

She had to take it. His fingers wrapped confidently around hers, and they stepped closer.

Heat all but singed their skin as they drew closer, but no ash floated in the air. "Look," Avery said. She pointed to her arm. "The hair isn't singeing."

Luca glanced at his own arms and gave her a small smile. "We're going to be OK."

They stepped forward, into the flames, and Avery gasped as they engulfed her.

Red surrounded them. Red in front of her. Red behind her. Red all around her.

Where was Luca? She grasped at the air, searching for him. When had she let go of his hand?

The red turned deeper until it was almost white. A blinding, white heat that blew all around her. Suddenly, a crackling black face erupted in front of her. The creature's eyes glowed, and its teeth were as sharp as razor blades. Avery stumbled backwards, scrambling to get away from the creature's grip. Tears choked her and she gasped for air. She couldn't breathe. Suffocation seemed like a terrible way to die.

And then it was gone. The fire disappeared, and the heat faded.

The jungle grew around her, just like it had since they arrived.

Except, the closer she looked the more she saw. These trees were different. This stream was different. The air itself was different.

Suddenly, everything in her brain lined up. The map. The visions. The demon prophecy.

The fire protecting this part of the jungle.

She sucked in a deep breath just as Luca stepped into the clearing. "Luca! I think I know what this place is."

33

Rae

Rae placed his hand on the dirt and closed his eyes. He whispered a prayer, deep and low. Evil had been brought in through Rafa's betrayal to the Father.

The earth vibrated and Rae prayed faster.

The vibrations stopped.

Peeling open one eye, he glanced at the ground.

Nothing. The dead plant was still dead, poisoned by whatever evil had found its way in.

He resituated his hand, then closed his eyes and prayed more fervently. The vibrations restarted and this time he extended his prayer for protection. Continued life. Guidance. When he opened his eyes, the dead plant had sprung anew. It bounced and swayed in the humid air, and Rae smiled.

No matter how the evil one tried, he would never gain access to the garden. He would not find the tree. Never again would he use it against the Father.

A shuffling and a crack sounded to his left. Standing from his place on the ground, Rae scanned the area. At first, he saw nothing, but then he froze. Hot dread seeped through him.

A man stumbled through the inner garden, staring at everything he passed, his mouth hanging wide.

The Miles man.

Rafa!

Rafa was the only explanation for how Miles had gotten inside.

Rae dashed behind Mr. Miles, following as quietly as he could as they moved through the jungle. Cutting him off would be easy; rerouting him would be the bigger issue.

Still, Rae could not force Mr. Miles to leave for good. He had to leave of his own choice, or he would continue returning.

Rae needed Avery. She was the only one who could turn her father back. She was the only one who could stop the wrath of the Father.

Mr. Miles moved slowly, taking in every tree, every flower, every animal with awe. His eyes practically glowed with excitement. While the rest of the group prepared to leave—and should have left, if Rafa had not confused the youth leader's trip across the jungle and doubled the time it took—Mr. Miles was in no hurry. He meandered between trees, strolled along the crystal stream, and even bent low as if he would drink the water.

Thank heavens he didn't. Water directly from the River of Life was not suitable to offer drink to a human. It was bad enough they were drinking from the small creeks that ran through the rest of the jungle.

Rae positioned himself behind Mr. Miles and to the right, then slowly, he projected the air currents toward the man. Closing his eyes, he held out his hands and blew out through his nostrils.

Mr. Miles didn't seem to notice, and he began moving closer to the perimeter of the garden. He stopped to finger a piece of fruit.

Rae projected further. If he pushed too hard, Mr. Miles was sure to notice. He obviously knew he was in a special place, and he would begin to wonder where the force was coming from.

Mr. Miles left the fruit hanging and continued exploring. He moved back toward the inside, away from the wall, and Rae ground his teeth. Miles headed straight for the tree.

Hadn't he known this wouldn't be easy? The elders had told him to be prepared for a day like today. Jacob had warned that not every century would be simple.

Rae's time to fight had come, he just hoped it did not come down to an actual fight.

He prayed quickly then darted behind a tree and worked to hide himself on Mr. Miles' left side. His eyes slid closed and he took a deep breath, then he pushed—not too hard, but harder than before. When he opened his eyes, Mr. Miles had moved back toward the outer edge. Rae moved a few trees closer and continued pushing. Mr. Miles stepped even closer to the wall.

One more push and he would be out. Once Rae had secured their home, he would be free to bind Mr. Miles and send him on his way. The human would never know where he had been, and he certainly would not remember what he had seen.

Taking a deep breath, he projected one last time. Mr. Miles lifted his foot. His body moved in sync to cover the six or eight inches needed to get to the outside. His foot headed toward the ground...

A commotion on the left drew Mr. Miles' attention and Rae growled. He jerked his gaze that way and froze.

Avery and her friend Luca stumbled into the clearing and gazed around with the same awe and wonder that was on Mr. Miles' face. Avery spoke to Luca in a low voice. It was too low for Mr. Miles to hear, but Rae heard it and winced.

She knew the truth, had figured it out for herself. But that also meant she could help.

Mr. Miles' eyebrows rose, showing his disbelief at seeing his daughter. He opened his mouth to speak, but a moment later two others stepped through the wall.

Rae sucked in a breath of frustration. This was impossible! How were they getting through? He would never be able to stop them all.

June gasped and cried, brushing at her skin and shaking. "Get it off! Get it off!" she screamed through her tears. Nothing crawled on her skin, and it was unscathed, though she likely felt like she was on fire. That could only mean one thing, but the girl was hardly his concern right now.

"Whoa!" Benny said. He didn't seem to notice June's distress. "What is this place?"

Avery glanced around, but she hadn't spotted Rae or her father yet. Her gaze finally landed back on Luca and she took a shaky breath. "I think we're in the Garden of Eden."

34

Avery

One tree stood out among the others. Avery wasn't sure how no one else had noticed it yet—it stood twice as high and twice as full as the others, and its fruit was as big as softballs.

Avery moved toward the tree without thinking. She had to get a closer look. All the while her brain screamed at her to *stop*! This couldn't be right. Could it?

The Garden of Eden had been locked to people thousands of years ago, after Adam and Eve had eaten the forbidden fruit. It was protected by angels with flames of fire.

Pieces clicked together in her mind, and she knew she'd been on the brink of it all along. Rae was—an angel? Then there was the wall of fire, the tree with the amazing looking fruit, and even the healing waters that seemed to point to the obvious. She'd searched for answers in her Bible, and her suspicions had been right. They had found the Garden of Eden from the Creation story. She turned slowly, taking in the beauty around her.

Rae stood to her far right, and Daddy stood just beyond him.

Avery gasped. "Daddy!"

He started toward her but Rae stepped out from

where he stood behind a tree.

Daddy pulled up short, staring at Rae in shock. "What—who are you?"

Rae looked to Avery, but she didn't speak. Rae could defend himself, and she was ready to hear what he had to say.

The second he paused, though, he had lost her attention. Her eyes roamed over the jungle—the garden—and she couldn't get enough. The trees were a shade of green she had only ever seen inside a crayon box, bright and vibrant. They grew perfectly portioned, their leaves shady but not quite overbearing. Beyond the trees, a stream flowed throw the garden. Bigger than a stream, it was more like a river. It ran right in the middle, cutting the garden in half, but that wasn't anything spectacular. What really caught her attention was the water inside the stream. It was blue, and it literally sparkled. Sunlight filtered through the canopy above, and the beams bounced off the water in glistening splendor.

Animals lounged in the garden, too, but they weren't animals Avery recognized. One looked like a cross between a hyena and a giraffe—a hyena's head on a short giraffe's body—and another animal resembled what could only be called a unicorn.

She spun around to Luca. "Are you seeing this?"

He stared beyond her, taking in the garden and all its glory. "Uh-huh."

"You cannot be here." Rae's voice broke through her thoughts. It didn't ruin the experience, though. Oddly enough, his voice felt melodic in this place, like a song. For the first time in years, she wanted to sing.

Avery stepped forward, closing the gap between them. "Are you an angel? You've been trying to help us all along."

Rae glanced around the group, his eyes darting between faces. A frown messed up the beauty of his face and she had the strangest desire to see him happy. Sadness didn't fit here.

"I have been trying to protect the sanctity of the garden, and that is all. Obviously I failed."

Daddy stepped between them, his face eager. "How did you find me, Avery? Did you figure it out on your own?"

Something surged across his face, something so close to pride that Avery started shaking. She swallowed hard and nodded. "I've suspected for a few days. There are so many clues, and with everything I've heard you say over the years, I definitely had my suspicions."

His grin spread across his face and he clasped her shoulders. "I always knew you had it in you!"

It was like the best dream she'd ever had. Daddy approved! He knew she'd been worth his time all along, she'd just needed to prove it. And here she was, doing just that.

He nodded and glanced around. "I had it pegged within a few days, and I knew I had to keep searching until I found it." He spread his arms out and looked around with a deep breath. "Look at it! It'll be the biggest archeological find of the millennium!"

Avery felt her excitement fade, and she recalled the temple and the prophecy. "What? Daddy, you can't tell anyone about this place." She spoke in hushed tones, almost like she was at a wedding. Disturbing the beauty around her was the last thing she wanted to do.

Daddy either didn't hear her or didn't care, and with sickening regret she admitted it was probably the second choice.

A deep laugh erupted from his chest, and he moved away from her and closer to the stream a few yards away. "Think about it! Scientists would go nuts testing this water. And those animals! Did you see them? Entirely new species. Why, we could name one after you, Avery!"

Avery stepped toward him, studying his face. His eyes burned with an inner fire, and while he seemed nuts, his eyes told her the truth. He was completely bent on going through with this. How was she supposed to stop him? Another thought nagged at her. She didn't have to stop him. She could help him. She could aid his efforts at broadcasting his big find, and he would be proud of her. He would love her.

"I cannot allow that." Rae's voice cracked and Avery turned toward him. She'd almost forgotten he was there, but his demeanor now surprised her. His eyes drooped and his shoulders sagged.

Deep inside, she suspected he wasn't sad that Daddy planned to introduce the world to this place; he was sad because he wasn't going to let Daddy get away with it.

What was Rae going to do with them all?

Fear knotted in her stomach and snapped her out of her crazy thoughts about helping Daddy. She rushed to Rae. "You won't hurt him, right? Angels can't hurt people, can they? We can get him out of here."

Luca stepped forward and nodded. "We will leave this place and never look back. Our group is ready to leave as we speak. They're waiting for our return."

Rae looked between them and shook his head. "I cannot be sure that everyone in your group feels the same way." He glanced again to Daddy.

Seconds ticked by as she considered what needed to be done. "Daddy, we have—" she started, but a noise drew her away.

Not a noise, more like a desperate cry.

Avery spun toward Benny and June.

Benny watched the whole thing unfold with wide eyes. His mouth dangled open.

But June knelt on the ground. Groans came from her throat and she bent toward the grass, holding her head in her hands.

Avery's heart clenched—she couldn't help it. The girl was obviously in agony. "What's wrong with her?"

"The Creator is not with her. She cannot comprehend the power of this place. It is overwhelming her."

"What's that supposed to mean?" Luca asked. "Do we need to get her out of here?"

Rae nodded once. "If she does not leave soon she will most likely die, though I could not say with certainty. I've rarely seen an actual human in the garden, let alone a lost human."

June? Dear sweet June who was always the first to respond with kindness and the first to cry tears of tenderness?

Unless her eyes were blue, of course. No wonder she responded so poorly to the demons of this place.

Demons! Memories of the black beetles made Avery shiver.

For they are the spirits of devils, working miracles, which go forth unto the kings of the earth and of the whole world, to gather them to the battle of that great day of God Almighty.

Avery spun back to Rae and stepped close to him.

"I saw him. I saw a demon as I came through the fire."

Rae's eyes clouded and he nodded. "Yes, I felt his presence. He could not latch onto you because God's spirit is inside of you. He latched onto her, instead."

Sorrow filled Avery as she glanced again at June. They had to save her. They had to save themselves.

"I don't understand any of this," Luca said. He stepped toward Rae, blocking Avery from the angel. Avery could hear the anger dripping from Luca's voice. "You show up like you want to help us, you tell us now you've been trying to keep us out, and yet we can't seem to leave. What's going on?"

Avery ignored Luca's words. Pieces clicked together in her mind, and she realized the truth behind the prophecy. A battle would come if she couldn't stop him. She was the only one who could stop Daddy. He was the one the jungle needed protection against.

Tears clogged her throat as she considered it. She couldn't stop him. He would never listen to her, even if she begged and pleaded. Worst of all, she would lose the pride she'd so newly earned.

Rae watched her curiously, and after a moment, he began speaking. "I am not alone here, as you know. Rafa brought you here. He wanted someone, anyone, to find this place. He felt it was divine when your father made his discoveries and was interested in staying.

"As I said, it was my goal to keep you out. I could do nothing to help you leave, because Rafa worked against me at every turn. Helping humans is not my assignment. My assignment is protecting the garden."

He stopped and swallowed hard. His eyes deepened, blazed, steeled. "You have seen what no human is allowed to see. I cannot allow the tale to be told."

"I won't tell!" Benny threw himself at Rae, falling at his feet.

Tears burned her eyes as she watched Benny beg for his life.

Benny continued. "I don't care what you do to us. Take us and drop us off in the middle of the arctic. Get us out of here. Make us forget. I don't care, just don't kill us."

June's moans grew louder, but Avery couldn't concentrate on her. "Wait, can you do that? Can you make us forget?"

Avery remembered Gabby and Katelyn's story. Her eyes widened. "You've done it before! Gabby and Katelyn found this place. It's where they saw you, isn't it? You led them away and made them forget."

"Do you think they made it through that fire?" Luca asked. His voice dripped with doubt.

But Avery was determined. "Yes. They mentioned the tree. They had to have seen it." She turned to look at the one tree. The beautiful tree.

The tree Daddy stood under at this very moment, his hand reached out to pluck the fruit.

"Daddy, no!" she screamed.

All eyes flashed toward him.

Rae was gone in a flicker of light.

Daddy's body flew through the air and landed with a thump against a tree trunk across the stream. He slumped toward the ground, blood pooling at the corner of his lip.

"Daddy!" Avery rushed toward him.

"Don't step in the water!" Rae shouted. He leapt forward and caught her.

Before she could protest, her feet lifted off the

ground, and for the briefest second she floated. She landed on the other side and Rae was gone. Ten feet away. Breathing hard.

She didn't have time to figure out this strange angel guy. Instead, she rushed to Daddy and wiped the blood from his lip. "He's still breathing," she said.

Luca raced to the edge of the stream. "Now is the time to get him out of here. He can't fight us. We'll take him back to our camp and we will leave." He turned to Rae, his nostrils flared. "You have to help us. You have to trust us."

Rae frowned again. He searched their faces. What could he possibly be looking for?

"Please!" Avery said. "He's hurt. We have to get him out of here, and that will take the threat away."

"I'll have to bind your minds. You will not remember any of this."

June groaned louder and started shaking.

Avery turned to Luca, then to Rae.

"Trust me," Luca said. "We don't want to remember any of this."

Finally, Rae nodded. Avery sighed in relief.

"You help June," Luca said to her. "I'll get your dad."

She launched across the water this time, careful to keep her feet from touching the water as she skipped large rocks. No need to get the angel all weirded out again.

June moaned and her head lolled back as Avery tried to help her stand. "What's happening?" Avery asked.

"She has lost consciousness," Rae said. "We do not have much time."

Avery's back strained as she tried to lift June to

her feet. "Benny, help."

Benny hurried over and slung June's other arm around his shoulders. "I can't believe any of this is happening."

"You won't have to believe it much longer," Avery said. "Let's move."

Luca had managed to throw Daddy over his shoulder, and Rae led him to a part of the stream that he could step over without touching the water. Luca reached them and nodded toward the place where they'd come through the wall of fire.

Avery turned and gasped. A guy stood directly in front of her. His dark hair stood on end, and his dark skin glistened with sweat. "Going somewhere so soon? I had hoped to give everyone the grand tour."

"Back away, Rafa!" Rae said. "Do you not think you have done enough?"

Rafa's eyebrows rose and he barked out a laugh. "Enough? No, brother, not nearly enough. The archeologist is going to broadcast our location to the world. This place will be swarming with people. Dirty, selfish, greedy people who care not for the sanctity of—well, of anything!" His face lit up with what Avery could only call glee. He was happy about all of this?

"What could you possibly gain from that?"

He turned to her, as if he were really seeing her for the first time. His eyes took her in. Made her want to squirm. Finally, he turned to Rae. "You can help me, my brother!"

"You lie," Rae said through gritted teeth. "And you are not my brother. Give up now, Rafa. Even if you manage to bring others here, the Father will not allow it. You will kill innocents."

The giddy look slid off Rafa's face and he scowled

at Rae. "Innocents? I don't care about them. It is my mission to destroy the innocents." He turned back to Avery and beat his chest. "Why should I care what happens to humans?"

Avery seethed inside, but what could she say?

June's body began shaking in Avery's arms, rattling her teeth. "Please let us pass. She'll die."

"Wonderful. It's precisely what I had in mind anyway." Rafa raised his arms and small black beetles erupted around them.

"You can't bring them in here!" Rae said. He moved toward Rafa, his nostrils flared and his eyes shooting flames of anger. "I cannot allow it!" He gave a twist of his wrists and the beetles scattered.

Rafa laughed. "Is that so? What are you going to do about it?"

Rae moved as fast as lightning. His hands shoved into Rafa's chest, sending Rafa backwards and into a tree with a loud *thump*. Rafa didn't stay down like Daddy had, though. He shot up like a bullet and came at Rae with hands formed into claws.

"This is pointless," Rae shouted. They wrestled on the floor of the garden. "The Creator will not let you win."

"You think not?" Rafa flipped Rae onto his back and positioned himself on top. Grabbing Rae's head, Rafa slammed him into the ground.

June's body seized up and she gasped, then she slumped again with a moan. Avery and Benny looked at each other.

"We have to get her out of here," Avery said. June wasn't the only person she was worried about. If this was any indication of the battle coming, Avery didn't want to stick around herself.

"They're distracted," Luca whispered. "Let's get out of here. If we hurry we might be able to make it back to camp before they notice."

Avery nodded. She took a deep breath and moved toward the exit of the garden. Black beetles swarmed them, only these weren't the small bugs from earlier. The huge creatures were as large as watermelons, and they skittered around them, above them, even over their shoes.

Luca kicked one, sending it flying. Thick beads of sweat popped out on his forehead and he grunted as he heaved Daddy higher on his shoulder.

"It's the demons tormenting June," Avery said. "They attract the beetles. What do we do now?"

"Can you carry her by yourself?" Benny asked.

Avery frowned. "I don't know. What are you thinking?"

Rafa flew past them and hurdled into a tree high above them. The tree splintered. He slid to the ground with a sickening thud. Rae was on top of him in an instant. "Evil will never consume the good, Rafa. It pains me that you never learned this."

Dirt smeared across Rafa's skin. Scratches lined his body. But no blood.

Avery looked to Benny again. "What's your plan?"

"Take her and get out. I can stay behind to distract these bug things."

"You can't stay, Benny! You don't know what they'll do."

But Benny shook his head. "It's better than all of us getting stuck here."

Avery turned to Luca for help, but his lips pressed together in a thin line. "It's worth a try."

Avery shook her head. She couldn't believe this

was happening.

Benny squirmed out of the hold June's arm had on his neck, and he helped reposition her lifeless body over Avery's form. Avery slumped under June's weight, but after a moment, she adjusted to the extra load and tried taking a shaky step. She nodded. "I think I can make it."

Benny gulped. "Then go. I'll try to get out as soon as I can."

If ever she had wanted to hug Benny it was today. "You don't have to do this, you know."

He shrugged. "Let me have my moment. No one else ever has before."

Her heart squeezed and she swallowed back tears. "OK. Thank you, Benny."

Taking a deep breath, she stepped toward the trees again. Luca moved slowly behind her, and the bugs swarmed. She did her best to ignore them. With Benny staying put, though, they didn't seem to protest her and Luca's movement as much.

They reached the edge of the tree line and Avery glanced back one last time.

The beetles crawled over Benny's body. Terror covered his face, but he stood perfectly still as a huge bug climbed on top of his head.

"Let's move," Luca said.

Avery nodded and turned to go, but Rafa appeared in front of her. "What's this? You thought you could go without my noticing?" He threw back his head and laughed. "You're taking my winning ticket away from me, and I just can't have that."

Rafa shoved Luca backwards. Under normal circumstances, the force of his shove would have sent Luca flying, but with Daddy in his arms, Luca toppled backwards and hit the ground hard. The air left his lungs in a grunt, and Avery screamed.

The dark angel didn't seem to notice her, though. He wanted Daddy. Daddy was the one who would tell the world about this place if given the chance. Daddy was the one who had unleashed the demon.

And Avery was the only one who could stop him.

Avery glanced at the way out. She had to save June first. She could slip through and save June's life, then slip back inside. But what if she got stuck outside the fire wall?

If only the right choice were as plain as the danger they were in.

Pressing her eyes closed, she whispered a prayer for help. Then she opened her eyes and stepped forward.

Stepping through the portal to the outer jungle felt like walking in a vacuum. The air sucked in behind her, and a terrible screech pierced the air. June's body shuddered.

Avery bent low and put June on the ground. "I'm sorry to leave you here, June." She brushed the hair out of June's eyes. Hopefully, June would wake up and make her way back to camp, but who knew what would happen?

Avery stood and turned back to the wall of fire that had reappeared. It didn't burn her this time. No heat blew across her skin, because she knew now it was all in her mind.

Taking a deep breath, she stepped back inside.

35

Luca

Squirming out from under Mr. Miles's body, Luca scrambled to his feet and scooted away from the crazed, dark angel. Rafa stared into Luca's eyes, waiting for Luca's move.

Luca didn't plan on moving, though. What could he do against a supernatural being?

His gaze darted to Mr. Miles who still lay unconscious on the ground. He couldn't leave Mr. Miles here. He would be dead by the end of the day if not sooner, and Avery would never forgive Luca.

"Not sure what to do, eh?" Rafa said. "You could follow your girlfriend back into the jungle. Of course, then Rae here would have to hunt you down. He can't let word get out about this place, you know."

"I will not let you have the human," Rae bit out. He stood to their left, panting and watching Rafa like a lion on the hunt. "None of them, in fact."

Rafa growled and rolled his eyes. "Stay out of this, will you? You can't beat me."

Luca stood perfectly still as the two angels restarted their fight. If only he were closer to getting out, he might try making a run for it. Benny still stood near the edge of the garden. Tears ran down his face as the bugs crawled all around him, but he didn't budge.

Luca winced. "Go!" he mouthed.

Benny shook his head.

Luca tried to wave at him, shooing him out, but Benny stayed put.

Luca's gaze pulled away when Avery stumbled back into the garden.

Stupid, brave girl! What was she doing?

He gritted his teeth and shook his head.

"Let the others go," Avery said.

Rafa and Rae didn't even offer her a glance.

"Get out of here," Luca hissed. "Both of you. Go!"

Avery lifted her chin. "No way. We're in this together."

He huffed and shook his head. So stubborn.

Mr. Miles groaned on the ground at Luca's feet. That got the angels' attention.

Rafa was at his side in a moment. "Is he finally waking up?"

"He won't help you," Avery said. "There is still some good left inside him."

Luca didn't argue, but he definitely disagreed. Mr. Miles would shout it from the rooftops if it would buy him the recognition. The sacredness of the place didn't matter to people like him. To people like Luca's own dad.

The urge to lash out built inside his soul. Dad hadn't cared about the sacredness of the church on the night he died. He hadn't cared about his family, either, or how his suicide would affect them.

Anger burst through him like hot lava. A loud shout erupted from his throat and he lunged at Rafa. The surprise was enough to knock Rafa backwards, but it only lasted a second. Rafa fought back, knocking Luca into a tree. The air left Luca's lungs, and he gasped for breath.

He wasn't done yet, though. Ever since Dad's death, Mr. Miles had looked at him differently. Looked at him like he was undeserving, like he would probably do the same thing as his old man one of these days. Mr. Miles had worked hard to put distance between Luca and Avery since then.

Luca growled and charged Rafa, but Rafa was too fast. He moved easily, letting Luca pass him by. Luca didn't wait to recharge. Sucking in a deep breath, he spun around and charged again. This time he hit Rafa straight on.

Rafa fell backwards and knocked his head against something hard. It wasn't a tree, though. Rae stood behind the dark angel. He wrapped his arms around Rafa's chest. Rafa struggled to break free, his face a mask of anger.

"Bah!" he yelled. "Get your hands off me!"

"I will not!" Rae shouted back.

Before Luca knew what was happening, Avery had rushed past him. She stood in front of Rafa and shouted. "I bind you from this moment forward, in the name of Jesus Christ! You will bring no further harm to my father or the rest of us. You will bring no further harm to this sacred garden. You are hereby banished for evermore!"

Rafa gave one last cry of anger as a bright light flashed, and then he was gone.

Avery slumped to the ground, shaking, while Rae gaped at her.

Luca stared at the space that had just held Rafa. The dark angel had disappeared, and now a spot of dead grass lay in his place.

Luca swallowed hard and glanced at Benny, who stared open-mouthed at Avery. The bugs had vanished along with Rafa.

Avery moaned from the ground, brining Luca back to reality. He rushed forward and wrapped her in his arms. "Are you OK? How did you do that?"

"I don't know," she gasped, still struggling to breathe. "I remembered the book, and I prayed for guidance. The words came out without my meaning for them to."

Mr. Miles groaned again.

Luca reluctantly let Avery go. "We need to go." The anger from earlier had vanished. For the first time ever, he'd let himself feel it. Bask in it. He'd ignored his pain for so long, he'd forgotten what it felt like to be free of it. And now he'd let it go. A deep, cleansing breath cleared his head, and he bent to heft Mr. Miles back onto his shoulder. "Let's move."

As he lifted Mr. Miles onto his shoulder, Mr. Miles moaned and his eyes fluttered open. At first, he glanced around in confusion, but then his eyes opened wide and he struggled to get out of Luca's grasp.

"What is this? We must bring back proof. We must document it all!"

The struggle was too much for Luca, and he stumbled backwards. He lost his grip and his feet began to slip, but then Avery came at him with an enormous stick.

The smack against Mr. Miles' head vibrated Luca's bones.

Avery dropped the stick with a thud as Mr. Miles went still once again. She breathed hard, tears streaming down her face. She had done it.

He knew she could, though it had cost her.

Benny waved at them and nodded toward the exit.

Avery's gaze moved to Rae. She swallowed and

stepped toward him. "Rae? Are you OK?"

Rae didn't move from his bowed position on the ground. His face pressed to the earth, and a slow, quiet chant rose. Rae was praying.

Luca shifted uncomfortably under Mr. Miles's weight. "We need to get out of here."

Avery finally looked at him. She nodded but still moved to Rae's side. She touched his shoulder. "Thank you. We'll go in peace, now. We will make sure no one tells."

Rae kept still, and this time Avery moved ahead of them all and rushed to get out. They stepped through the invisible wall and the air around them changed.

June lay in the jungle, shaking uncontrollably.

"She's having another seizure," Benny said.

"That's not good," Luca said. "How do we get her back?"

"Once she stops we can carry her," Benny said.

They waited a few moments until the shaking stopped, and then Benny and Avery bent to lift her into their arms. Once they were positioned comfortably, they started back for the camp.

Luca couldn't get the images from his mind. The Garden of Eden? No way. Angels? Unlikely.

This place was more than he'd ever imagined when they found themselves stranded all those days ago. And if he couldn't get the images out of his mind, he was pretty sure Avery and Benny couldn't either, but no one mentioned it.

They made their way back to camp in silence.

36

Avery

They arrived back at camp just as darkness fell across the desert. Avery's body shook with exhaustion as she and Benny lowered June to the floor of one of the shelters.

"What happened to her?" Erin asked.

The others swarmed around them.

Avery glanced at Luca before speaking. "We got lost. She must have overheated, and she passed out. Then she had a seizure."

"Was it like before?" Erin asked. She immediately moved to check June's vital signs.

Avery had almost forgotten about the earlier seizure. "Yeah, I guess it was like that."

Erin nodded as she continued to work.

"What about him?" Chad nodded to Daddy.

Luca lowered Daddy to the sandy ground. "He's the reason we went in to start with. We found him, but he'd been hurt. He hasn't woken up yet, but he's breathing."

Erin moved immediately to her next patient. "Benny, can you bring the medical supplies from the back of the van?"

"Yeah. Sure." Benny's shoulders slumped as he moved slowly toward the van. Poor guy was exhausted.

"Hey loser, think you could speed it up?" Bradley asked.

Luca spun around and scowled at Bradley. "He's got more guts than you'll ever have. Leave him alone."

Bradley must have seen something in Luca's eyes, because he stepped back, frowning.

Avery almost smiled. Almost.

Benny returned with the box and Erin began digging through it. She came out with gauze to clean Daddy's bleeding lip and head.

Avery winced. She'd done that to him, busted his forehead. But it was the only way to get him out of the garden. They'd had to leave before Rae changed his mind.

Erin's voice snapped her out of her daydream. "We need water. Someone found your backpack when we went swimming in the creek. Somehow, it'd been knocked into the water. It's over by the fire now."

Avery didn't question the explanation, just rushed to the bag of waters and returned with two bottles for Erin to use. She held the water to each of the patients' lips and poured a few drops. Daddy and June seemed to respond, but they remained unconscious.

"I think they're going to be OK," Erin said. "We'll get them help first thing tomorrow."

But Erin had no idea what they'd both been through. The things—the beings—who had tormented them. How could June ever recover after being tormented by a demon?

Erin worked furiously and Avery paused. Erin had recovered from whatever tormented her. If Erin could do it, maybe Daddy and June could, as well.

"Maybe we should leave now," Luca said, pulling Avery from her thoughts.

Avery knew the darkness would prevent them from making much progress, but she couldn't blame Luca. She wanted to get out of there, too. Now. Before Rae changed his mind about letting them go so easily.

"First light," Chad said. "A very wise guy put that idea in my head."

Luca managed a small smile and nod, but Avery knew it cost him. "You got it, boss."

"Let's get some rest. We'll be ready to ride as soon as the sun peeks out in the morning," Chad said.

The group broke up and went to their sleeping quarters.

Avery moved toward the van, but Luca grabbed her arm.

"Are you OK?"

Was she? Her whole body hadn't stopped shaking since she cast Rafa from the garden. Her mind reeled at the thought. Where had she come up with such an idea? Finally, she shrugged and gave him a small smile. "Sure. What about you? You're the one who got into a fist fight with an angel. And for my dad, no less."

He shrugged. "I was doing it more for you than him. I'd do anything for you. You know that, right?"

Did she?

She ran through everything that had happened since coming here. She'd seen visions, dealt with her fears of rejection, and faced her father—and all in a few days. Luca had been by her side the entire time, no matter if she'd abandoned him three months ago.

Of course, he would do anything for her. Daddy wasn't right, not even most of the time. Hadn't her heart told her that for years? The desire to have someone take care of her, to have someone want to take care of her, had been so unfulfilled for so long, she'd just latched on to the idea that if she was perfect enough for Daddy then he'd eventually come around.

Maybe he would never come around.

Luca was her friend. Her very best friend.

She swallowed her fears and took his hand. "Yes, I know that. Thank you."

He wove his fingers into hers and squeezed gently. "You're not going to forget it before we get back home, are you?"

Tears burned her eyes and she forced out a smile. "No. I won't forget it."

"Good."

"What do we do about Daddy, though? He's sure to remember."

Luca glanced away, frowning. Finally, he looked back to her. "I hate to say it, but he hit his head. We'll use that against him."

Avery winced. It hurt to agree with Luca on this point. She didn't want to accuse her own father of seeing things—of being crazy—but she agreed. "OK."

He brushed her cheek and tingles raced down her neck. "I'll see you in the morning."

She nodded and watched as he slipped away to his own shelter. Taking a shaky breath, she climbed into the van. There was no way she'd get a decent night's sleep. It was going to be a long eight hours.

Morning sunlight irritated her eyes as she peeled them open the next morning. She rubbed her gritty eyes and looked around. Had she actually fallen asleep?

The others scurried around the van, packing supplies and getting ready to split.

They were leaving! Avery bolted from the van, her

heart pounding a hundred miles a minute. This had to work. She wasn't sure how, but it had to.

Daddy lay sleeping in the open, near the logs at the fire, but June sat awake and alert. Erin kneeled in front of her, holding up four fingers.

"How are you?" Avery asked when she'd made her way over.

June shrugged. "I can't remember anything, but I see we found your dad."

"Yeah, we did. Thanks for going with us." Avery studied her friend—she was sure she could call her that now. If what Rae said was true, June didn't have God in her life. Did June even realize it? She went to church and played the part, but had she really never come to know God herself?

"I'm going to get you some aspirin before we leave," Erin said. "Sit tight."

Avery scooted closer and took June's hand. "You had a tough time in there."

June nodded. "I just remember not feeling well. I felt," she paused, seeming to struggle for the right word. "Scared. I felt scared."

"What had you afraid?"

"I was afraid I was going to die. It was like I could see the flames of hell all around me."

Most likely it was the flames of the wall of fire around the garden, but Avery didn't mention it.

"Avery, I think I'm going to hell."

So Rae had been right.

Avery smiled. "That's not too hard to fix, you know, if you're willing."

June didn't return the smile. Instead, she nodded quickly. "Yes. I'm willing. Will you help me? Will you pray with me?"

"Of course," Avery said. She bowed her head and prayed a simple prayer with June—a prayer for forgiveness and salvation.

When they finished, June's green eyes shined with tears. "Thank you, Avery. I want to tell everyone as soon as we get home."

"I think that would be lovely." Avery squeezed her hands. "But first we have to actually get home."

June finally smiled and nodded. "Right."

Daddy moaned from his place in the sand. At least someone had spread a few shirts out before leaving him there for the night. He rolled over and coughed, then tried to sit up.

Avery rushed to his side. "Take it easy, Daddy. You're hurt." She helped him sit the rest of the way. What would he say about everything?

He frowned and looked around. "My head hurts."

She bit her lip. "You hurt your head." Or, more accurately, she had hurt his head.

"How did I get out here? I was in the jungle." His frown deepened. "You were there, too. What's going on, Avery?"

"You hit your head." Luca's voice sounded behind her and she spun around. "You'll probably be confused for a while."

Something flashed in Daddy's eyes, and he scowled. "I am not confused."

Avery sucked up her fears and patted his hand. "It'll be fine, Daddy. We're going to get you home and checked out at the hospital."

"I'm not going anywhere!" He tried to stand, but he wobbled before he even got to his knees. He scowled again but kept quiet.

"Let's load up!" Chad called.

Avery sucked in a tight breath. "This is it," she said.

Luca nodded. He called Chad and Bradley, and the three of them helped Daddy to a seat in the front row. Fitting thirty people inside a fifteen passenger van wasn't easy, but no one complained. Well, except Daddy.

Sam climbed into the driver's seat and cranked the engine. Avery let out a quick sigh of relief when the thing started. He gave the gas pedal a few taps, and the engine revved. "It seems the gas lines are doing well," he said.

Another sigh of relief.

Avery glanced at Luca and held her breath. He held her gaze as the van lurched in the sand. They pulled away slowly and nothing went wrong. Avery gripped her seat and watched out the window as the jungle faded into the distance.

Finally, Luca smiled. "Ready to go home?"

She nodded. "Yeah. I want to put everything that happened here behind me."

He reached out and took her hand. "Not everything, I hope."

She smiled as the van rolled on, and she took a deep breath. This trip hadn't been anything like she'd expected, but somehow she knew it had turned out exactly as it was supposed to. Finally, she shook her head and squeezed his fingers. "No. I won't forget everything. I promise."

~*~

It took hours to make it to a town, and another day to make arrangements to leave Iraq. The entire two weeks had passed while they were stranded in the jungle—the Garden. The mission organization accepted their story easily enough. They'd been blown off course by a sandstorm, and gotten stranded in the desert.

As far as most of the group knew, it was exactly what had happened. Only she knew differently, just as Luca and Benny did. And Daddy.

He was already making plans for a dig in Iraq. While no one believed his story of what he'd seen in the jungle, he seemed to know it was truth. He hadn't spoken more than three words to Avery since they arrived home the month before.

Luca knocked on her door just as she finished brushing her teeth. She raced to answer it, and he smiled and shoved his hands in his pocket. "Ready?"

"Yep." She grabbed her purse and followed him out. Tonight he was coming to youth group with her. She hadn't even asked him to, he'd just decided it on his own.

They climbed inside his beat up car, and started down the road. "Erin said we'd be splitting up tonight—girls in one group, guys in the other."

He kept his eyes on the road and nodded, and she turned toward the windshield as well. Things were good with Luca, and even good with the others. While she wasn't best buds with any of the girls, they didn't treat her like she had the plague anymore.

"Did you hear from June? She texted me and said she got a clear checkup from her oncologist."

Luca glanced at her. "That's great. I hadn't heard."

Avery smiled. It *was* great news. Even if she hadn't become close friends with the other girls, she and June kept in constant contact.

They drove a few minutes in silence, but it was comfortable silence. Warm. Happy.

They stopped at a red light, and just before it turned green, Luca reached over and took her hand. He squeezed it softly and heat crept into her stomach. His eyes stayed on the road, and Avery acted like it was nothing, but as they pulled away she couldn't stop her smile. Her start over had turned into a get-back-on-track, and at least for today, things were good.

Thank you for purchasing this Watershed Books title.
For other inspirational stories, please visit our on-line
bookstore at www.pelicanbookgroup.com.

For questions or more information, contact us at
customer@pelicanbookgroup.com.

Watershed Books
Make a Splash!™
an imprint of Pelican Ventures Book Group
www.PelicanBookGroup.com

Connect with Us
www.facebook.com/Pelicanbookgroup
www.twitter.com/pelicanbookgrp

To receive news and specials, subscribe to our bulletin
http://pelink.us/bulletin

May God's glory shine through
this inspirational work of fiction.

AMDG